# HUNTING THE SNARK
# AND OTHER SHORT NOVELS

*Mike Resnick*

**Five Star • Waterville, Maine**

Five Star First Edition Science Fiction and Fantasy Series.

Published in 2002 in conjunction with Tekno Books and Ed Gorman.

Set in 11 pt. Plantin.

Printed in the United States on permanent paper.

**Library of Congress Cataloging-in-Publication Data**

Resnick, Michael D.
   Hunting the snark and other short novels / Mike Resnick.
     p.  cm. — (Five Star first edition science fiction and fantasy series)
     Contents: Hunting the snark—Redchapel—Bwana—Seven views of Olduvai Gorge.
    ISBN 0-7862-3878-X (hc : alk. paper)
    1. Science fiction, American. I. Title. II. Series.
PS3568.E698 H87 2002
  813'.54—dc21                     2001055738

To Carol, as always,
And to Marty Greenberg—
occasionally my editor,
occasionally my partner,
always my friend.

# TABLE OF CONTENTS

Introduction . . . . . . . . . . . . . . . . . . . . . . . . 7

Hunting the Snark . . . . . . . . . . . . . . . . . . . . 10

Redchapel. . . . . . . . . . . . . . . . . . . . . . . . . 74

Bwana . . . . . . . . . . . . . . . . . . . . . . . . . . 118

Seven Views of Olduvai Gorge . . . . . . . . . . . . . 176

# INTRODUCTION

Hi. I'm Mike Resnick, and I'd like to welcome you to my worlds. (That's the nice part of being a science fiction writer. Other writers can only introduce you to their characters, but a science fiction writer has all time and space to play with, and I try my best to make use of it.)

The first story in the book, "Hunting the Snark," came about because Gardner Dozois, my good friend and the award-winning editor of *Isaac Asimov's Science Fiction Magazine*, knew I had taken a number of trips to Africa and was editing a series of classic reprints about African hunting. So, in the middle of a crowded room, where it was very difficult to say No, he challenged me to write "the ultimate science fiction hunting story".

So I agreed—and promptly forgot about it. Then, a year later, Gardner started nagging me for the story. And nobody nags like Gardner. I made a couple of false starts, and then one day I remembered Lewis Carroll's wonderful poem, "The Hunting of the Snark," and suddenly I had a story to tell after all. The ending is all my own (and rather typical of my kind of ending), but the rest is a true collaboration with Carroll, whom I have always admired for his talent and now admire even more since he became the only one of my many collaborators not to ask for half the money.

The story was nominated for a Hugo and a Nebula, science fiction's two highest awards, and won a lesser award called the HOmer.

Next up is "Redchapel." I have written a number of alternate histories starring that most colorful and accomplished of all Americans, Teddy Roosevelt. And they are all rather depressing. Roosevelt succeeded at just about every task he ever put his hand to—writing, law enforcement, politics, war, ornithology, taxidermy, hunting, exploring—and of course, if you are doing an *alternate* history, such a man tends to lose in the end.

I wanted Teddy to win one for a change—and one day I remembered that about thirty years ago I had written an article about Jack the Ripper, and had suggested who the Ripper might be. In all the years since it appeared, no one had followed up on it or made fictional use of it, so I decided that it was time for Teddy to hunt down the Ripper. The story was nominated for a Hugo.

The third story is "Bwana," one of the stories that went to make up the Kirinyaga saga (which, to my surprise, became the most-honored story-cycle in science fiction history.) Only one Kirinyaga story failed to win an award of some kind, and that was "Bwana" (though it was nominated for a couple of minor ones.) As such, it has appeared far less often than any of the others, and I'm happy to offer it up to you.

The fourth and final story, "Seven Views of Olduvai Gorge," is probably the most successful I've ever written. It was commissioned by another dear friend, Kristine Kathryn Rusch, who was then editing *The Magazine of Fantasy and Science Fiction*. She knew I was going on a safari to Botswana and Zimbabwe in 1990, and promised to buy any story I could come up with. I came back with a simple one—the future safari that appears all in italics in the middle of "Seven Views"—but the more I thought about it, the more nuances and variations occurred to me, and Kris, displaying truly remarkable patience and forbearance, waited almost three years for me to write and deliver the story.

I think it was worth the wait. "Seven Views of Olduvai Gorge" won the Hugo, the Nebula, the HOmer, and the *Science Fiction Chronicle* Poll in America, then went on to win Spain's Ignotus Award, France's Prix Ozone, Croatia's Futura Award, and also won the Universitat Polytecnica de Catalunya's Grand Prize.

"Hunting the Snark" and "Bwana" take place on other worlds; the other two take place on Earth. "Redchapel" takes place in 1888; the others take place in the future. One is narrated by a witch doctor, another by an alien. One borrows from poetry, one from history.

I think the above paragraph goes a long way toward explaining why I have an ongoing love affair with science fiction. I hope this book can encourage you to have one, too.

—Mike Resnick

# HUNTING THE SNARK

Believe me, the last thing we ever expected to find was a Snark.

And I'm just as sure we were the last thing he ever expected to meet.

I wish I could tell you we responded to the situation half as well as he did. But maybe I should start at the beginning. Trust me: I'll get to the Snark soon enough.

My name's Karamojo Bell. (Well, actually it's Daniel Mathias Bellman. I've never been within five thousand light years of the Karamojo district back on Earth. But when I found out I was a distant descendant of the legendary hunter, I decided to appropriate his name, since I'm in the same business and I thought it might impress the clients. Turned out I was wrong; in my entire career, I met three people who had heard of him, and none of them went on safari with me. But I kept it anyway. There are a lot of Daniels walking around; at least I'm the only Karamojo.)

At that time I worked for Silinger & Mahr, the oldest and best-known firm in the safari business. True, Silinger died 63 years ago and Mahr followed him six years later and now it's run by a faceless corporation back on Deluros VIII, but they had better luck with their name than I had with mine, so they never changed it.

We were the most expensive company in the business, but we were worth it. Hundreds of worlds have been hunted out over the millennia, but people with money will always pay to have first crack at territory no one else has set foot on or even seen. A couple of years ago the company purchased a ten-planet hunting concession in the newly-opened Albion Cluster, and so many of our clients wanted to be the first to hunt virgin worlds that we actually held drawings to see who'd get the privilege. Silinger & Mahr agreed to supply one professional hunter per world and allow a maximum of four clients per party, and the fee was (get ready for it!) twenty million credits. Or eight million Maria Theresa dollars, if you don't have much faith in the credit—and out here on the Frontier, not a lot of people do.

We pros wanted to hunt new worlds every bit as much as the clients did. They were parceled out by seniority, and as seventh in line, I was assigned Dodgson IV, named after the woman who'd first charted it a dozen years ago. Nine of us had full parties. The tenth had a party of one—an incredibly wealthy man who wasn't into sharing.

Now, understand: I didn't take out the safari on my own. I was in charge, of course, but I had a crew of twelve blue-skinned humanoid Dabihs from Kakkab Kastu IV. Four were gunbearers for the clients. (I didn't have one myself; I never trusted anyone else with my weapons.) To continue: one was the cook, three were skinners (and it takes a lot more skill than you think to skin an alien animal you've never seen before without spoiling the pelt), and three were camp attendants. The twelfth was my regular tracker, whose name—Chajinka—always sounded like a sneeze.

We didn't really need a pilot—after all, the ship's navigational computer could start from half a galaxy away and land on top of a New Kenya shilling—but our clients were paying for luxury, and Silinger & Mahr made sure they got it. So in addition to the Dabihs, we also had our own personal pilot, Captain Kosha Mbele, who'd spent two decades flying one-man fighter ships in the war against the Sett.

The hunting party itself consisted of four business associates, all wealthy beyond my wildest dreams if not their own.
There was Willard Marx, a real estate magnate who'd developed the entire Roosevelt planetary system; Jaxon Pollard,
who owned matching chains of cut-rate supermarkets and
upscale bakeries that did business on more than a thousand
worlds; Philemon Desmond, the CEO of Far London's
largest bank—with branches in maybe 200 systems—and his
wife, Ramona, a justice on that planet's Supreme Court.

I don't know how the four of them met, but evidently
they'd all come from the same home world and had known
each other for a long time. They began pooling their money in
business ventures early on, and just kept going from one success to the next. Their most recent killing had come on
Silverstrike, a distant mining world. Marx was an avid hunter
who had brought trophies back from half a dozen worlds, the
Desmonds had always wanted to go on safari, and Pollard,
who would have preferred a few weeks on Calliope or one of
the other pleasure planets, finally agreed to come along so
that the four of them could celebrate their latest billion
together.

I took an instant dislike to Marx, who was too macho by
half. Still, that wasn't a problem; I wasn't being paid to enjoy
his company, just to find him a couple of prize trophies that
would look good on his wall, and he seemed competent
enough.

The Desmonds were an interesting pair. She was a pretty
woman who went out of her way to look plain, even severe; a
well-read woman who insisted on quoting everything she'd
read, which made you wonder which she enjoyed more,
reading in private or quoting in public. Philemon, her husband, was a mousy little man who drank too much, drugged
too much, smoked too much, seemed in awe of his wife, and

actually wore a tiny medal he'd won in a school track meet some thirty years earlier—probably a futile attempt to impress Mrs. Desmond, who remained singularly unimpressed.

Pollard was just a quiet, unassuming guy who'd lucked into money and didn't pretend to be any more sophisticated than he was—which, in my book, made him considerably more sophisticated than his partners. He seemed constantly amazed that they had actually talked him into coming along. He'd packed remedies for sunburn, diarrhea, insect bites, and half a hundred other things that could befall him, and jokingly worried about losing what he called his prison pallor.

We met on Braxton II, our regional headquarters, then took off on the six-day trip to Dodgson IV. All four of them elected to undergo DeepSleep, so Captain Mbele and I put them in their pods as soon as we hit light speeds, and woke them about two hours before we landed.

They were starving—I know the feeling; DeepSleep slows the metabolism to a crawl, but of course it doesn't stop it or you'd be dead, and the first thing you want to do when you wake up is eat—so Mbele shagged the Dabihs out of the galley, where they spent most of their time, and had it prepare a meal geared to human tastes. As soon as they finished eating, they began asking questions about Dodgson IV.

"We've been in orbit for the past hour, while the ship's computer has been compiling a detailed topographical map of the planet," I explained. "We'll land as soon as I find the best location for the base camp."

"So what's this world like?" asked Desmond, who had obviously failed to read all the data we'd sent to him.

"I've never set foot on it," I replied. "No one has." I smiled. "That's why you're paying so much."

"How do we know there's any game to be found there,

then?" asked Marx pugnaciously.

"There's game, all right," I assured him. "The Pioneer who charted it claims her sensors pinpointed four species of carnivore and lots of herbivores, including one that goes about four tons."

"But she never landed?" he persisted.

"She had no reason to," I said. "There was no sign of sentient life, and there are millions of worlds out there still to be charted."

"She'd damned well better have been right about the animals," grumbled Marx. "I'm not paying this much to look at a bunch of trees and flowers."

"I've hunted three other oxygen worlds that Karen Dodgson charted," I said, "and they've always delivered what she promised."

"Do people actually hunt on chlorine and ammonia worlds?" asked Pollard.

"A few. It's a highly specialized endeavor. If you want to know more about it after the safari is over, I'll put you in touch with the right person back at headquarters."

"I've hunted a couple of chlorine worlds," interjected Marx.

*Sure you have,* I thought.

"Great sport," he added.

When you have to live with your client for a few weeks or months, you don't call him a braggart and a liar to his face, but you do file the information away for future reference.

"This Karen Dodgson—she's the one the planet's named for?" asked Ramona Desmond.

"It's a prerogative of the Pioneer Corps," I answered. "The one who charts a world gets to name it anything he or she wants." I paused and smiled. "They're not known for their modesty. Usually they name it after themselves."

14

"Dodgson," she said again. "Perhaps we'll find a Jabberwock, or a Cheshire Cat, or even a Snark."

"I beg your pardon?" I said.

"That's was Lewis Carroll's real name: Charles Dodgson."

"I've never heard of him," I replied.

"He wrote *Jabberwocky* and *The Hunting of the Snark*, along with the Alice books." She stared at me. "Surely you've read them."

"I'm afraid not."

"No matter," she said with a shrug. "It was just a joke. Not a very funny one."

In retrospect, I wish we'd found a Jabberwock.

*"Just the place for a Snark!" the Bellman cried,*
*As he landed his crew with care;*
*Supporting each man on the top of the tide*
*By a finger entwined in his hair.*

Dodgson IV was lush and green, with huge rolling savannahs, thick forests with trees growing hundreds of feet high, lots of large inland lakes, a trio of freshwater oceans, an atmosphere slightly richer than Galactic Standard, and a gravity that was actually a shade lighter than Standard.

While the Dabihs were setting up camp and erecting the self-contained safari Bubbles near the ship, I sent Chajinka off to collect possible foodstuffs, then took them to the ship's lab for analysis. It was even better than I'd hoped.

"I've got good news," I announced when I clambered back out of the ship. "There are at least seventeen edible plant species. The bark of those trees with the golden blossoms is also edible. The water's not totally safe, but it's close enough so that if we irradiate it it'll be just fine."

"I didn't come here to eat fruits and berries or whatever the hell Blue Boy found out there," said Marx gruffly. "Let's go hunting."

"I think it would be better for you and your friends to stay in camp for a day while Chajinka and I scout out the territory and see what's out there. Just unwind from the trip and get used to the atmosphere and the gravity."

"Why?" asked Desmond. "What's the difference if we go out today or tomorrow?"

"Once I see what we're up against, I'll be able to tell you which weapons to take. And while we know there are carnivores, we have no idea whether they're diurnal or nocturnal or both. No sense spending all day looking for a trophy that only comes out at night."

"I hadn't thought of that." Desmond shrugged. "You're the boss."

I took Captain Mbele aside and suggested he do what he could to keep them amused—tell them stories of past safaris, make them drinks, do whatever he could to entertain them while Chajinka and I did a little reconnoitering and learned what we'd be up against.

"It looks pretty normal to me," said Mbele. "A typical primitive world."

"The sensors say there's a huge biomass about two miles west of here," I replied. "With that much meat on the hoof, there should be a lot of predators. I want to see what they can do before I take four novices into the bush."

"Marx brags about all the safaris he's been on," complained Mbele. "Why not take the Great White Hunter with you?"

"Nice try," I said. "But I make the decisions once we're on the ground. You're stuck with him."

"Thanks a lot."

16

"Maybe he's been on other safaris, but he's a novice on Dodgson IV, and as far as I'm concerned that's all that counts."

"Well, if it comes to that, so are you."

"I'm getting paid to risk my life. He's paying for me to make sure he gets his trophies and doesn't risk *his*." I looked around. "Where the hell did Chajinka sneak off to?"

"I think he's helping the cook."

"He's got his own food," I said irritably. "He doesn't need ours." I turned in the direction of the cooking Bubble and shouted: "Chajinka, get your blue ass over here!"

The Dabih looked up at the sound of my voice, smiled, and pointed to his ears.

"Then get your goddamned t-pack!" I said. "We've got work to do."

He smiled again, wandered off, and returned a moment later with his spear and his t-pack, the translating mechanism that allowed Man and Dabih (actually, Man and just about anything, with the proper programming) to converse with one another in Terran.

"Ugly little creature," remarked Mbele, indicating Chajinka.

"I didn't pick him for his looks."

"Is he really that good?"

"The little bastard could track a billiard ball down a crowded highway," I replied. "And he's got more guts than most Men I know."

"You don't say," said Mbele in tones that indicated he still considered Dabihs one step up—if that—from the animals we had come to hunt.

*"His form is ungainly—his intellect small—"*
*(So the Bellman would often remark)—*
*"But his courage is perfect! And that, after all,*

*Is the thing that one needs with a Snark. "*

I'm not much for foot-slogging when transportation is available, but it was going to take the Dabihs at least a day to assemble the safari vehicle and there was no sense hanging around camp waiting for it. So off we went, Chajinka and me, heading due west toward a water hole the computer had mapped. We weren't out to shoot anything, just to see what there was and what kind of weaponry our clients would need when we went out hunting the next morning.

It took us a little more than an hour to reach the water hole, and once there we hid behind some heavy bush about fifty yards away from it. There was a small herd of brown-and-white herbivores slaking their thirst, and as they left, a pair of huge red animals, four or five tons apiece, came down to drink. Then there were four or five more small herds of various types of grass-eaters. I had just managed to get comfortable when I heard a slight scrabbling noise. I turned and saw Chajinka pick up a slimy five-inch green worm, study its writhing body for a moment, then pop it into his mouth and swallow it. He appeared thoughtful for a moment, as if savoring the taste, then nodded his head in approval, and began looking for more.

Once upon a time that would have disgusted me, but I'd been with Chajinka for more than a decade and I was used to his eating habits. I kept looking for predators, and finally asked if he'd spotted any.

He waited for the t-pack to translate, then shook his head. "Night eaters, maybe," he whispered back.

"I never saw a world where *all* the carnivores were nocturnal," I answered. "There have to be some diurnal hunters, and this is the spot they should be concentrating on."

"Then where are they?"

"You're the tracker," I said. "You tell me."

He sighed deeply—a frightening sound if you're not used to Dabihs. A few of the animals at the water hole spooked and ran off thirty or forty yards, raising an enormous cloud of reddish dust. When they couldn't spot where the noise had come from, they warily returned to finish drinking.

"You wait here," he whispered. "I will find the predators."

I nodded my agreement. I'd watched Chajinka stalk animals on a hundred worlds, and I knew that I'd just be a hindrance. He could travel as silently as any predator, and he could find cover where I would swear none existed. If he had to freeze, he could stand or squat motionless for up to fifteen minutes. If an insect was crawling across his face, he wouldn't even shut an eye if it was in the insect's path. So maybe he regarded worms and insects as delicacies, and maybe he had only the vaguest notion of personal hygiene, but in his element— and we were in it now—there was no one of any species better suited for the job.

I sat down, adjusted my contact lenses to Telescopic, and scanned the horizon for the better part of ten minutes, going through a couple of smokeless cigarettes in the process. Lots of animals, all herbivores, came by to drink. Almost too many, I decided, because at this rate the water hole would be nothing but a bed of mud in a few days.

I was just about to start on a third cigarette when Chajinka was beside me again, tapping me on the shoulder.

"Come with me," he said.

"You found something?"

He didn't answer, but straightened up and walked out into the open, making no attempt to hide his presence. The animals at the water hole began bleating and bellowing in panic and raced off, some low to the ground, some zig-zagging with every stride, and some with enormous leaps. Soon all of them vanished in the thick cloud of dust they had raised.

I followed him for about half a mile, and then we came to it: a dead catlike animal, obviously a predator. It had a tan pelt, and I estimated its weight at 300 pounds. It had the teeth of a killer, and its front and back claws were clearly made for rending the flesh of its prey. Its broad tail was covered with bony spikes. It was too muscular to be built for sustained speed, but its powerful shoulders and haunches looked deadly efficient for short charges of up to one hundred yards.

"Dead maybe seven hours," said Chajinka. "Maybe eight."

I didn't mind that it was dead. I minded that its skull and body were crushed. And I especially minded that there'd been no attempt to eat it.

"Read the signs," I said. "Tell me what happened."

"Brown cat," said Chajinka, indicating the dead animal, "made a kill this morning. His stomach is still full. He was looking for a place to lie up, out of the sun. Something killed him."

"*What* killed him?"

He pointed to some oblong tracks, not much larger than a human's. "This one is the killer."

"Where did he go after he killed the brown cat?"

He examined the ground once more, then pointed to the northeast. "That way."

"Can we find him before dark?"

Chajinka shook his head. "He left a long time ago. Four, five, six hours."

"Let's go back to the water hole," I said. "I want you to see if he left any tracks there."

Our presence frightened yet another herd of herbivores away, and Chajinka examined the ground.

Finally he straightened up. "Too many animals have come and gone."

"Make a big circle around the water hole," I said. "Maybe a quarter mile. See if there are any tracks there."

He did as I ordered, and I fell into step behind him. We'd walked perhaps half the circumference when he stopped.

"Interesting," he said.

"What is?"

"There were brown cats here early this morning," he said, pointing to the ground. "Then the killer of the brown cat came along—you see, here, his print overlays that of a cat—and they fled." He paused. "An entire family of brown cats—at least four, perhaps five—fled from a single animal that hunts alone."

"You're sure he's a solitary hunter?"

He studied the ground again. "Yes. He walks alone. Very interesting."

It was more than interesting.

There was a lone animal out there that was higher on the food chain than the 300-pound brown cats. It had frightened away an entire pod of large predators, and—this was the part I didn't like—it didn't kill just for food.

Hunters read signs, and they listen to their trackers, but mostly they tend to trust their instincts. We'd been on Dodgson IV less than five hours, and I was already getting a bad feeling.

"I kind of expected you'd be bringing back a little something exotic for dinner," remarked Jaxon Pollard when we returned to camp.

"Or perhaps a trophy," chimed in Ramona Desmond.

"I've got enough trophies, and you'll want to shoot your own."

"You don't sound like a very enthusiastic hunter," she said.

"You're paying to do the hunting," I replied. "My job is to back you up and step in if things get out of hand. As far as I'm concerned, the ideal safari is one on which I don't fire a single shot."

"Sounds good to me," said Marx. "What are we going after tomorrow?"

"I'm not sure."

"You're not sure?" he repeated. "What the hell were you doing all afternoon?"

"Scouting the area."

"This is like pulling teeth," complained Marx. "What did you find?"

"I think we may have found signs of Mrs. Desmond's Snark, for lack of a better name."

Suddenly everyone was interested.

"A Snark?" said Ramona Desmond delightedly. "What did it look like?"

"I don't know," I replied. "It's bipedal, but I've no idea how many limbs it has—probably four. More than that is pretty rare in large animals anywhere in the galaxy. Based on the depth of the tracks, Chajinka thinks it may go anywhere from 250 to 400 pounds."

"That's not so much," said Marx. "I've hunted bigger."

"I'm not through," I said. "In a land filled with game, it seems to have scared the other predators out of the area." I paused. "Well, actually, that could be a misstatement."

"You mean it hasn't scared them off?" asked Ramona, now thoroughly confused.

"No, they're gone. But I called them *other* predators, and I don't know for a fact that our Snark is a predator. He killed a huge, catlike creature, but he didn't eat it."

"What does that imply?" asked Ramona.

I shrugged. "I'm not sure. It could be that he was defending his territory. Or . . ." I let the sentence hang while I considered its implications.

"Or what?"

"Or he could simply enjoy killing things."

"That makes two of us," said Marx with a smile. "We'll go out and kill ourselves a Snark tomorrow morning."

"Not tomorrow," I said firmly.

"Why the hell not?" he asked pugnaciously.

"I make it a rule never to go after dangerous game until I know more about it than it knows about me," I answered. "Tomorrow we'll go out shooting meat for the pot and see if we can learn a little more about the Snark."

"I'm not paying millions of credits to shoot a bunch of cud-chewing alien cattle!" snapped Marx. "You've found something that practically screams 'Superb Hunting!' I vote that we go after it in the morning."

"I admire your enthusiasm and your courage, Mr. Marx," I said. "But this isn't a democracy. I've got the only vote that counts, and since it's my job to return you all safe and sound at the end of this safari, we're not going after the Snark until we know more about it."

He didn't say another word, but I could tell that at that moment he'd have been just as happy to shoot me as the Snark.

Before we set out the next morning, I inspected the party's weapons.

"Nice laser rifle," I said, examining Desmond's brand new pride and joy.

"It ought to be," he said. "It cost fourteen thousand

credits. It's got night sights, a vision enhancer, an anti-shake stock . . ."

"Bring out your projectile rifle and your shotgun, too," I said. "We have to test all the weapons."

"But I'm only going to use *this* rifle," he insisted.

I almost hated to break the news to him.

"In my professional opinion, Dodgson IV has a B3 biosystem," I said. "I already registered my findings via subspace transmission from the ship last night." He looked confused. "For sport hunting purposes, that means you have to use a non-explosive-projectile weapon with a maximum of a .450 grain bullet until the classification is changed."

"But—"

"Look," I interrupted. "We have fusion grenades that can literally blow this planet apart. We have intelligent bullets that will find an animal at a distance of ten miles, respond to evasive maneuvering, and not contact the target until an instant kill is guaranteed. We've got molecular imploders that can turn an enemy brigade into jelly. Given the game we're after, none of them would qualify as sport hunting. I know, we're only talking about a laser rifle in your case, but you don't want to start off the safari by breaking the law, and I'm sure as a sportsman you want to give the animal an even break."

He looked dubious, especially about the even break part, but finally he went back to his Bubble and brought out the rest of his arsenal.

I gathered the four of them around me.

"Your weapons have been packed away for a week," I said. "Their settings may have been affected by the ship's acceleration, and this world's gravity is different, however minimally, from your own. So before we start, I want to give everyone a chance to adjust their sights." *And,* I added to myself, *let's see if any of you can hit a non-threatening target at 40 yards, just so I'll know what I'm up against.*

"I'll set up targets in the hollow down by the river," I continued, "and I'll ask you to come down one at a time." *No sense letting the poorer shots get humiliated in front of the better ones—always assuming there* are *any better ones.*

I took a set of the most basic targets out of the cargo hold. Once I reached the hollow, I placed four of them where I wanted them, activated the anti-grav devices, and when they were gently bobbing and weaving about six feet above the ground, I called for Marx, who showed up a moment later.

"Okay, Mr. Marx," I said. "Have you adjusted your sights?"

"I *always* take care of my weapons," he said as if the question had been an insult.

"Then let's see what you can do."

He smiled confidently, raised his rifle, looked along the sights, pulled the trigger, and blew two targets to pieces, then repeated the procedure with his shotgun.

"Nice shooting," I said.

"Thanks," he replied with a look that said: *of course* I'm a crack shot. I told you so, didn't I?

Desmond was next. He raised his rifle to his shoulder, took careful aim, and missed, then missed three more times.

I took the rifle, lined up the sights, and fired. The bullet went high and to the right, burying itself in a tree trunk. I adjusted the sights and took another shot. This time I hit a target dead center.

"Okay, try it now," I said, handing the rifle back to Desmond.

He missed four more times. He missed sitting. He missed prone. He missed using a rest for the barrel. Then he tried the shotgun, and missed twice more before he finally nailed a target. Then, for good measure, he totally misused his laser rifle, trying to pinpoint the beam rather than sweep the area, and missed yet again. We were both relieved when his session ended.

His wife was a little better; she hit the target on her third try with the rifle and her second with the shotgun. She swept the area with her laser rifle, wiping out all the remaining targets.

Pollard should have been next, but he didn't show up, and I went back to camp to get him. He was sitting down with the others, sipping a cup of coffee.

"You're next, Mr. Pollard," I said.

"I'm just going to take holos," he replied, holding up his camera.

"You're sure, Jaxon?" asked Desmond.

"I don't think I'd enjoy killing things," he replied.

"Then what the hell are you doing here?" demanded Marx.

Pollard smiled. "I'm here because you nagged incessantly, Willard. Besides, I've never been on a safari before, and I enjoy taking holographs."

"All right," I said. "But I don't want you wandering more than twenty yards from me at any time."

"No problem," said Pollard. "I don't want *them* killing me any more than I want to kill *them*."

I told his gunbearer to stay behind and help with the camp and the cooking. You'd have thought I'd slapped him in the face, but he agreed to do as he was ordered.

We clambered into the vehicle and got to the water hole in about half an hour. Within five minutes Marx had coolly and efficiently brought down a pair of spiral-horned tan-and-brown herbivores with one bullet each. Then, exercising his right to name any species that he was the first to shoot, he dubbed them Marx's Gazelles.

"What now?" asked Desmond. "We certainly don't need any more meat for the next few days."

"I'll send the vehicle back to camp for the skinners. They'll bring back the heads and pelts as well as the best cuts of meat, and I'll have them tie the rest of the carcasses to some nearby trees."

"Why?"

"Bait," said Marx.

"Mr. Marx is right. *Something* will come along to feed on them. The smell of blood might bring the catlike predators back. Or, if we're lucky, maybe the Snark will come back and we'll be able to learn a little more about him."

"And what do *we* do in the meantime?" asked Desmond in petulant tones.

"It's up to you," I said. "We can stay here until the vehicle returns, we can march back to camp, or we can footslog to that swamp about four miles to the north and see if there's anything interesting up there."

"Like a Snark?" asked Ramona.

"Five Men and four Dabihs walking across four miles of open savannah aren't about to sneak up and surprise anything. But we're not part of the ecological system. None of the animals will be programmed to recognize us as predators, so there's always a chance—if he's there to begin with—that the Snark will stick around out of curiosity or just plain stupidity."

It was the answer they wanted to hear, so they decided to march to the swamp. Pollard must have taken fifty holos along the way. Desmond complained about the heat, the humidity, the terrain, and the insects. Ramona stuck a chip that read the text of a book into her ear and didn't utter a word until we reached the swamp. Marx just lowered his head and walked.

When we got there we came upon a small herd of herbivores, very impressive-looking beasts, going about 500 pounds apiece. The males possessed fabulous horns, perhaps 60 inches long, with a triple twist in them. The horns looked like they were made of crystal, and they acted as a prism, separating the sunlight into a series of tiny rainbows.

"My God, look at them!" said Pollard, taking holographs as fast as he could.

"They're magnificent!" whispered Ramona Desmond.

"I'd like one of those," said Marx, studying the herd.

"You took the gazelles," I noted. "Mr. Desmond has first shot."

"I don't want it," said Desmond nervously.

"All right," I said. "Mrs. Desmond, you have first shot."

"I'd never kill anything so beautiful," she replied.

"No," muttered Desmond so softly that she couldn't hear him. "You'd just throw them into jail."

"Then it's Mr. Marx's shot," I said. "I'd suggest you take the fellow on the far right. He doesn't have the longest horns, but he's got the best-matched set. Let's get a little closer." I turned to the others as Marx took his rifle from his gunbearer and loaded it. "You stay here."

I signaled to Chajinka to take a circuitous approach. Marx, displaying the proper crouching walk, followed him, and I brought up the rear. (A hunter learns early on *never* to get between a client and the game. Either that, or he keeps a prosthetic ear company in business.)

When we'd gotten to within thirty yards, I decided we were close enough and nodded to Marx. He slowly raised his rifle and took aim. I could tell he was going for a heart shot rather than take the chance of ruining the head. It was a good strategy, always assuming that the heart was where he thought it was.

Marx took a deep breath, let it out slowly, and began squeezing the trigger.

And just as he did so, a brilliantly colored avian flew past, shrieking wildly. The horned buck jumped, startled, just as Marx's rifle exploded. The rest of the herd bolted in all directions at the sound of the shot, and before Marx could get off a second shot the buck bellowed in pain, spun around, and vanished into the nearby bush.

"Come on!" said Marx excitedly, jumping up and running after the buck. "I know I hit him! He won't get far!"

I grabbed him as he hurtled past. "You're not going anywhere, Mr. Marx!"

"What are you talking about?" he demanded.

"There's a large dangerous wounded animal in the bush," I said. "I can't let you go in after it."

"I'm as good a shot as you are!" he snapped. "It was just a fluke that that goddamned bird startled it. You know that!"

"Look," I said. "I'm not thrilled going into heavy bush after a wounded animal that's carrying a pair of five-foot swords on its head, but that's what I get paid to do. I can't look for him and keep an eye on you as well."

"But—"

"You say you've been on safari before," I said. "That means you know the rules."

He muttered and he cursed, but he *did* know the rules, and he rejoined the rest of the party while Chajinka and I vanished into the bush in search of our wounded prey.

The swamp smelled of rotting vegetation. We followed the blood spoor on leaves and bushes through two hundred yards of mud that sucked at the Dabih's feet and my boots, and then, suddenly, it vanished. I saw a little hillock a few yards off to the right, where the grass was crushed flat, small branches were broken, and flowers were broken off their stems. Chajinka studied the signs for a full minute, then looked up.

"The Snark," he said.

"What are you talking about?"

"He was hiding, watching us," answered Chajinka. He pointed to the ground. "The wounded animal lay down here. You see the blood? The Snark was over there. Those are his tracks. When the animal lay down, the Snark saw it was too weak to get up again, but still dangerous. He circled behind it. See—here is where he went. Then he leaped upon it and killed it."

"How?"

Chajinka shrugged. "I cannot tell. But he lifted it and carried it off."

"*Could* he lift an animal that big?"

"He did."

"He can't be more that a few hundred yards ahead of us," I said. "What do you think? Can we catch up with him?"

"You and I? Yes."

Every now and then, when my blood was up, Chajinka had to remind me that I wasn't hunting for my own pleasure. Yes, was the implication, he and I could catch up with the Snark. Marx might not be a hindrance. But there was no way we could take Pollard and the Desmonds through the swamp, keep an eye out for predators, and hope to make up any ground on the Snark—and of course I couldn't leave them alone while we went after the Snark with Marx.

"All right," I said with a sigh. "Let's get back and tell them what happened."

Marx went ballistic. He ranted and cursed for a good three minutes, and by the end of it I felt he was ready to declare a blood feud against this trophy thief.

When he finally calmed down, I left Chajinka behind to see if he could learn anything more about the Snark while the rest of us began marching back to the water hole, where the vehicle was waiting for us.

*"We have sailed many months, we have sailed many weeks,*
*(Four weeks to the month you may mark),*
*But never as yet ('tis your Captain who speaks)*
*Have we caught the least glimpse of a Snark!"*

Mbele had himself a good laugh when we got back to camp, hot and tired and hungry.

"You keep talking about the Snark as if it exists!" he said in amusement. "It's an imaginary beast in a children's poem."

"Snark is just a convenient name for it," I said. "We can call it anything you like."

"Call it absent," he said. "No one's seen it."

"Right," I said. "And I suppose when you close your eyes, the whole galaxy vanishes."

"I never thought about it," admitted Mbele. "But it probably does." He paused thoughtfully. "At least, I certainly hope so. It makes me feel necessary."

"Look!" I exploded. "There's a dead 300-pound killer cat out there, and a missing antelope that was even bigger!" I glared at him. "*I* didn't kill one and steal the other. Did *you?*"

He swallowed his next rejoinder and gave me a wide berth for the rest of the day.

Chajinka trotted into camp the next morning and signaled to me. I walked over and joined him.

"Did you learn anything?" I asked.

"It is an interesting animal," he said.

31

I grimaced, for as everyone knows, the Dabihs are masters of understatement.

*"Come, listen, my men, while I tell you again*
*The five unmistakeable marks*
*By which you may know, wheresoever you go,*
*The warranted genuine Snarks. "*

I gathered the hunting party around me.

"Well," I announced, "we know a little more about the Snark now than we did yesterday." I paused to watch their reactions. Everyone except Desmond seemed interested; Desmond looked like he wished he were anywhere else.

"Chajinka has been to the tree where we tied the dead meat animals," I continued.

"And?" said Marx.

"The ropes were untied. Not cut or torn apart or bitten through; untied. So we know that the Snark either has fingers, or some damned effective appendages. And some meat was missing from the carcasses."

"All right," said Ramona. "We know he can untie knots. What else?"

"We know he's a carnivore," I said. "We weren't sure about that yesterday."

"So what?" asked Marx. "There are millions of carnivores in the galaxy. Nothing unique about that."

"It means he won't stray far from the game herds. They're his supermarket."

"Maybe he only has to eat once every few months," said Marx, unimpressed.

"No," I said. "That's the third thing we've learned: he's got to eat just about as often as we do."

"How do we know that?" asked Ramona.

"According to Chajinka, he approached the meat very cautiously, but his tracks show that he trotted away once he'd eaten his fill. The trail disappeared after a mile, but we know that he trotted that whole distance."

"Ah!" said Ramona. "I see."

"I sure as hell don't," complained her husband.

"Anything that can sustain that pace, that kind of drain on its energy, has to eat just about every day." I paused. "And we know a fourth thing."

"What is that?" she asked.

"He's not afraid of us," I said. "He had to know we were the ones who killed those meat animals. Our tracks and scent were all over the place, and of course there were the ropes. He knows that we're a party of at least nine—five, if you discount Chajinka and the three gunbearers, and he has no reason to discount them. And yet, hours after learning all that, he hasn't left the area." I paused. "That leads to a fifth conclusion. He's not very bright; he didn't understand that Marx's gun was what wounded the animal he killed yesterday—because if he realized we could kill from a distance, he'd *be* afraid of us."

"You deduce all that just from a few tracks and the signs that Chajinka saw?" asked Desmond skeptically.

"Reading signs and interpreting what they mean is what hunting's all about," I explained. "Shooting is just the final step."

"So do we go after him now?" asked Marx eagerly.

I shook my head. "I've already sent Chajinka back out to see if he can find the creature's lair. If he's like most carnivores, he'll want to lie up after he eats. If we know where to look for him, we'll save a lot of time and effort. It makes more sense to wait for Chajinka to report back, and then go after the Snark in the morning."

"It seems so odd," said Ramona. "We've never seen this creature, and yet we've already reasoned out that he's incredibly formidable."

"Of course he's formidable," I said.

"You say that as if *everything* is formidable," she said with a condescending smile.

"That's the first axiom on safari," I replied. "Everything bites."

"If this thing is as dangerous as you make it seem," said Desmond hesitantly, "are we permitted to use more . . . well, sophisticated weapons?"

"Show a little guts, Philemon," said Marx contemptuously.

"I'm a banker, not a goddamned Alan Quatermain!" shot back Desmond.

"If you're afraid, stay in camp," said Marx. "Me, I can't wait to get him in my sights."

"You didn't answer my question, Mr. Bell," persisted Desmond.

Mbele pulled out the Statute Book and began reading aloud. "Unless, in the hunter's judgment, the weapons you are using are inadequate for killing the prey, you must use the weapons that have been approved for the world in question."

"So if he presents a serious threat, we can use pulse guns and molecular imploders and the like?"

"Have you ever seen a molecular imploder in action?" I asked. "Aim it at a 50-story building and you turn the whole thing into pudding in about three seconds."

"What about pulse guns?" he persisted.

"There's not a lot of trophy left when one of those babies hit the target," I said.

"We need *something,* damn it!" whined Desmond.

"We have more than enough firepower to bring down any

animal on this planet," I said, getting annoyed with him. "I don't mean to be blunt, but there's a difference between an inadequate hunter and an inadequate weapon."

"You can say that again!" muttered Marx.

"That was *very* blunt, Mr. Bell," said Desmond, getting up and walking to his Bubble. His wife stared at him expressionlessly, then pulled out her book and began reading.

"That's what you get for being honest," said Marx, making no attempt to hide his amusement. "I just hope this Snark is half the creature you make it out to be."

*I'll settle for half,* I thought uneasily.

Chajinka, who was sitting on the hood of the safari vehicle, raised his spear, which was my signal to stop.

He jumped down, bent over, examined the grasses for a few seconds, then trotted off to his left, eyes glued to the ground.

I climbed out and grabbed my rifle.

"You wait here," I said to the four humans. The Dabih gunbearers, who clung to handles and footholds on the back of the vehicle when it was moving, had released their grips and were now standing just behind it.

"Whose shot it is?" asked Marx.

"Let me think," I said. "You shot that big buck yesterday, and Mrs. Desmond killed the boar-like thing with the big tusks just before that. So Mr. Desmond has the first shot today."

"I'm not getting out of the vehicle," said Desmond.

"It's against regulations to shoot from the safety of the vehicle," I pointed out.

"Fuck your regulations and fuck you!" hollered Desmond. "I don't want the first shot! I don't want *any* shot! I don't even know what the hell I'm doing on this stupid safari!"

"Goddammit, Philemon!" hissed Marx fiercely.

"What is it?" asked Desmond, startled.

"If there was anything there, Mr. Desmond," I explained, trying to control my temper, "you just gave it more than ample reason to run hell for leather in the opposite direction. You *never* yell during a hunt."

I walked away in disgust and joined Chajinka beneath a small tree. He was standing beside a young dead herbivore whose skull had been crushed.

"Snark," he said, pointing to the skull.

"When?" I asked.

He pulled back the dead animal's lips to examine its gums, felt the inside of its ears, examined other parts for a few seconds.

"Five hours," he said. "Maybe six."

"The middle of the night."

"Yes."

*"Its habit of getting up late you'll agree*
*That it carries too far, when I say*
*That it frequently breakfasts at five-o'clock tea,*
*And dines on the following day."*

"Can you pick up his trail?" I asked Chajinka.

He looked around, then gave the Dabih equivalent of a frown. "It vanishes," he said at last, pointing to a spot ten feet away.

"You mean some animals obliterated his tracks after he made them?"

He shrugged. "No tracks at all. Not his, not anyone's."

"Why not?"

He had no answer.

I stared at the ground for a long moment. "Okay," I said at last. "Let's get back to the vehicle."

He resumed his customary position on the hood, while I sat behind the control panel and thought.

"Well?" asked Marx. "Did it have something to do with the Snark?"

"Yeah," I said, still puzzled by the absence of any tracks. "He made a kill during the night. His prey was an animal built for what I would call evasive maneuvering. That means he's got excellent nocturnal vision and good motor skills."

"So he's a night hunter?" asked Ramona.

"No, I wouldn't say that," I replied. "He killed the crystal-horned buck at midday, so like most predators he's also an opportunist; when a meal is there for the taking, he grabs it. Anyway, if we can't find his lair, we're probably going to have to build a blind, sit motionless with our guns, hang some fresh bait every evening, and hope it interests him."

"That's not *real* hunting!" scoffed Marx.

"There's no way we can go chasing after him in the dark," I responded.

"I'm not chasing *anything* in the dark!" said Desmond adamantly. "You want to do it, you do it without me."

"Don't be such a coward!" said Marx.

"Fuck you, Willard!" Desmond retorted.

"Bold words," said Marx. "Why don't you take some of that bravery and aim it at the animals?"

"I hate it here!" snapped Desmond. "I think we should go back to camp."

"And do what?" asked Marx sarcastically.

"And consider our options," he replied. "It's a big planet. Maybe we could take off and land on one of the other continents—one without any Snarks on it."

"Nonsense!" said Marx. "We came here to hunt big game.

Well, now we've found it."

"I don't know *what* we've found," said Desmond, halfway between anger and panic, "and neither do you."

"That's what makes it such good sport and so exciting," said Marx.

"Exciting is watching sports on the holo," Desmond shot back. *"This* is *dangerous."*

"Same damned thing," muttered Marx.

We spent the next two days searching unsuccessfully for any sign of the Snark. For a while I thought he had moved out of the area and considered moving our base camp, but then Chajinka found some relatively fresh tracks, perhaps three hours old. So we didn't move the camp after all—but we also didn't find the creature.

Then, on the third afternoon of the search, as we were taking a break, sitting in the shade of a huge tree with purple and gold flowers, we heard a strange sound off in the distance.

"Thunder?" asked Marx.

"Doesn't seem likely," replied Pollard. "There's not a cloud in the sky."

"Well, it's *something,*" continued Marx.

Ramona frowned. "And it's getting closer. Well, louder, anyway."

On a hunch, I set my lenses to Telescopic, and it was a damned lucky thing I did.

*"Everybody! Up into the tree—fast!"* I shouted.

"But—"

"No arguments! Get going!"

They weren't the most agile tree-climbers I'd ever encountered, but when they were finally able to see what I had seen, they managed to get clear of the ground in one hell of a hurry. A minute later a few thousand Marx's Gazelles thundered past.

I waited for the dust to settle, then lowered myself to the ground and scanned the horizon.

"Okay, it's safe to come down now," I announced.

"Why didn't we climb into the vehicle?" asked Ramona, getting out of the tree and checking her hands for cuts.

"It's an open vehicle, Mrs. Desmond," I pointed out. "You could have wound up with a fractured skull as they jumped over it—or with a gazelle in your lap if one of them was a poor jumper."

"Point taken."

"What the hell would cause something like that?" asked Pollard, staring after the stampeding herd as he brushed himself off.

"I'd say a predator made a sloppy kill, or maybe blew one entirely."

"How do you figure that?"

"Because this is the first time we've seen a stampede . . . so we can assume that when they're killed quickly and efficiently, the gazelles just move out of the predator's range and then go back to grazing. It's when the predator misses his prey, or wounds it, and then races after it into the middle of the herd that they panic."

"You think it's one of the big cats?" asked Pollard.

"It's possible."

"I'd love to get some holos of those cats on a kill."

"You may get your wish, Mr. Pollard," I said. "We'll backtrack to where the stampede started and hope we get lucky."

"That suits me just fine," said Marx, patting his rifle.

We headed southwest in the vehicle until the terrain became too rough, then left it behind and started walking as the landscape changed from hilly and tree-covered to heavily forested. Chajinka trotted ahead of us, eyes on the ground, spotting things even I couldn't see, and finally he came to a stop.

"What it is?" I asked, catching up with him.

He pointed straight ahead into the dense foliage. "He is there."

"He?"

"The Snark," he said, pointing to a single track.

"How deep is the cover?" I asked. "How do you know he didn't run right through it?"

He pointed to the bushes, which were covered with thorns. "He cannot run through this without pain."

"You've never seen him," said Ramona, joining us. "How do you know?"

"If it did not rip his flesh, he would be a forest creature, created by God to live here," answered Chajinka, as if explaining it to a child. "But we know that he hunts plains game. A forest dweller with thick, heavy skin and bones could not move swiftly enough. So this is not his home—it is his hiding place."

I thought there was a good chance that it was more than his hiding place, that it could very well be his fortress. It was damned near impenetrable, and the forest floor was covered with dry leaves, so no one was going to sneak up on him without giving him plenty of warning.

"What are we waiting for?" asked Marx, approaching with Desmond. He stopped long enough to take his rifle from his gunbearer.

"We're waiting until I can figure out the best way to go about it," I responded.

"We walk in and blow him away," said Marx. "What's so hard about that?"

I shook my head. "This is *his* terrain. He knows every inch of it. You're going to make a lot of noise walking in there, and the way the upper terraces of the trees are intertwined, I've got a feeling that it could be dark as night 600 yards into the forest."

"So we'll use infra-red scopes on our guns," said Marx.

I kept staring at the thick foliage. "I don't like it," I said. "He's got every advantage."

"But *we've* got the weapons," persisted Marx.

"With minimal visibility and maneuverability, they won't do you much good."

"Bullshit!" spat Marx. "We're wasting time. Let's go in after him."

"The four of you are my responsibility," I replied. "I can't risk your safety by letting you go in there. Within a couple of minutes you could be out of touch with me and with each other. You'll be making noise with every step you take, and if I'm right about the light, before long you could be standing right next to him without seeing him. And we haven't explored any Dodgson forests yet—he might not be the only danger. There could be everything from arboreal killer cats to poisonous insects to 50-foot-long snakes with an attitude."

"So what do you propose?" asked Marx.

"A blind makes the most sense," I said. "But it could take half a day to build one, and who the hell knows where he'll be by then?" I paused. "All right. The three of you with weapons will spread out. Mr. Pollard, stand well behind them. Chajinka and I will go into the bush and try to flush him out."

"I thought you said it was too dangerous," said Ramona.

"Let me amend that," I answered. "It's too dangerous for amateurs."

"If there's a chance that he can harm you, why don't we just forget about it?" she continued.

"I appreciate your concern," I began, "but—"

"I'm not being totally altruistic. What happens to us if he kills you?"

"You'll return to base camp and tell Mbele what happened. He'll radio a subspace message to headquarters, and Silinger & Mahr will decide whether to give you a refund or take you to another planet with a new hunter."

"You make it sound so . . . so businesslike," she said distastefully.

"It's my business," I replied.

"Why did you ever become a hunter?"

I shrugged. "Why did you become a judge?"

"I have a passion for order," she said.

"So do I," I replied.

"You find order in killing things?"

"I find order in Nature. Death is just a part of it." I paused. "Now, Mr. Marx," I said, turning back to him, "I want you to . . ."

He wasn't there.

"Where the hell did he go?" I demanded.

No one seemed to know, not even Chajinka. Then his gunbearer approached me.

"Boss Marx went *there*." He pointed to the forest, then ruefully held up the back-up rifle. "He did not wait for me."

"*Shit!*" I muttered. "It's bad enough that I've got to go in after the Snark! Now I stand a hell of a good chance of getting blown away by that macho bastard!"

"Why would he shoot you?" asked Ramona.

"He'll hear me before he sees me," I answered. "He's running on adrenaline. He'll be sure I'm the Snark."

"Then stay out here."

"I wish I could," I said truthfully. "But it's my job to protect him whether he wants me to or not."

That particular argument became academic about five seconds later, when we heard a shot, and then a long, agonized scream.

A *human* scream.

"You two stand about 200 yards apart," I said to the Desmonds. "Shoot anything that comes out of there that doesn't look like me or a Dabih!" Then, to Chajinka: "Let's go!"

The Dabih led the way into the forest. Then, as it started getting thicker and darker, we lost Marx's trail. "We're more likely to find him if we split up," I whispered. "You go left, I'll go right."

I kept my gun at the ready, wishing I'd inserted my infrared lenses into my eyes that morning. After a minute I couldn't hear Chajinka any more, which meant when I finally heard footsteps I was going to have to hold my fire until I could tell whether it was the Dabih or the Snark.

It's no secret that hunters hate going into the bush after a wounded animal. Well, let me tell you something: going into the bush after an *un*wounded animal is even less appealing. Sweat ran down into my eyes, insects crawled inside my shoes and socks and up my shirtsleeves, and my gun seemed to have tripled in weight. I could barely see ten feet in front of me, and if Marx had yelled for help from 50 yards away, I probably would be five minutes locating him.

But Marx was past yelling for help. I was suddenly able to make out the figure of a man lying on the ground. I approached him cautiously, seeing Snarks—whatever they looked like—behind every tree.

Finally I reached him and knelt down to examine him. His throat had been slashed open, and his innards were pouring out of a gaping hole in his belly. He was probably dead before he hit the ground.

*"Chajinka!"* I hollered. There was no response.

I called his name every thirty seconds, and finally, after about five minutes, I heard a body shuffling through the thick bush, its translated, monotone voice saying, "Don't shoot! Don't shoot!"

"Get over here!" I said.

He joined me a moment later. "Snark," he said, looking at Marx's corpse.

"For sure?" I asked.

"For sure."

"All right," I said. "Help me carry his body back out of here."

Then, suddenly, we heard two rifle shots.

"Damn!" I bellowed. "He's broken out!"

"Perhaps he will be dead," said Chajinka, leading the way back out of the forest. "There were two shots."

When we finally got into the open, we found Philemon Desmond sitting on the ground, hyper-ventilating, his whole body shaking. Ramona and Pollard stood a few yards away, staring at him—she with open contempt, he with a certain degree of sympathy.

"What happened?" I demanded.

"He burst out of the woods and came right at me!" said Desmond in a shaky voice.

"We heard two shots. Did you hit him?"

"I don't think so." He began shaking all over. "No, I definitely didn't."

"How the hell could you miss?" I shouted. "He couldn't have been twenty yards away!"

"I've never killed anything before!" Desmond yelled back.

I scanned the hilly countryside. There was no sign of the Snark, and there had to be a good five hundred hiding places just within my field of vision.

"Wonderful!" I muttered. "Just wonderful!"

*The Bellman looked uffish, and wrinkled his brow.*
*"If only you'd spoken before!*
*It's excessively awkward to mention it now,*
*With the Snark, so to speak, at the door!"*

We dragged Marx's body out of the forest and loaded it into the back of the safari vehicle.

"My God!" whined Desmond. "He's dead! He was the only one of us who knew the first damned thing about hunting, and he's dead! We've got to get out of here!"

"He was also a friend," said Ramona. "You might spare a little of your self-pity for *him*."

"Ramona!" said Pollard harshly.

"I'm sorry," she said with a total lack of sincerity.

Pollard had been staring at Marx's body since we brought it out of the forest. "Jesus, he's a mess!" he said at last. "Did he suffer much?"

"No," I assured him. "Not with wounds like those—he would have gone into shock immediately."

"Well, we can be thankful for that, I suppose," said Pollard. He finally tore his eyes away from the body and turned to me. "What now?"

"Now it's not a matter of sport any more," I said, morbidly wondering whether the authorities would revoke my license for losing a client, or simply suspend it. "He's killed one of us. He's got to die."

"I thought that was the whole purpose of the safari."

"The purpose was a sporting stalk, with the odds all on the game's side. Now the purpose is to kill him as quickly and efficiently as we can."

"That sounds like revenge," noted Ramona.

"Practicality," I corrected her. "Now that he knows how easy it is to kill an armed man, we don't want him to get into the habit."

"How do you stop him?"

"There are ways," I said. "I'll use every trick I know—and I know a lifetime's worth of them—before he has a chance to kill again." I paused. "Now, so I'll know which traps to set, I want you to tell me what he actually looks like."

"Like a huge red ape with big glaring eyes," said Pollard.

"No," said Ramona. "He looked more like a brown bear, but with longer legs."

"He was sleek," offered Pollard.

Ramona disagreed again. "No, he was shaggy."

"Wonderful," I muttered. "I trust you at least took a couple of holos, Mr. Pollard?"

He shook his head. "I was so surprised when he burst out of there that I totally forgot the camera," he admitted shamefacedly.

"Well, that's an enormous help," I said disgustedly. I turned to Desmond. "How about you?"

"I don't know," he whimpered. Suddenly he shuddered. "He looked like Death!"

"You must forgive Philemon," said Ramona, with an expression that said *she* wasn't about to forgive him. "He's really very good at investments and mergers and even hostile takeovers. He's just not very competent at *physical* things." She patted his medal. "Except running."

Marx had a wife and three grown children back on Roosevelt III, and his friends felt sure they'd want him shipped home, so we put his body in a vacuum container and stuck it in the cargo hold.

After that was done, Chajinka and I went to work. We set

seven traps, then went back to camp and waited.

Early the next morning we went out to see what we'd accomplished.

That was when I learned that the Snark had a sardonic sense of humor.

Each of the traps contained a dead animal. But lest we mistakenly think that *we* had anything to do with it, each one had its head staved in.

The son of a bitch was actually mocking us.

*"For the Snark's a peculiar creature, that won't*
*Be caught in a commonplace way.*
*Do all that you know, and try all that you don't:*
*Not a chance must be wasted today!"*

I awoke the next morning to the sound of vaguely familiar alien jabbering. It took me a minute to clear my head and identify what I was hearing. Then I raced out of my Bubble and almost bumped into Chajinka, who was running to meet me.

"What's going on?" I demanded.

He responded in his native tongue.

"Where's your t-pack?" I asked.

He jabbered at me. I couldn't understand a word of it.

Finally he pulled me over to the area where the Dabihs ate and slept, and pointed to the shapeless pile of metal and plastic and computer chips. Sometime during the night the Snark had silently entered the camp and destroyed all the t-packs.

I kept wondering: was he just lucky in his choice, or could he possibly have *known* how much we needed them?

Mbele, awakened by the same sounds, quickly emerged from his Bubble.

"What the hell is going on?" he asked.

"See for yourself," I said.

"Jesus!" he said. "Can any of the Dabihs speak Terran?"

I shook my head. "If they could, they wouldn't need t-packs, would they?"

"Was it the Snark?"

I grimaced. "Who else?"

"So what do you do now?"

"First, I try to figure out whether it was mischief or malice, and whether he had any idea what havoc it would cause."

"You think he might be a little smarter than your average bear in the woods?"

"I don't know. He lives like an animal, he acts like an animal, and he hunts like an animal. But in a short space of time he's killed Marx, and he's seen to it that the five remaining Men can't communicate with the twelve Dabihs." I forced a wry smile to my mouth. "That's not bad for a dumb animal, is it?"

"You'd better wake the others and let them know what's happened," said Mbele.

"I know," I said. I kicked one of the broken t-packs up against a tree. "Shit!"

I woke the Desmonds and Pollard and told them what had occurred. I thought Philemon Desmond might faint. The others were a little more useful.

"How long ago did this happen?" asked Pollard.

"Chajinka could probably give you a more accurate estimate, but I can't speak to him. My best guess is about two hours."

"So if we go after him, he's two hours ahead of us?"

"That's right."

"We'd better kill him quickly," said Ramona. "He could come back any time, now that he knows where our camp is."

"Give me a laser rifle," added Pollard. "I haven't fired a gun since I was a kid at camp, but how the hell hard can it be to sweep the area with a beam?"

"You look a little under the weather, Mr. Desmond," I said. "Perhaps you'd like to stay in camp."

Actually, he looked incredibly grateful for the out I'd given him. Then his wife ruined it all by adding that he'd just be in the way.

"I'm going," he said.

"It's really not necessary," I said.

"I paid. I'm going."

And that was that.

"There's no sense taking gunbearers," I said as the four of us walked to the safari vehicle. "We can't talk to them, and besides, the rules don't apply in this case. If we see him, we'll take him from the safety of the vehicle, and it'll give you something solid to rest your rifles on while you're sweeping the area." They climbed onto their seats. "Wait here a minute."

I went back, found Mbele, and told him that we were going after the Snark, and that he should use the Dabihs to set up some kind of defensive perimeter. Then I signaled to Chajinka to join me. A moment later he had taken his customary position on the hood of the vehicle, and we were off in pursuit of the Snark.

The trail led due northeast, past the savannah, toward rolling country and a large, lightly forested valley. Two or three times I thought we'd spot him just over the next hill, but he was a cagey bastard, and by mid-afternoon we still hadn't sighted him.

As dusk fell Chajinka couldn't read the signs from the vehicle, so he jumped off and began trotting along, eyes glued to the ground. When we entered the valley, he was following

49

the trail so slowly that Ramona and Pollard got out and walked along with him while I followed in the vehicle and Desmond stayed huddled in the back of it.

*But the valley grew narrow and narrower still,*
*And the evening got darker and colder,*
*Till (merely from nervousness, not from good will)*
*They marched along shoulder to shoulder.*

Night fell with no sign of the Snark. I didn't want to chance damaging the vehicle by driving over that terrain in the dark, so we slept until sunrise, and then drove back to base camp, reaching it just before noon.

Nobody was prepared for the sight that awaited us.

The eleven Dabihs we'd left behind were sprawled dead on the ground in grotesquely contorted positions, each with his throat shredded or his intestines ripped out. Dismembered arms and legs were everywhere, and the place was swimming in blood. Dead staring eyes greeted us accusingly, as if to say: "Where were you when we needed you?"

The stench was worse than the sight. Ramona gagged and began vomiting. Desmond whimpered and curled up into a fetal ball on the floor of the vehicle so he wouldn't have to look at the carnage. Pollard froze like a statue; then, after a moment, he too began vomiting.

I'd seen a lot of death in my time. So had Chajinka. But neither of us had ever seen anything remotely like this. There hadn't been much of a struggle. It doesn't take a 400-pound predator very long to wipe out a bunch of unarmed 90-pound Dabihs. My guess was that it was over in less than a minute.

"What the hell happened here?" asked Pollard, gesturing weakly toward all the blood-soaked dismembered bodies when he finally was able to speak.

*"The method employed I would gladly explain,*
*While I have it so clear in my head.*
*If I had but the time and you had but the brain—*
*But much yet remains to be said."*

"Where's Mbele?" I asked, finally getting past the shock of what I was looking at and realizing that he wasn't among them.

Before anyone could answer, I raced to the hatch and entered the ship, rifle at the ready, half-expecting to be pounced on by the Snark at any moment.

I found what was left of Captain Mbele in the control room. His head had been torn from his body, and his stomach was ripped open. The floor, the bulkheads, even the viewscreen were all drenched with his blood.

"Is he there?" called Ramona from the ground.

"Stay out!" I yelled.

Then I searched every inch of the ship, looking for the Snark. I could feel my heart pounding as I explored each section, but there was no sign of him.

I went back to the control room and began checking it over thoroughly. The Snark didn't know what made the ship work, or even what it was, but he knew it belonged to his enemies, and he did a lot of damage. Some of it—to the pilot's chair and the DeepSleep pods and the auxiliary screens—didn't matter. Some of it—to the fusion ignition and the navigational computer and the subspace radio—mattered a *lot*.

I continued going through the ship, assessing the damage. He'd ripped up a couple of beds in his fury, but the most serious destruction was to the galley. I had a feeling that nothing in it would ever work again.

I went back outside and confronted the party.

"Did you find Captain Mbele?" asked Ramona.

"Yes. He's in the ship." She started walking to the hatch. I grabbed her arm. "Trust me: you don't want to see him."

"That's it!" screamed Desmond. "We were crazy to come here! I want out! Not tomorrow, not later! *Now!*"

"I second the motion," agreed Ramona. "Let's get the hell off this planet before it kills any more of us."

"That's not possible," I said grimly. "The Snark did some serious damage to the ship."

"How long will it take to fix it?" asked Pollard.

"If I was a skilled spacecraft mechanic with a full set of tools and all the replacement parts I needed, maybe a week," I answered. "But I'm a hunter who doesn't know how to fix a broken spaceship. I wouldn't know where to begin."

"You mean we're stranded?" asked Ramona.

"For the time being," I said.

"What do you mean, 'for the time being'?" shrieked Desmond hysterically. "We're here forever! We're dead! We're all dead!"

I grabbed him and shook him, and when he wouldn't stop screaming I slapped him, hard, on the face.

"That won't help!" I said angrily.

"We'll never get off this goddamned dirtball!" he bleated.

"Yes we will," I said. "Mbele had to check in with Silinger & Mahr every week. When they don't hear from us, they'll send a rescue party. All we have to do is stay alive until they get here."

"They'll never come!" moaned Desmond. "We're all going to die!"

"Stop your whining!" I snapped. *This is just what I needed now,* I thought disgustedly; *we're surrounded by dismembered corpses, the very ground is soaked with blood, the Snark's probably still nearby, and this asshole is losing it.* "We have work to do!" They all looked at me. "I want the three of you to start digging a mass grave for the eleven Dabihs. When that's done, I want us to burn everything—every tree, every bush, everything—to get rid of the smell of blood so it doesn't attract any predators. What we can't burn, we'll bury."

"And what are *you* going to be doing?" demanded Desmond, who had at least regained some shred of composure.

"I'm going to bring what's left of Mbele out of the ship and clean up all the blood," I said bluntly. "Unless you'd rather do it." I thought he was going to faint. "Then, if I can make myself understood to Chajinka, he and I will try to secure the area."

"How?" asked Ramona.

"We got some devices that are sensitive to movement and body heat. Maybe we can rig up some kind of alarm system. Chajinka and I can hide them around the perimeter of the camp. If we finish before you do, we'll pitch in and help with the grave. Now get busy—the sooner we finish, the sooner we can lock ourselves in the ship and decide on our next move."

"*Is* there a next move?" asked Pollard.

"Always," I replied.

It took me almost four hours to clean Mbele's blood and innards from the control room. I put what was left of him into a vacuum pouch, then hefted it to my shoulder and carried it outside.

I found Chajinka helping with the grave. I called him over and showed him, with an elaborate pantomime, what I had in mind, and a few moments later we were planting the sensing devices around the perimeter of our camp. I saw no reason to stay in the Bubbles with such a dangerous enemy on the loose, so I collapsed them and moved them back into the cargo hold. The grave still wasn't done, so Chajinka and I helped finish the job. Desmond wouldn't touch any of the corpses, and Ramona looked like she was going be get sick again, so the Dabih, Pollard and I dragged the corpses and spare body parts to the grave. I added the pouch containing Mbele's remains, and after we four humans and Chajinka filled it in, I read the Bible over it.

"Now what?" asked Ramona, dirty and on the verge of physical collapse.

"Now we burn everything, bury any remaining dried blood, and then we move into the ship," I said.

"And just wait to be rescued?"

I shook my head. "It could be weeks, even a month, before a rescue party arrives. We're going to need meat, and since we've no way to refrigerate it with the galley destroyed, it means we'll probably have to go hunting every day, or at least every other day."

"I see," she said.

"And I'm going to kill the Snark," I said.

"Why don't we just wait for the rescue party and not take any chances?" suggested Ramona fearfully.

"It's killed thirteen beings who were under my protection," I said grimly. "I'm going to kill him if it's the last thing I do."

"Maybe Philemon should give you his laser rifle," Ramona suggested. "He's not very good with it anyway."

Desmond glared at her, but made no reply.

"He may need it," I said. "Besides, I'm happy with my own weapon."

"Where will you hunt for it?" asked Pollard.

"Right in this general area," I answered. "He has no reason to leave it."

"We can't just sit around like bait and wait for him!" whined Desmond. "In all the time we've been on the planet you've never even seen him—but he's killed Marx and Mbele and our Dabihs. He comes into camp whenever he wants! He sabotages our t-packs and our ship! We'll need an army to kill him!"

"If he comes back, you'll be safe inside the ship," I said.

"Locking himself in the ship didn't help Captain Mbele," noted Ramona.

"He didn't close the hatch. As I read the signs, he saw what was happening and raced into the ship for a gun. The Snark caught him before he found it." I paused. "He knew better than to be out here without a weapon."

"So now it's *his* fault that this monster killed him?" shouted Desmond. "Let's not blame the hunter who fucked up! Let's blame the victim!"

That's when I lost it. "One more word out of you and there'll be another killing!" I shouted back at him.

Pollard stepped between us. "Stop it!" he snapped. "The creature's out there! Don't do his work for him!"

We both calmed down after that, and finally went into the ship. There was no food, but everyone was so physically and emotionally exhausted that it didn't matter. Half an hour later we were all sound asleep.

Each morning Chajinka and I walked across the scorched, empty field that had so recently been covered with vegetation. We would climb into the safari vehicle and prepare to go out to bag the day's food—and even though there was no longer any place to hide near the ship, I constantly had the uneasy feeling that *he* was watching us, measuring our strength, biding his time.

We never went more than four miles from camp. I didn't shoot the choicest animals, just the closest. Then we'd cut off the strips of meat we thought we'd need and leave the carcass for the scavengers. We'd return to camp, and after breakfast we'd set out on foot to look for signs of the Snark.

I knew he was nearby, knew it as surely as I knew my own name, but we couldn't find any physical sign of him. I warned the others not to leave the ship without their weapons, preferably not to leave it at all, and under no circumstance were they to go more than thirty yards away from it unless they were in my company.

By the fifth day after the massacre everyone was getting tired of red meat, so I decided to take Chajinka down to the river, and see if we could spear a few fish.

"Can I come with you?" asked Ramona, appearing just inside the hatch. "I'm starting to feel distinctly claustrophobic."

I couldn't see any reason why not. Hell, she was safer with Chajinka and me than back at the ship.

"Bring your rifle," I said.

She disappeared inside the ship, then emerged with a laser rifle a moment later.

"I'm ready."

"Let's go," I said.

We marched through heavy bush to the river.

"All the local animals must come down here to drink," noted Ramona. "Wouldn't it be easier to do your hunting right here rather than go out in the safari vehicle each morning?"

"We'd attract too many scavengers," I explained. "And since Chajinka and I come down here twice a day to bring water back to the ship, why cause ourselves any problems?"

"I see." She paused. "Are there any carnivores in the river —the kind that might eat a human?"

"I haven't seen any," I replied. "But I sure as hell wouldn't recommend taking a swim."

When we reached the river, Chajinka grabbed a large

branch and beat the water. When he was sure it was safe, he waded out, thigh-deep, and held his spear above his head, poised to strike, while we watched him in total silence. He stayed motionless for almost two full minutes, then suddenly stabbed the water and came away with a large, wriggling fish.

He grinned and said something that I couldn't understand, then clambered onto the bank, picked up a rock, and smashed it down on the fish's head. It stopped moving, and he went back into the water.

"Two more and we'll have our dinner," I remarked.

"He's really something," she said. "Where did you find him?"

"I inherited him."

"I beg your pardon?"

"He was the tracker for the hunter I apprenticed under," I explained. "When he retired, he left me his client list—and Chajinka."

Suddenly there was a yell of triumph from Chajinka. He held up his spear, and there was a huge fish, maybe 25 pounds, squirming at the end of it. The Dabih himself didn't weigh much more than 85 pounds, the current was strong and the footing was slippery. Suddenly he fell over backward and vanished beneath the surface of the water.

He emerged again a second later, but without the spear and the fish. I saw them floating downstream a good ten yards from him. There was no sense telling him where to look; he couldn't understand a word I said without a t-pack. So I waded into the water and went after the spear myself. It became chest-deep very quickly, and I had to fight the current, but I finally reached the spear and waded back to shore. Chajinka climbed out a moment later with an embarrassed grin on his face. He made another incomprehensible comment, then brained the fish as he had done with the first one.

"See?" I said sardonically. "Even fishing can be exciting with you're on safari."

There was no answer. I spun around. Ramona Desmond was nowhere to be seen.

*So the Snark pronounced sentence, the Judge being quite*
*Too nervous to utter a word.*
*When it rose to its feet, there was silence like night,*
*And the fall of a pin might be heard.*

I squatted down next to her corpse. There was no blood; he'd noiselessly broken her neck and left her where she'd fallen.

"He was watching us the whole time," I said furiously. "He waited until she was alone, then grabbed her and pulled her into the bush." A chilling thought occurred to me. "I wonder who's hunting who?"

Chajinka muttered something incomprehensible.

"All right," I said at last. "Let's take her back to camp."

I lifted Ramona's body to my shoulder and signaled him to follow me.

Desmond raced out of the ship when he saw us. He began flagellating himself and pulling tufts of his hair out, screaming nonsense words at the top of his lungs.

"What the hell is happening?" asked Pollard, clambering out through the hatch. Then he saw the body. He had to work to keep his voice under control. "Oh, Jesus! Oh, Jesus!" he kept repeating. When he'd finally calmed down, he said, "It's more than an animal! It's like some vengeful alien god come to life!"

Chajinka went into the cargo hold and emerged with a shovel.

Pollard stared at Desmond, who was still raving. "I'll help with the grave."

"Thanks," I said. "I think I'd better get Desmond to his cabin and give him a sedative."

I walked over and put a hand on his shoulder.

"It was *your* fault!" he screamed. "*You* were supposed to protect her and you let it kill her!"

I couldn't deny it, so I just kept urging him gently toward the ship.

And then, between one second and the next, he snapped. I could see it in his face. His eyes went wide, the muscles in his jaw began twitching, even the tenor of his voice changed.

"That thing is going to learn what it means to kill the wife of the most powerful man on Far London!" He looked off into the bush and hollered: "I'm Philemon Desmond, goddammit, and I'm through being terrified by some ignorant fucking beast! Do you hear me? It's over! You're dead meat!"

"Come on, Mr. Desmond," I said softly, pushing him toward the ship.

"Who the hell are you?" he demanded, and I could tell that he really didn't recognize me.

I was about to humor him with an answer when everything went black and the ground came up to meet me.

*And the Banker, inspired with a courage so new*
*It was a matter for general remark,*
*Rushed madly ahead and was lost to their view*
*In his zeal to discover the Snark.*

Pollard sloshed some water on my face. I gasped for breath, then sat up and put a hand to my head. It came away covered with blood.

"Are you all right?" he asked, kneeling down next to me, and I saw that Chajinka was behind him.

"What happened?"

"I'm not sure," he said. "We were just starting to dig the grave when I heard Desmond suddenly stop gibbering. Then he whacked you on the head with something, and ran off."

"I never saw it coming," I groaned, blinking my eyes furiously. "Where did he go?"

"I don't know." He pointed to the southwest. "That way, I think."

*"Shit!"* I said. "The Snark is still in the area!"

I tried to get to my feet, but was overwhelmed by pain and dizziness, and sat back down, hard.

"Take it easy," he said. "You've probably got a hell of a concussion. Where's the first aid kit? Maybe I can at least stop the bleeding."

I told him where to find it, then concentrated on trying to focus my eyes.

When Pollard returned and began working on my head, I asked, "Did you see if he at least took his laser rifle with him?"

"If he didn't have it when he hit you, he didn't stop to get it."

"Goddammit!"

"I guess that means he doesn't have it."

"Wonderful," I muttered, wincing as he did something to the back of my head. "So he's unarmed, running through the bush, and screaming at the top of his lungs."

"All done," said Pollard, standing up. "It's not a pretty job, but at least the bleeding's stopped. How do you feel?"

"Groggy," I said. "Help me up."

Once I was on my feet, I looked around. "Where's my rifle?"

"Right here," said Pollard, picking it up and handing it to me. "But you're in no shape to go after Desmond."

"I'm not going after Desmond," I mumbled. "I'm going

after *him!*" I signaled Chajinka to join me and set off unsteadily to the southwest. "Lock yourself in the ship."

"I'll finish burying Ramona first."

*"Don't!"*

"But—"

"Unless you're prepared to fend him off with a shovel if he shows up, do what I said."

"I can't leave her body out for the scavengers," Pollard protested.

"Take her with you. Spray her with the preservatives we use for trophies and stash her in the cargo hold. We'll bury her when I get back."

"*If* you get back," he corrected me. "You look like you can barely stand on your feet."

"I'll be back," I promised him. "I'm still a hunter, and he's still just an animal."

"Yeah—he's just an animal. That's why there's just you, me and Chajinka left alive."

Desmond didn't get very far—not that I ever expected him to. We found him half a mile away, his skull crushed. I carried him back to camp and buried him next to his wife.

"That bastard's been one step ahead of us from the start," said Pollard bitterly as we sat down next to the ship and slaked our thirst with some lukewarm water. Chajinka sat a few yards away, motionless as a statue, watching and listening for any sign of the Snark.

"He's smarter than I thought," I admitted. "Or luckier."

"Nothing is that lucky," said Pollard. "He must be intelligent."

"Absolutely," I agreed.

Pollard's eyes went wide. "Wait a minute!" he said sharply. "If you *knew* he was intelligent, what the hell were we doing hunting him in the first place?"

"There's a difference between intelligence and sentience," I said. "We know he's intelligent. We don't know that he's sentient."

He looked puzzled. "I thought they were the same thing."

I shook my head. "Back on Earth, chimpanzees were intelligent enough to create crude tools, and to pass that knowledge on from one generation to the next—but no one ever claimed they were sentient. The fact that the Snark can hide his trail, spot my traps and elude us makes him intelligent. It doesn't make him sentient."

"On the other hand, it doesn't prove he's *not* sentient," said Pollard stubbornly.

"No, it doesn't."

"So what do we do?"

"We kill him," I answered.

"Even if he's sentient?"

"What do you do when someone murders fifteen sentient beings?" I said. "If he's a Man, you execute him. If he's an animal, you track him down and kill him. Either way, the result is the same."

"All right," said Pollard dubiously. "We kill him. How?"

"We leave the ship and go after him."

"Why?" he demanded. "We're safe in the ship!"

"Tell that to Mbele and the Desmonds and the Dabihs," I shot back. "As long as we stay here, he knows where we are and we don't know where *he* is. That means he's the hunter and we're the prey. If we leave camp and pick up his trail before he picks up ours, we go back to being the hunters again." I got to my feet. "In fact, the sooner we start, the better."

He wasn't happy about it, but he had no choice but to come along, since the alternative was to remain behind alone.

After we loaded the vehicle I patted the hood, waited for Chajinka to jump onto it, and then we drove to the spot where we'd found Desmond's body.

The Dabih picked up the trail, and we began tracking the Snark. I wanted him so bad I could taste it. It wasn't just revenge for all the Men and Dabihs he'd killed. It wasn't even a matter of professional pride. It was because I knew this was my last hunt, that I'd never get my license back after losing fifteen sentient beings who were under my protection.

The trail led back to the camp, where the Snark had watched us bury Desmond's body. It had kept out of sight until we drove off, and then began moving in a northwesterly direction. We tracked it until late afternoon, when we found ourselves about eight miles from the ship.

"There's no sense going back for the night," I told Pollard. "We might never pick up the trail again."

"Isn't he likely to double back to the camp?"

"Not while we're out here, he isn't," I said with absolutely certainty. "This isn't a hunt any longer—it's a war. Neither of us will quit until the other's dead."

He looked at me much the way I'd looked at Desmond earlier in the day. Finally he spoke up: "We can't track him at night."

"I know," I replied. "We'll each keep watch for three hours—you, me and Chajinka—and we'll start again as soon as it's light enough."

I sat the first watch, and I was so keyed up that I couldn't get to sleep, so I sat through Pollard's watch as well before I woke Chajinka and managed a three-hour nap. As soon as it was light, we started following the trail again.

By noon we were approaching a small canyon. Then, suddenly, I saw a flicker of motion off in the distance. I stopped the vehicle and activated my Telescopic lenses.

He was more than a mile away, and he had his back to us, but I knew I'd finally gotten my first look at the Snark.

*Erect and sublime, for one moment of time,*
*In the next, that wild figure they saw*
*(As if stung by a spasm) plunge into a chasm,*
*While they waited and listened in awe.*

I drove to the edge of the canyon. Chajinka hopped off the hood, and Pollard and I joined him a moment later.

"You're sure you saw him?" asked Pollard.

"I'm sure," I said. "Bipedal. Rust-colored. Looks almost like a cross between a bear and a gorilla, at least from this distance."

"Yeah, that's him all right." He peered down into the canyon. "And he climbed down there?"

"That's right," I said.

"I assume we're going after him?"

"There's no reason to believe he'll come out anywhere near here," I said. "If we wait, we'll lose him."

"It's looks pretty rocky," he said. "Can we pick up his trail?"

"Chajinka will find it."

Pollard sighed deeply. "What the hell," he said with a shrug. "I'm not going to wait here alone while the two of you go after him. I figure I'll be safer with you—providing I don't break my neck on the terrain."

I motioned for Chajinka to lead the way down, since he was far more sure-footed than any human. He walked along the edge of the precipice for perhaps fifty yards, then came to a crude path we were able to follow for the better part of an hour. Then we were on the canyon floor next to a narrow stream where we slaked our thirst, hoping the water wouldn't make us too sick, as we'd left the irradiation tablets back at the ship.

We rested briefly, then took up the hunt again. Chajinka was able to find a trail where I would have sworn none existed. By early afternoon the floor of the canyon was no longer flat, and we had to follow a winding path over and around a series of rock formations. Pollard was game, but he was out of shape. He kept falling behind, actually dropping out of sight a couple of times, which forced us to stop and wait for him to catch up.

When he dropped behind yet again, I wanted to ask him if he needed a break. I didn't dare shout and give away our position to the Snark, so I compromised by signaling Chajinka to slow his pace until Pollard caught up with us.

He didn't—and after a few minutes we went back to see what was the matter.

I couldn't find him. It was like he had vanished off the face of the planet.

*They hunted till darkness came on, but they found*
*Not a button, or feather, or mark,*
*By which they could tell that they stood on the ground*
*Where the Baker had met with the Snark.*

We spent half an hour looking for Pollard. There was no trace of him, and eventually we were forced to admit that somehow the Snark had turned back on his trail and circled around us or hid and waited for us to pass by. Either way, it was obvious that he'd managed to get Pollard.

I knew it was futile to keep looking for him, so I signaled Chajinka to continue searching for the Snark. We hiked over the rocky canyon floor until at last we came to a steep wall.

"We go up, or we go back," I said, looking at the wall.

"Which will it be?"

He stared at me expectantly, waiting for me to signal him which way to go.

I looked back the way we'd come, then up in the direction of the path we were following—

—and as I looked up, I saw a large object hurtling down toward me!

I pushed Chajinka out of the way and threw myself to my left, rolling as I hit the ground. The object landed five feet away with a bone-jarring *thud!*—and I saw that it was Pollard's body.

I looked up, and there was the Snark standing on a ledge, glaring down at me. Our eyes met, and then he turned and began racing up the canyon wall.

"Are you all right?" I asked Chajinka, who was just getting to his feet.

He brushed himself off, then made a digging motion and looked questioningly at me.

We didn't have any shovels, and it would take hours to dig even a shallow grave in the rocky ground using our hands. If we left Pollard's body where it was, it would be eaten by scavengers—but if we took the time to bury him, we'd lose the Snark.

*"Leave him here to his fate—it is getting so late!"*
*The Bellman exclaimed in a fright.*
*"We have lost half the day. Any further delay,*
*And we sha'n't catch a Snark before night."*

When we got halfway up the wall, I stopped and looked back. Alien raptors were circling high in the sky. Then the first of them landed next to Pollard and began pulling away bits of his flesh. I turned away and concentrated on the Snark.

It took an hour to reach the top, and then Chajinka spent a few minutes picking up the Snark's trail again. We followed it for another hour, and the landscape slowly changed, gradually becoming lush and green.

And then something strange happened. The trail suddenly became easy to follow.

Almost *too* easy.

We tracked him for another half hour. I sensed that he was near, and I was ready to fire at anything that moved. The humidity made my hands sweat so much that I didn't trust them not to slip on the stock and barrel, so I signaled Chajinka that I wanted to take a brief break.

I took a sip from my canteen. Then, as I leaned against a tree, wiping the moisture from my rifle, I saw a movement half a mile away.

It was *him!*

I pulled my rifle to my shoulder and took aim—but we were too far away. I leaped to my feet and began running after him. He turned, faced me for just an instant, and vanished into the bush.

When we got to where he'd been, we found that his trail led due north, and we began following it. At one point we stopped so I could remove a stinging insect from inside my boot—and suddenly I caught sight of him again. He roared and disappeared again into the heavy foliage as I raced after him.

It was almost as if the son of a bitch was *taunting* us, and I wondered: is he leading us into a trap?

And then I had a sudden flash of insight.

Rather than leading us *into* a trap, was he leading us *away* from something?

It didn't make much sense, but somewhere deep in my gut it felt right.

"*Stop!*" I ordered Chajinka.

He didn't know the word, but the tone of my voice brought him up short.

I pointed to the south. "This way," I said.

The Dabih frowned and pointed toward the Snark, saying something in his own tongue.

"I know he's there," I said. "But come this way anyway."

I began walking south. I had taken no more than four or five steps when Chajinka was at my side, jabbering again, and pulling my arm, trying to make me follow the Snark.

"No!" I said harshly. It certainly wasn't the word, so it must have been the tone. Whatever the reason, he shrugged, looked at me as if I was crazy, and fell into step behind me. He couldn't very well lead, since there was no trail and he didn't know where we were going. Neither did I, for that matter, but my every instinct said the Snark didn't want me going this direction, and that was reason enough to do it.

We'd walked for about fifteen minutes when I heard a hideous roar off to my left. It was the Snark, much closer this time, appearing from a new direction. He showed himself briefly, then raced off.

"I *knew* it!" I whispered excitedly to Chajinka, who just looked confused when I continued to ignore the Snark.

As we kept moving south, the Snark became bolder and bolder, finally getting within a hundred yards of us, but never showing himself long enough for me to get a shot off.

I could feel Chajinka getting tenser and tenser, and finally, when the Snark roared from thirty yards away, the little Dabih raised his spear above his head and raced after him.

"*No!*" I cried. "He'll kill you!"

I tried to grab him, but he was much too quick for me. I followed him into the eight-foot-high grass-like vegetation. It was a damned stupid thing to do: I couldn't see Chajinka, I couldn't see the Snark, and I had no room to maneuver or even sidestep if there was a charge. But he was my friend—probably, if I was honest, my *only* friend—and I couldn't let him face the Snark alone.

Suddenly I heard the sounds of a scuffle. There was some growling, Chajinka yelled once, and then all was silent.

I went in the direction I thought the sounds had come from, pushing the heavy grasses aside. Then I was making my way through thornbush, and the thorns ripped at my arms and legs. I paid no attention, but kept looking for Chajinka.

I found him in a clearing. He'd put up the fight of his life—his wounds attested to that—but even with his spear he was no match for a 400-pound predator. He recognized me, tried to say something that I wouldn't have understood anyway, and died just as I reached his side.

I knew I couldn't stay in the heavy bush with the Snark still around. This was *his* terrain. So I made my way back to the trail and continued to the south. The Snark roared from cover, but didn't show himself.

After another quarter mile I came to a huge tree with a hollow trunk. I was about to walk around it when I heard a high-pitched whimpering coming from inside it. I approached it carefully, my rifle ready, the safety off—

—and suddenly the Snark broke out of cover no more than fifteen yards away and charged me with an ear-splitting roar.

He was on me so fast that I didn't have time to get off a shot. He swiped at me with a mighty paw. I ducked and turned away, but the blow caught me on the shoulder and sent me flying. I landed on my back, scrambled to my feet, and saw him standing maybe ten feet away. My rifle was on the ground right next to him.

He charged again. This time I was ready. I dove beneath his claws, rolled as I hit the ground, got my hands on my weapon, and got off a single shot as he turned to come at me again.

"Got you, you bastard!" I yelled in triumph.

At first I thought I might have hit him too high in the chest to prove fatal, but he collapsed instantly, blood spurting from the wound—and I noticed that he had a festering wound on his side, doubtless from Marx's shot a week ago. I watched him for a moment, then decided to "pay the insurance," the minimal cost of a second bullet, to make sure he didn't get back up and do any damage before he died. I walked over to stick the muzzle of my rifle in his ear, found that I didn't have a clear shot, and reached out to nudge his head around with my toe.

I felt something like an electric surge within my head, and suddenly, though I'd never experienced anything remotely like it before, I knew I was in telepathic communication with the dying Snark.

*Why did you come to my land to kill me?* he asked, more puzzled than angry.

I jumped back, shocked—and lost communication with him. Obviously it could only happen when we were in physical contact. I squatted down and took his paw in my hands, and felt his fear and pain.

Then he was dead, and I stood up and stared down at him, my entire universe turned upside down—because during the brief moment that I had shared his thoughts, I learned what had *really* happened.

The Snark's race, sentient but non-technological, was never numerous, and had been wiped out by a virulent disease. Through some fluke, he alone survived it. The others had died decades ago, and he had led a life of terrifying loneliness ever since.

He knew our party was on Dodgson IV the very first day

we landed. He was more than willing to share his hunting ground with us, and made no attempt to harm us or scare us off.

He had thought the killing of the crystal-horned buck was a gift of friendship; he didn't understand that he was stealing Marx's trophy because the concept of trophies was completely alien to him. He killed Marx only after Marx wounded him.

Even then he was willing to forgive us. Those dead animals we found in my traps were his notion of a peace offering.

He couldn't believe that we really wanted to kill him, so he decided he would visit the camp and try to communicate with us. When he got there, he mistook the Dabihs' t-packs for weapons and destroyed them. Then, certain that this would be seen as an act of aggression even though he hadn't harmed anyone, he left before we woke up.

He came back to try one last time to make peace with us. This time he made no attempt to enter the camp unseen. He marched right in, fully prepared to be questioned and examined by these new races. But what he *wasn't* prepared for was being attacked by the Dabihs. Fighting in self-defense, he made short work of them. Mbele raced into the ship, either to hide or to get a weapon. He knew first-hand what Marx's weapon had done to him at fifty yards, and he didn't dare let Mbele shoot at him from the safety of the ship, so he raced into it and killed him before he could find a weapon.

After that it was war. He didn't know why we wanted to kill him, but he no longer doubted that we did . . . and while there was a time when he would have welcomed an end to his unhappy, solitary existence, he now had a reason, indeed a driving urge, to stay alive at all costs . . .

. . . because he wasn't a *he* at all; he was an *it*. The Snark was an asexual animal that reproduced by budding. Its final thought was one of enormous regret, not that it would die, for it understood the cycles of life and death, but that now its offspring would die as well.

I stared down at the Snark's body, my momentary feeling of triumph replaced by an overwhelming sense of guilt. What I had thought was my triumph had become nothing less than genocide in the space of a few seconds.

I heard the whimpering again, and I walked back to the hollow tree trunk and looked in. There, trembling and shrinking back from me, was a very small, very helpless version of the Snark.

I reached out to it, and it uttered a tiny, high-pitched growl as it huddled against the back of the trunk.

I spoke gently, moved very slowly, and reached out again. This time it stared at my hand for a long moment, and finally, hesitantly, reached out to touch it. The instant we made contact I was able to feel its all-encompassing terror.

*Do not be afraid, little one,* I said silently. *Whatever happens, I will protect you. I owe you that much.*

Its fear vanished, for you cannot lie when you are telepathically linked, and a moment later it emerged from its hiding place.

I looked off into the distance. Men would be coming soon. The rescue party would touch down in the next week or two. They'd find Marx's body in the hold, and they'd exhume the Desmonds and Mbele and the eleven Dabihs. They'd read the Captain's diary and know that all this carnage was caused by an animal called a Snark.

And since they were a hunting company, they'd immediately outfit a safari to kill the Snark quickly and efficiently. No argument could possibly deter them, not after losing an entire party of Men and Dabihs.

But they would be in for a surprise, because *this* Snark not only knew the terrain, but knew how Men thought and acted, and was armed with Man's weapons.

The infant reached out to me and uttered a single word. I tried to repeat it, laughed at how badly I mispronounced it, took the tiny creature in my arms, and went off into the bush to learn a little more about being a Father Snark while there was still time.

*In the midst of the word he was trying to say,*
*In the midst of his laughter and glee,*
*He had softly and suddenly vanished away—*
*For the Snark was a Boojum, you see.*

# REDCHAPEL

an alternate history in which Theodore Roosevelt, Esq. encounters the hideous fiend known only as Jack the Ripper

> *"From Hell, Mr. Lusk—*
> *Sir, I send you half the Kidne I took from one woman,*
> *prasarved it for you tother piece I fried and ate it was very nise*
> *I may send you the bloody knif that too it out if you only wate a*
> *whil longer*
> *signed Catch me when yu can Mishter Lusk"*
>
> *—Jack the Ripper*
> *October 16, 1888*

> *"I have not a particle of sympathy with the sentimentality*
> *—as I deem it, the mawkishness—which overflows with foolish*
> *pity for the criminal and cares not at all for the victim of the*
> *criminal."*
>
> *—Theodore Roosevelt*
> *Autobiography*
> *The date was September 8, 1888*

A hand reached out of the darkness and shook Roosevelt by the shoulder.

He was on his feet in an instant. His right hand shot out, crunching against an unseen jaw, and sending his assailant crashing against a wall. He crouched low, peering into the shadows, trying to identify the man who was clambering slowly to his feet.

"What the devil happened?" muttered the man.

"My question precisely," said Roosevelt, reaching for his pistol and training it on the intruder. "Who are you and what are you doing in my room?"

A beam of moonlight glanced off the barrel of the gun.

"Don't shoot, Mr. Roosevelt!" said the man, holding up his hands. "It's me—John Hughes!"

Roosevelt lit a lamp, keeping the gun pointed at the small, dapper man. "You haven't told me what you're doing here."

"Besides losing a tooth?" said Hughes bitterly as he spit a tooth into his hand amid a spray of blood. "I need your help."

"What is this all about?" demanded Roosevelt, looking toward the door of his hotel room as if he expected one of Hughes' confederates to burst through the door at any moment.

"Don't you remember?" said Hughes. "We spoke for more than an hour last night, after you addressed the Royal Ornithological Society."

"What has this got to do with birds?" said Roosevelt. "And you'd better come up with a good answer. I'm not a patient man when I'm rudely awakened in the middle of the night."

"You don't remember," said Hughes accusingly.

"Remember *what?*"

Hughes pulled out a badge and handed it to the American. "I am a captain of the London Metropolitan Police. After your speech we talked and you told me how you had single-handedly captured three armed killers in your Wild West."

Roosevelt nodded. "I remember."

"I was most favorably impressed," said Hughes.

"I hope you didn't wake me just to tell me that."

"No—but it was the fact that you have personally dealt with a trio of brutal killers that made me think—hope, actually—that you might be able to help me." Hughes paused awkwardly as the American continued to stare at him. "You *did* say that if I ever needed your assistance . . ."

"Did I say to request it in the middle of the night?" growled Roosevelt, finally putting his pistol back on his bed table.

"Try to calm yourself. Then I'll explain."

"This is as calm as I get under these circumstances." Roosevelt took off his nightshirt, tossed it on the four-poster bed, then walked to an ornate mahogany armoire, pulled out a pair of pants and a neatly folded shirt, and began getting dressed. "Start explaining."

"There's something I want you to see."

"At this hour?" said Roosevelt suspiciously. "Where is it?"

"It's not far," said Hughes. "Perhaps a twenty-minute carriage ride away."

"What is it?"

"A body."

"And it couldn't wait until daylight?" asked Roosevelt.

Hughes shook his head. "If we don't have her in the morgue by daylight, there will be panic in the streets."

"I'm certainly glad you're not given to exaggeration," remarked Roosevelt sardonically.

"If anything," replied the small Englishman seriously, "that was an understatement."

"All right. Tell me about it."

"I would prefer that you saw it without any preconceptions."

"Except that it could cause a riot if seen in daylight."

"I said a panic, not a riot," answered Hughes, still without smiling.

Roosevelt buttoned his shirt and fiddled with his tie.

"What time is it, anyway?"

"6:20 A.M."

"The sun's not an early riser in London, is it?"

"Not at this time of year." Hughes shifted his weight awkwardly.

"Now what's the matter?"

"We have a crisis on our hands, Mr. Roosevelt. I realize that I have no legal right to enlist your help, but we are quite desperate."

"Enough hyperbole," muttered Roosevelt, slipping on his coat.

"You *really* hunted down those murderers in a blizzard?" said Hughes suddenly.

"The Winter of the Blue Snow," said Roosevelt, nodding his head briskly. "Doubtless exaggerated by every dime novelist in America."

"But you *did* bring them back, alone and unarmed," persisted the Englishman, as if Roosevelt's answer was the most important thing in his life.

"Yes . . . but I knew the territory, and I knew who and where the killers were. I don't know London, and I assume the identity of the killer you're after is unknown."

"So to speak."

"I don't understand," said Roosevelt, adjusting his hat in front of a mirror.

"We don't know who he is. All we know is that he calls himself Saucy Jack."

The two men approached the police line behind the Black Swan. The night fog had left the pavement damp, and there was a strong smell of human waste permeating the area. Chimneys spewed thick smoke into the dawn sky, and the sound of a horse's hooves and a cart's squeaking wheels could be heard in the distance.

"Sir?" asked one of the constables, looking from Hughes to Roosevelt.

"It's all right, Jamison," said Hughes. "This is Theodore Roosevelt, a colleague from America. He is the man who brought Billy the Kid and Jesse James to justice."

Constable Jamison stepped aside immediately, staring at the young American in awe.

"Now, why did you say that, John?" asked Roosevelt in low tones.

"It will establish respect and obedience much faster than if I told him you were an expert on birds."

The American sighed. "I see your point." He paused. "Just what am I supposed to be looking at?"

"It's back here," said Hughes, leading him behind the building to an area that had been temporarily lit by flaming torches.

They stopped when they were about ten feet away. There was a mound beneath a blood-drenched blanket.

"Steel yourself, Mr. Roosevelt," said Hughes.

"After all the monographs I've written on taxidermy, I don't imagine you can show me anything that can shock me," answered Roosevelt.

He was wrong.

The blanket was pulled back, revealing what was left of a middle-aged woman. Her throat had been slit so deeply that she was almost decapitated. A bloody handkerchief around her neck seemed to be the only thing that stopped her head from rolling away.

Her belly was carved open, and her innards were pulled out and set on the ground just above her right shoulder. Various internal organs were mutilated, others were simply missing.

"What kind of creature could do something like this?" said Roosevelt, resisting the urge to retch.

"I was hoping you might be able to tell *us,*" said Hughes.

Roosevelt tore his horrified gaze from the corpse and turned to Hughes. "What makes you think I've ever encountered anything like this before?"

"I don't know, of course," said Hughes. "But you *have* lived in America's untamed West. You have traveled among the aboriginal savages. You have rubbed shoulders with frontier cowboys and shootists. Americans are a simpler, more brutal people—barbaric, in ways—and I had hoped . . ."

"I take it you've never been to America."

"No, I haven't."

"Then I shall ignore the insult, and only point out that Americans are the boldest, bravest, most innovative people on the face of the Earth."

"I assure you I meant no offense," said Hughes quickly. "It's just that we are under enormous pressure to bring Saucy Jack to justice. I had hoped that you might bring some fresh insight, some different methodology . . ."

"I'm not a detective," said Roosevelt, walking closer to the corpse. "There was never any question about the identities of the three killers I went after. As for *this* murder, there's not much I can tell you that you don't already know."

"Won't you try?" said Hughes, practically pleading.

Roosevelt squatted down next to the body. "She was killed from behind, of course. She probably never knew the murderer was there until she felt her jugular and windpipe being severed."

"Why from behind?"

"If I were trying to kill her from in front, I'd stab her in a straightforward way—it would give her less time to raise her hand to deflect the blade. But the throat was slit, not punctured. And it had to be the first wound, because otherwise she would have screamed and someone would have heard her."

"What makes you think someone didn't?"

Roosevelt pointed to the gaping hole in the woman's abdomen. "He wouldn't have had the leisure to do *that* unless he was sure no one had seen or heard the murder." The American stood up again. "But you know all that."

"Yes, we do," said Hughes. "Can you tell us anything we *don't* know?"

"Probably not. The only other obvious fact is that the killer had some knowledge of anatomy."

"This hardly looks like the work of a doctor, Mr. Roosevelt," said Hughes.

"I didn't say that it was. But it was done by someone who knew where the various internal organs belonged, or else he'd never have been able to remove them in the dark. Take a look. There's no subcutaneous fat on the ground, and he didn't waste his time mutilating muscle tissue."

"Interesting," said Hughes. "Now that *is* something we didn't know." He smiled. "I think we should be very grateful that you are a taxidermist as well as an ornithologist." He covered the corpse once more, then summoned another constable. "Have her taken to the morgue. Use the alleyways and discourage onlookers."

The constable saluted and gathered a team of policemen to move the body.

"I assume we're through here," said Roosevelt, grateful that he no longer had to stare at the corpse.

"Yes. Thank you for coming."

Roosevelt pulled his timepiece out of a vest pocket and opened it.

"No sense going back to sleep. Why don't you come back to the Savoy with me and I'll buy breakfast?"

"I've quite lost my appetite, but I will be happy to join you for a cup of tea and some conversation, Mr. Roosevelt."

"Call me Theodore." He shook his head. "Poor woman. I wonder who she was?"

Hughes pulled a notebook out of his pocket. "Her name was Annie Chapman. She was a Whitechapel prostitute."

"Whitechapel?"

"Whitechapel is the section of the city we are in."

Roosevelt looked around, truly seeing it for the first time, as the sun began burning away the fog. "I hope New York never has a slum like this!" he said devoutly.

"Wait until New York has been around as long as London, and it will have this and worse," Hughes assured him.

"Not if I have anything to say about it," said Roosevelt, his jaw jutting out pugnaciously as he looked up and down the street.

Hughes was surprised by the intensity of the young man's obvious belief in himself. As they stared at the broken and boarded windows, the drunks lying in doorways and on the street, the mangy dogs and spavined cats and fat, aggressive rats, the endless piles of excrement from cart horses, the Englishman found himself wondering what kind of man who could view a woman's mutilated corpse with less distaste than he displayed toward surroundings that Hughes took for granted.

They climbed into Hughes' carriage, and the driver set off for the Savoy at a leisurely trot. Before long they were out of Whitechapel, and, Roosevelt noted, the air instantly seemed to smell fresher.

Roosevelt had eaten the last of his eggs, and was concentrating on his coffee when an officer entered the dining room and approached Hughes.

"I'm sorry to interrupt, sir," he said apologetically, "but they said at the Yard that this is of the utmost urgency."

He handed a small envelope to Hughes, who opened it and briefly looked at what it contained.

"Thank you," said Hughes.

"Will there be anything else, sir?" asked the officer. "Any reply?"

"No, that will be all."

The officer saluted, and when he left Hughes turned back to Roosevelt.

"What are your plans now, Theodore?"

"I have two more speeches to give on ornithology," answered Roosevelt, "and one on naval warfare, and then I board the boat for home on Friday."

"Let me tell you something about the murder you saw today," began Hughes.

"Thank you for letting me finish my breakfast first," said Roosevelt wryly.

"We have a madman loose in Whitechapel, Theodore," continued Hughes.

"That much is obvious."

"We knew that before today," said Hughes.

Roosevelt looked up. "This wasn't his first victim?"

"It was at least his second." Hughes paused. "It's possible that he's killed as many as five women."

"How can he still be at large?"

"We can't watch every Whitechapel prostitute every minute of the day and night."

"He only kills prostitutes?"

"Thus far."

"Were they all this brutally mutilated?"

"The last one—a girl named Polly Nichols—was. The first three suffered less grievous damage, which is why we cannot be sure they were all killed by the same hand."

"Well, you've got your work cut out for you," said Roosevelt. "I certainly don't envy you." He paused. "Have you any suspects so far?"

Hughes frowned. "Not really."

"What does that mean?"

"Nothing."

Roosevelt shrugged. "As you wish. But the subject of Saucy Jack is closed. Either you confide in me or I can't help."

Hughes looked around the half-empty dining room, then lowered his voice. "All right," he said in little more than a whisper. "But what I tell you must go no farther than this table. It is for you and you alone."

Roosevelt stared at him with open curiosity. "All right," he said. "I can keep a secret as well as the next man."

"I hope so."

"You sound like you're about to name Queen Victoria."

"This is not a joking matter!" whispered Hughes angrily. "I am convinced that the man who has been implicated is innocent, but if word were to get out . . ."

Roosevelt waited patiently.

"There are rumors, undoubtedly spread about by anarchists, that are little short of sedition," continued Hughes. "Scandalous behavior within one's own class is one thing— but murders such as you witnessed this morning . . . I simply cannot believe it!" He paused, started to speak, then stopped. Finally he looked around the room to make certain no one was listening. "I can't give you his name, Theodore. Without proof, that would be tantamount to treason." He lowered his voice even more. "He is a member of the Royal Family!"

"Every family's got its black sheep," said Roosevelt with a shrug.

Hughes stared at him, aghast. "Don't you understand what I'm telling you?"

"You think royalty can't go berserk just as easily as common men?"

"It's unthinkable!" snapped Hughes. He quickly glanced around the room and lowered his voice again. "This is not Rome, and our Royals are not Caligula and Nero." He struggled to regain his composure. "You simply do not comprehend the gravity of what I am confiding in you. If even a hint that we were investigating this slander were to get out, the government would collapse overnight."

"Do you really think so?" asked Roosevelt.

"Absolutely." The small, dapper policeman stared at Roosevelt. "I would like to enlist your aid in uncovering the *real* murderer before these vile rumors reach a member of the force who cannot keep his mouth shut."

"I don't believe you were listening to me," said Roosevelt. "My ship leaves on Friday morning."

"Without you, I'm afraid."

Roosevelt frowned. "What are you talking about?"

Hughes handed the envelope he'd been given across the table to Roosevelt.

"What is this?" demanded Roosevelt, reaching for his glasses.

"A telegram from your President Cleveland, offering us your services in the hunt for the madman."

Roosevelt read the telegram twice, then crumpled it up in a powerful fist and hurled it to the floor.

"Grover Cleveland doesn't give a tinker's damn about your murderer!" he exploded.

Hughes looked nervously around the room, and gestured the American to keep his voice down.

"He just wants to keep me from campaigning for his

Republican opponent!"

"Surely you will not disobey the request of your president!"

"I can if I choose to!" thundered Roosevelt. "He's my president, not my king, a difference that I gather was lost on you when you manipulated him into sending this!" He glowered at the telegram that lay on the floor. "I knew he was worried about Harrison, but this is beyond the pale!"

"I apologize," said Hughes. "I wanted a fresh outlook so badly, I seem to have overstepped my . . ."

"Oh, be quiet," Roosevelt interrupted him. "I'm staying."

"But I thought you said—"

"Americans rise to challenges. I'll rise to this one. I'm just annoyed at the way you went about securing my services." He frowned again. "I'll show that corrupt fool in the White House! I'll solve your murder *and* get back to the States in time to help Ben Harrison defeat him in the election!"

"You'll stay?" said Hughes. "I can't tell you what this means! And of course, I'll help you in any way I can."

"You can start by checking me out of this palace and finding me a room in Whitechapel."

"In *Whitechapel?*" repeated Hughes with obvious distaste. "My dear Theodore, it simply isn't done."

"Well, it's about to *get* done," said Roosevelt. "I saw the way the onlookers stared at you, as if you were the enemy, or at least a foreign power. If they're going to learn to trust me, then I've got to live like they do. I can't look for a killer until dinnertime, then come back to the Savoy, don a tuxedo, and mingle with the rich and the powerful until the next morning."

"If you insist."

"I do. I just want time to send a wire to my wife Edith, explaining why I won't be on the ship when it docks."

"We can send for her, if—"

"American men do not put their wives in harm's way," said Roosevelt severely.

"No, of course not," said Hughes, getting hastily to his feet. "I'll send my carriage by for you in an hour. Is there any other way I can assist you?"

"Yes. Gather all the newspaper articles and anything else you have on these murders. Once I've got a room in Whitechapel, I'll want all the material sent there."

"You can have everything we've got on Saucy Jack."

"Some name!" snorted Roosevelt contemptuously.

"Well, he does seem to have acquired another one, though it's not clear yet whether he chose it himself or the press gave it to him."

"Oh?"

"Jack the Ripper."

"Much more fitting," said Roosevelt, nodding his head vigorously.

*My Dearest Edith:*

*I'm having Mr. Carlson hand deliver this letter to you, to explain why I'm not aboard the ship.*

*Let me first assure you that I'm in perfect health. My extended stay here is due to a pair of conscienceless culprits—the President of the United States and someone known only as Jack the Ripper.*

*The latter has embarked on a rampage of murder that would shock even our own Western shootists such as Doc Holliday and Johnny Ringo. You do not need to know the details, but believe me when I say that this fiend must be brought to justice.*

*An officer from Scotland Yard has read of my experiences in the Dakota Bad Lands and asked Grover Cleveland to "loan" me to the British until these murders have been solved—and Cleveland pounced on such an excuse to remove me from the upcoming campaign.*

*With luck, I'll have things sorted out and solved in time to see Ben Harrison give his victory speech in a little less than two months.*

*My best to Alice and little Ted.*
*Your Theodore*

Roosevelt sat on a rickety wooden chair, his back to the window, thumbing through Hughes' files.

It was clear that Polly Nichols was a Ripper victim. He doubted that the three who preceded her—Emma Smith, Ada Wilson, and Martha Tabram—were. They'd been brutally murdered, but the *modus operandi* differed appreciably from the two most recent killings.

The files were very circumspect about the Royal who had come under suspicion, but Roosevelt deduced that it was Prince Eddy, more formally Albert Victor, son of the Prince of Wales and, quite possibly, the future King of England.

Roosevelt put the papers down, leaned back on his chair, and closed his eyes. It just didn't make any sense. It would be as if Grover Cleveland had walked into a Washington slum and killed a pair of women and no one had recognized him. It was true that Prince Eddy was a dissolute and depraved man, and Roosevelt held him in total contempt—but there was just no way he could walk fifty yards in any direction, in or out of Whitechapel, without being recognized.

He removed his spectacles, rubbed his eyes, and then stood up. It was time to stop hypothesizing and go out and meet the residents of the area. He needed to talk to them, get to know them, and learn *their* opinions, which, he was sure, would be worth more than the police's.

He walked over to a decrepit coat rack, then paused and smiled. He crossed the room to his steamer trunk, opened it, and a few moments later was dressed in the fringed buckskin he wore at his Dakota ranch. (It had been designed by his favorite New York haberdasher, since all the Dakotans were busily trying to look like New Yorkers.) He took off his shining black shoes and pulled on a pair of well-worn boots. Then he tucked a knife and a pistol into his belt.

He considered a coonskin hat, but decided to wear a Stetson instead. He looked at himself in the fly-specked mirror and grinned in approval. As long as he was going to be identified as an American the moment he opened his mouth, he might as well dress like one.

He walked out the door of his shabby building, and was immediately aware that he had become an object of notoriety. Every pedestrian within sight stopped to stare at him. Even horse-drawn carriages slowed down as they passed by.

He grinned at them, waved, and began making his way to the Black Swan, next to where Annie Chapman's body had been found. A number of curious onlookers had followed him, and most of them entered the tavern when he did.

He walked up to the bar, staring approvingly at his image in the mirror that faced him.

"I didn't know the circus had come to Whitechapel!" laughed a burly man who was standing a few feet away.

Roosevelt smiled and extended his hand. "Theodore Roosevelt. Pleased to meet you."

"Hey, you're a yank!" said the man. "Ain't never met one before." He paused and frowned. "Don't rightly know if I like yanks."

"Them the duds you fight Indians in, guv?" asked another.

"We don't fight Indians any more," answered Roosevelt.

"Killed 'em all, did you?"

"No. Now we live side by side with them."

"I heard they was all killers," said the burly man. "They go around cuttin' people's heads off."

"Most of them are pretty decent people," said Roosevelt, seeing an opportunity to bring up the subject he wanted to discuss. "And even the bad ones couldn't hold a candle to your Saucy Jack."

"Old Jack?" said the burly man with a shrug. "He's off the deep end, he is. Mad as a hatter and ten times as vicious."

"Has anyone here seen him?" asked Roosevelt.

"The only people what's seen him is lying in the morgue chopped up in bits and pieces," said a woman.

"They say he eats their innards," offered another, looking scared as she downed her drink.

"He only goes after women," added the burly man. "Men either fight too hard or don't taste so good."

"Maybe your women should go armed," suggested Roosevelt.

"What good would it do?" responded a woman. "If you're with a John, you don't need no weapon—and if you find you're with old Jack, you ain't got time to use it."

"That's muddled thinking," said Roosevelt.

"Who are you to come in here and tell us how to think?" said the burly man pugnaciously.

"I'm a friend who wants to help."

"Not if you don't live in Whitechapel, you ain't," said the man. "We ain't got no friends except for them what's stuck here."

"You didn't give me a chance to answer," said Roosevelt. "Yes, I live in Whitechapel."

"I ain't never seen you around," said a man from the back of the tavern.

"Me neither," chimed in another.

"I just arrived."

"This ain't a place where you 'arrive,' yank," said the burly man. "It's a place where you get dumped while the rest of London pisses on you."

"Bloody right!" said another of the women, "I'll bet the coppers are probably cheering for old Jack. Every time he strikes, there's less of us for them to worry about."

"If the police won't hunt him down, we'll have to do it ourselves," said Roosevelt.

"What do you mean—*ourselves?*" said the burly man. "You ain't one of us! What do you care?"

"All right-thinking men should care," responded Roosevelt. "There's a crazed killer out there. We have to protect society and bring him to the bar of justice."

"What kind of man dresses like a dandy and wants to hunt down Jack the Ripper? It just don't make no sense." He glared at the American. "You sure you ain't a writer for one of them magazines—them penny dreadfuls, here to make a hero out of old Jack?"

"I told you: I want to hunt him down."

"And when he jumps you, you'll point out that it's not fair to hit a man with spectacles!" guffawed the burly man.

Roosevelt removed his glasses, folded them carefully, and set them down on the bar.

"There are many things I don't need glasses for," he said, jutting out his chin. "You're one of them."

"Are you challenging me to a fight, yank?" said the burly man, surprised.

"Personally, I'd much rather fight the Ripper," said Roosevelt. "But it's up to you."

The man suddenly laughed and threw a huge arm around Roosevelt's shoulders. "I like your nerve, yank! My name's

Colin Shrank, and you and me are going to be great friends!"

Roosevelt grinned. "That suits me just fine. Let me buy you a drink."

"A pint of ale!" Shrank yelled to the bartender. He turned back to Roosevelt. "You're here too early, yank. Old Jack, he only comes out at night."

"But I see a number of ladies here, and at least some of them must be prostitutes," said Roosevelt.

"They ain't hardly ladies," said Shrank with a laugh, "and they're here because he's got 'em too scared to work at night, which is the proper time for their particular business."

"Too bloody true!" chimed in one of the women. "You ain't gettin' *me* out after dark!"

"I don't even feel safe in the daylight," said another.

"Did anyone here know Polly Nichols or Annie Chapman?" asked Roosevelt.

"I knew Annie," said the bartender. "Came here near every night to find a new bloke. Nice lady, she was."

"Why would she go off with the Ripper?" asked Roosevelt.

"Well, she didn't know it was the Ripper, now did she?" answered the bartender.

Roosevelt shook his head. "Everyone in Whitechapel knows that prostitutes are at risk, so why would Annie go out with someone she didn't know?"

"There's thousands of men come here every night," answered one of the prostitutes. "Maybe tens of thousands. What're the odds any one of them is Jack the Ripper?"

"It ain't *our* fault," said another. "We're just out to make a living. It's the police and the press and all them others. They don't care what happens here. They'd burn Whitechapel down, and us with it, if they thought they could get away with it."

A heavyset woman entered the tavern, walked right up to

the bar, and thumped it with her fist.

"Yeah, Irma," said the bartender. "What'll it be?"

"A pint," she said in a deep voice.

"Hard night?"

"Four of 'em." She shook her head disgustedly. "You'd think they'd learn. They never do."

"That's what they've got you for," said the bartender.

She grimaced and took her beer to a table.

"What was that all about?" asked Roosevelt.

"Irma, she's a midwife," answered Shrank.

"She delivered four babies last night?"

Shrank seemed amused. "She cut four of 'em out before they became a bother."

"A *midwife* performs abortions?" said Roosevelt, surprised. "Don't you have doctors for that?"

"Look around you, yank. There's ten times as many rats as people down here. A gent's got to be as well-armed as you if he don't want to get robbed. Women are being sliced to bits by a monster and no one does nothing about it. So you tell me: why would a doctor work here if he could work anywhere else?"

"No one cares about Whitechapel," said Irma bitterly.

"Well, they'd better *start* caring," said Roosevelt. "Because if this butcher isn't caught, you're going to be so awash in blood that you might as well call it Redchapel."

"Redchapel," repeated Shrank. "I like that! Hell, if we change the name, maybe they'd finally pay attention to what's going on down here."

"Why do you think he's going to kill again?" asked the bartender.

"If his motive is to kill prostitutes, there are still hundreds of them left in Whitechapel."

"But everyone knows he's crazy," said Shrank. "So maybe

he never had no motive at all."

"All the more reason for him to strike again," said Roosevelt. "If he had no reason to start, then he also has no reason to stop."

"Never thought of that," admitted Shrank. He gave Roosevelt a hearty slap on the back. "You got a head on your shoulders, yank! What do you do back in America?"

"A little of everything," answered Roosevelt. "I've been a politician, a rancher, a Deputy Marshall, a naturalist, an ornithologist, a taxidermist, and an author."

"That's a hell of a list for such a young bloke."

"Well, I have one other accomplishment that I'm glad you didn't make me show off," said Roosevelt.

"What was that?"

Roosevelt picked his glasses up from the bar and flashed Shrank another grin. "I was lightweight boxing champion of my class at Harvard."

*My Dearest Edith:*

*I must be a more formidable figure than I thought. No sooner do I agree to help apprehend Jack the Ripper than he immediately goes into hiding.*

*I have spent the past two weeks walking every foot of the shabby slum known as Whitechapel, speaking to everyone I meet, trying to get some information—any information—about this madman who is making headlines all over the world. It hasn't been productive—though in another way it has, for it has shown me how not to govern a municipality, and I suspect the day will come when that will prove very useful knowledge indeed.*

*I know America has its rich and its poor, its leaders and its followers, but any man can, through his own sweat and skills, climb to the top of whatever heap he covets. I find England's class system stifling, and I keep wondering where America would be if, for example, Abraham Lincoln had been forced to remain the penniless frontiersman he had been born. We have Negroes who were born into slavery who will someday hold positions of wealth and power, and while slavery is a shameful blot on our history, it was a system that men of good will and reason eventually destroyed. I see no such men attempting to bring about the necessary changes in British society.*

*I walk through Whitechapel, and I can envision what a handful of Americans, with American know-how and American values, could do to it in five years' time. And yet I fear it is doomed to remain exactly what it is until the buildings finally collapse of their own decrepitude.*

*I have made some friends among the residents, many of whom have been extremely hospitable to an alien. (Yes, I know I was well treated by the Royal Society, but I came there with a reputation as an expert. I came to Whitechapel only as an outsider. And yet I find I prefer to rub shoulders with the common man on this side of the ocean, even as I have always done at home.)*

*One special friend is a day laborer (who seems to labor as infrequently as possible) named Colin Shrank, who has been my guide down the fog-shrouded streets and filthy alleys of Whitechapel. As I say, we've discovered no useful information, but at least I now feel I have a reasonably thorough working knowledge of the geography of the place, a knowledge I will be only too happy to expunge the moment I return to our beloved Sagamore Hill.*

> *My best to Alice and little Ted.*
> *Your Theodore*

Roosevelt opened a letter, tossing the envelope carelessly on the bar of the Black Swan.

"Another note from your pal Hughes?" asked Shrank.

Roosevelt nodded. "He's through asking who the Ripper is. Now he just wants to know if he's through killing women."

Shrank shrugged. "Could be."

Roosevelt shook his head. "I doubt it. I think he takes too much joy in killing and disemboweling helpless women."

"Up against a man with a knife like that, they're *all* helpless," offered Shrank.

"Not so, Colin." Roosevelt looked around the tavern, and his gaze came to rest on Irma, the burly midwife. "The women he's attacked have all been on the slender side. If he went after someone like Irma here, he might have a real battle on his hands."

"I'm no prostitute!" snapped Irma indignantly. "I honor the Bible and the Commandments!"

"No offense intended," said Roosevelt quickly. "I was just suggesting that perhaps being a prostitute is not the Ripper's sole criterion, that maybe he goes after women he knows he can dispatch quickly."

"Why quickly, if he's having such a good time?" asked the bartender.

"Secrecy is his ally," answered Roosevelt. "He can't butcher them unless he kills them before they can scream. That means they can't struggle for more than a second or two."

"Ever been anything like him in America?" asked Shrank.

"Not to my knowledge. Certainly not in our cities, where such crimes would not go unnoticed and unreported."

"They gets noticed and reported, all right," said a woman. "Just no one cares, is all."

Roosevelt looked out the window. "It's starting to get dark." He walked to the door. "Come on, Colin. It's time to make our rounds."

"You go alone tonight," said Shrank, taking a drink of his ale.

"Aren't you feeling well?"

"I feel fine. But I been walking those damned bloody streets with you every night since he chopped Annie Chapman. It's been raining all day, and the wind bites right through my clothes to my bones, so I'm staying here. If you spot him, give a holler and I'll join you."

"Stick around, Theodore," added the bartender. "He ain't out there. Hell, he's probably got his throat sliced on the waterfront."

Roosevelt shook his head. "If I can save a single life by patrolling the streets, then I have no choice but to do it."

"That's the coppers' job," insisted Shrank.

"It's the job of every civic-minded citizen who cares about the safety of Whitechapel," replied Roosevelt.

"That lets you out. You ain't no citizen."

"Enough talk," said Roosevelt, standing at the door, hands on hips. "You're sure you won't come with me?"

"I can't even keep up with you in *good* weather," said Shrank.

Roosevelt shrugged. "Well, I can't stand here talking all night."

He turned and walked out into the fog for another fruitless night of hunting for the Ripper.


Roosevelt felt a blunt object poking his shoulder. He sat up, swinging wildly at his unseen assailant.

"Stop, Theodore!" cried a familiar voice. "It's me—John Hughes."

Roosevelt swung his feet to the floor. "You're lucky I didn't floor you again."

"I learned my lesson the first time," said Hughes, displaying a broom. "The handle's two meters long."

"All right, I'm awake," said Roosevelt. "Why are you here?"

"Jack the Ripper has struck again."

"*What?*" yelled Roosevelt, leaping to his feet.

"You heard me."

"What time is it?" asked Roosevelt as he threw his clothes on.

"About 3:30 in the morning."

"It's Sunday, right?"

"That's correct."

"Damn! I only went to bed about half an hour ago! Where did it happen?"

"In a little court off Berner Street," said Hughes. "And this time he was interrupted."

"By whom?"

"We're not sure."

"That doesn't make sense."

"Come with me, and I'll explain."

Roosevelt finished dressing. "Let's go."


"There it is," said Hughes as he and Roosevelt stared at the woman's body. The head lay in a pool of blood. "He cut her throat and slashed her face, but there's no other damage. He'd pulled her dress up and was just about to cut her belly open when he was interrupted."

"What makes you think he was interrupted?" asked Roosevelt. "Why couldn't he just have stopped for some other reason?"

"Because those two gentlemen"—Hughes pointed at a pair of locals who were speaking with two officers—"heard the scuffle and approached from different directions. We don't know which one startled him—for all we know, he might have heard them both—but he suddenly took flight. They saw the body, realized what had happened, and gave chase."

"For how long?"

Hughes shrugged. "Three or four blocks, before they knew for sure they'd lost him."

"Did they get a glimpse of him?" persisted Roosevelt. "Any kind of description at all?"

Hughes shook his head. "But one of them, Mr. Packer, alerted us, and the body was still warm and bleeding when we found it. We couldn't have missed him by five minutes." He paused. "We've got a hundred men scouring every street and alley in Whitechapel. With a little luck we may find him."

"May I speak to the two witnesses?" asked Roosevelt.

"Certainly."

Hughes accompanied Roosevelt as the American approached the men. "This is Mr. Roosevelt," he announced. "Please answer his questions as freely as you would answer mine."

Roosevelt walked up to the taller of the two men. "I only have a couple of questions for you. The first is: how old are you?"

"34," said the man, surprised.

"And how long have you lived in Whitechapel?"

"All my life, guv."

"Thank you."

"That's all you want to know?" asked the man.

"That's all," said Roosevelt. He turned to the smaller man. "Could you answer the same two questions, please?"

"I'm 28. Ain't never been nowhere else." He paused. "Well, I took the missus to the zoo once."

"Thank you. I have no further questions." He shook the smaller man's hand, then walked back to look at the corpse again. "Have you identified her yet?"

Hughes nodded. "Elizabeth Stride. Long Liz, they called her."

"A prostitute, of course?"

"Yes."

"When was the last time anyone saw her alive?"

"She was seen at Bricklayers Tavern just before midnight," answered Hughes.

"With a customer?"

"Yes, but she'd already serviced him. He has an alibi for the time of the murder."

"Which was when?"

"About 45 minutes ago." Hughes looked off into the fog. "I wonder if he's still out there?"

"If he is, I'm sure that—"

He was interrupted by a woman's scream.

"Where did *that* come from?" demanded Hughes.

"I don't know, sir," said one of the policemen. "Either straight ahead or off to the left. It's difficult to tell."

He turned back to Roosevelt. "What do you . . . *Theodore!!!*"

But the American was already racing into the fog, gun in hand.

"Follow him!" shouted Hughes to his men.

"But—"

"He's a hunter! I trust his instincts!"

They fell into stride behind Roosevelt, who ran through the darkness until he reached Church Passage. He leaned forward in a gunfighter's crouch and peered into the fog.

"It came from somewhere near here," he whispered as Hughes finally caught up with him. "Where does this thing lead?" he asked, indicating the narrow passage.

"To Mitre Street."

"Let's go," said Roosevelt, moving forward silently. He traversed the passage, emerged on Mitre Street, spotted a bulky object in an open yard, and quickly ran over to it.

"Damn!" muttered Hughes as he joined the American. "Another one!"

"Post a man to watch the body and make sure no one touches anything," said Roosevelt. "The Ripper can't be more than a minute ahead of us."

He trotted off down Mitre Street. The police began using their whistles to identify each other, and soon the shrill noise became almost deafening. Roosevelt had gone a short distance when he heard a faint moaning coming from a recessed doorway. He approached the source warily, gun in hand.

"Who are you?" he demanded.

"Thank God it's you, sir!" said a familiar voice, and as he moved closer he realized that it was Irma, the midwife. He lit a match and saw a large bruise over her left temple.

"What happened?"

"I was coming back from Elsie Bayne's when I heard a woman scream. Then a bloke dressed all in black run down the street and bowled me over." She was overcome by a sudden dizziness.

"Did you see his features?"

"He had crazy eyes," said Irma. "The kind what gives you nightmares."

"What color were they?"

"I don't know," she said helplessly. "It's dark."

"How tall was he?"

"Taller than you, sir," she replied. "Much taller. And thin. Like a skeleton, he was!"

"Was there anything, however small, that you can remember?" demanded Roosevelt. "Think hard. It's important."

"All I know is he wore black gloves."

"No distinguishing marks?"

"Just the wound."

"Wound?" said Roosevelt, pouncing on the word. "What wound?"

"On his cheek. It was dripping blood, it was."

"Which cheek?"

"I don't remember."

"Please try."

She frowned as if trying to recall, then whimpered in pain. "I don't know, sir." She looked down the street, where some bobbies were approaching them. "He done sliced another one, didn't he, sir?"

The American nodded. "Not far from here."

"These poor women!" sobbed Irma, starting to cry. "When will it stop?"

Roosevelt stood up. "You're our only eyewitness," he said. "The police artist may want to speak to you later."

"But I done told you what I know!"

"Other details may come back to you. Try to cooperate with him."

She nodded her head while rubbing her tears away with a filthy coat sleeve, and Roosevelt turned to the nearest officer. "When she feels strong enough, take her to the nearest hospital." He turned and walked rapidly back to the latest victim.

"He really did a job on this one, sir," said one of the policemen, staring down at the corpse.

The woman's throat had been slit from ear to ear. The Ripper had then opened her up from neck to groin and gutted her like a fish. Each of her internal organs lay on the ground, neatly arranged in a seemingly meaningless pattern. A piece of her apron had been cut away; the Ripper had evidently used it to wipe his knife.

"Jesus!" said another officer, staring in fascination. "I never saw anyone sliced up like this!"

"You're the taxidermist, Theodore," said Hughes, joining them. "Can you tell if anything's missing?"

Roosevelt studied the organs. "A kidney, I think."

"I'll have the police surgeon make sure," said Hughes. He paused. "If you're right, then we have to ask the question: as crazy as he is, *why* would he steal her kidney?"

"I'd hate to know the answer to that one, sir," said one of the policemen.

"Does anyone know who she is?" asked Roosevelt.

"If she's got any identification on her, it's too blood-soaked to read it," replied Hughes. "We'll ask around. We should know by morning."

Roosevelt walked away from the corpse, then signaled Hughes to join him.

"What is it, Theodore?"

"I wanted to speak where we couldn't be overheard," replied Roosevelt. "I'm sure you'll be happy to know that we can definitely eliminate Prince Eddy from the list of suspects."

"I am, of course," said Hughes. "But how do you know?"

"I've met him," said Roosevelt. "He's a weak man, ravaged by disease. He could barely grip my hand."

"Are you saying he's too weak to have killed these women?" asked Hughes, looking unconvinced.

"Anyone can kill an unsuspecting victim with a knife," responded the American.

"Well, then?"

"Your two witnesses," said Roosevelt. "They were 28 and 34 years old, in the prime of life. They were healthy, and neither was carrying any excess weight. And they know their way around Whitechapel." Roosevelt paused. "How could such an ill man, especially one who doesn't know the area, outrun them? Remember, they said they chased him for three or four blocks. The Albert Victor I met couldn't have run for *one* block, let alone four."

"Thank you, Theodore," said Hughes, obviously relieved. "You've lifted an enormous burden from me."

"Forget about him, and concentrate on what we *do* know," said the American. "For example, we know that the Ripper has an intimate knowledge of Whitechapel or he couldn't have evaded his pursuers. In fact, he evaded pursuit twice in one night, because we couldn't have been 60 seconds behind him at the site of *this* murder, and he vanished like an Apache in the Arizona hills."

"He probably ducked into a building after he bumped into the midwife," said Hughes.

"How would he know which ones were unlocked if he didn't know the area like the back of his hand? Whatever else he may or may not be, the Ripper is a resident of Whitechapel."

"Blast!" muttered Hughes. "That probably clears a second suspect as well."

"Oh?"

"A Dr. Thomas Neill Cream. But he wouldn't know Whitechapel any better than Prince Eddy. Furthermore, he's quite fat. I doubt that he could have outrun *any*one."

Roosevelt stared off into the distance, frowning.

"Is something wrong, Theodore?"

"Of course something's wrong," said Roosevelt irritably. "That madman has butchered two more women right under our noses." He continued looking into the fog and frowning. "And I'm missing something."

"What?"

He frowned again. "I don't know. But it's something I *should* know, something I'm sure I've overlooked."

"Can I be of any assistance?" asked Hughes.

Roosevelt remained motionless for another moment, then shrugged and shook his head.

The morgue wagon arrived, Hughes began supervising the removal of the corpse, and Roosevelt went back to his room where he replayed the events of the evening over and over in his mind, looking for the detail he had missed.

*My Dearest Edith:*

*They identified the evening's second victim, a poor prostitute named Catherine Eddowes. I know I said I would be coming home shortly, but I cannot leave while this fiend remains at large.*

*There is no question that he will strike again, but when and where is almost impossible to predict. There seems to be no pattern to his murders until after he has dispatched his victim, and then the pattern is one that I shall not distress you by describing.*

*There was absolutely nothing I could do to prevent the four murders, but I have the uneasy feeling that I have the ability right now to prevent any further killings, if I could but see the tree rather than the forest. I am certain I know something that might lead to his apprehension, yet I have no idea what that knowledge may be.*

*Ah, well, there is no need to worry you with my problems. I shall be on the first ship home after this dreadful affair has been brought to a successful conclusion, hopefully in time to make a speech or two on Ben Harrison's behalf, and then perhaps we'll take Alice and little Ted on a vacation to Yosemite or the Yellowstone.*

*Your Theodore*

"Where were you last night?" demanded Roosevelt when he entered the Black Swan on the morning of October 1.

"Right here," answered Colin Shrank. "You think I sliced them two women?"

"I just want to know what time you went home," said Roosevelt.

"Two o'clock or so."

"The first of them wasn't killed until almost three."

"Well, it weren't me!" snapped Shrank. "I didn't kill no bloody women!"

"I never said you did," said Roosevelt.

"Then why all the questions?"

"Because the one night you didn't make the rounds with me, the Ripper claimed two more victims. I think I should at least inquire after your whereabouts."

"Where was *you?*" shot back Shrank.

"I was in bed when Elizabeth Stride was murdered, but I was in Captain Hughes' company when Catherine Eddowes was killed," replied Roosevelt.

"So are you saying I done it or not?" said Shrank belligerently, his hands balled into massive fists.

Roosevelt stared long and hard at the man, then sighed. "No, I'm not."

"Good!" said Shrank. "And just to show there's no hard feelings, I'll let you buy me a pint of ale."

Roosevelt nodded to the bartender. "And I'll take a cup of coffee."

"Ain't got no coffee, Mr. Roosevelt," said the bartender. "How about a cup of tea?"

"That'll do," said Roosevelt, walking over to a table and sitting down.

"Now we're friends again, what made you decide I *ain't*

the Ripper?" asked Shrank.

"Your education."

"What education?" laughed Shrank. "I ain't never been to school in my life!"

"*That* education," said Roosevelt. "If you killed someone, could you find the spleen?"

"What's a spleen?"

"How about the pancreas?"

"Never heard of them."

"Point to where you think my lungs are."

Shrank pointed.

"There's your answer," said Roosevelt. "The Ripper knows where those organs are."

"How do you know I'm not lying?" said Shrank.

"Where would you have learned?"

"Maybe I read it in a book."

"Can you read?"

Suddenly Shrank laughed aloud. "Not a word!"

Roosevelt smiled. "One more reason why you're not the Ripper."

"One *more?*" repeated Shrank. "What was the first?"

"I've seen you get winded *walking* three blocks. The Ripper *ran* for at least half a mile last night and eluded some very fit pursuers."

"Then why'd you come in asking questions like that?"

"I'm just being thorough."

"I thunk we was friends—mates, you might say," said Shrank.

"We are. But if you were the Ripper, that wouldn't stop me from putting you away."

"At least you give a damn. I can't say as much for the rest of 'em."

"You mean the police?" responded Roosevelt. "You misjudge them. They've got hundreds of men working on the case."

"Only because the press keeps goading 'em," said Shrank. "But they don't care about us or Whitechapel. They'll catch the Ripper and then cross us off the map again."

"What do you think would make them do something about Whitechapel?" asked Roosevelt.

"It'll sound balmy—but as long as Saucy Jack's around, they pay attention to us. Maybe having him ain't such a bad thing after all." Shrank laughed bitterly. "He slices up another 40 or 50 women, they might clean this place up and turn it into Hyde Park."

"No," said the bartender with a smile. "Mayfair."

"You really think so?" asked Roosevelt.

"Nobody paid no attention to us before the Ripper, Mr. Roosevelt, and that's a fact," said the bartender.

"That's a very interesting outlook," said Roosevelt. "But I'll keep trying to catch him anyway."

"Maybe old Jack is really your pal Hughes," offered Shrank. "Y'know, he's always the first one at the body."

Roosevelt shook his head. "I was with him when the second woman was killed last night."

"It's a puzzle, all right."

"There are a *lot* of puzzles in this case," said Roosevelt.

"You mean, besides who is he?" said Shrank.

"Yes," said Roosevelt. He frowned again. *For example,* he thought, *why would he have walked off with Catherine Eddowes' kidney?*

It took 16 days for Roosevelt to get his answer. Then Hughes summoned him and showed him a crudely scrawled message that had been sent to George Lusk, the head of the Whitechapel Vigilance Committee.

*"From Hell, Mr. Lusk—*

*Sir, I send you half the Kidne I took from one woman,*
*prasarved it for you tother piece I fried and ate it was very nise*
*I may send you the bloody knif that too it out if you only wate a*
*whil longer*

*signed Catch me when yu can Mishter Lusk"*

—*Jack the Ripper*
*October 16, 1888*

"Well, at least now we know why the kidney was missing," said Hughes. A look of disgust crossed his face. "Do you really think he ate it?"

Roosevelt shrugged. "Who knows? He's certainly *capable* of eating it." He stared at the letter. "Does the handwriting match the previous messages?"

Hughes nodded. "It's the same man, all right."

Roosevelt lowered his head in thought for a moment. "All right," he said. "Here's what you must do. Make copies of that letter and give it to every newspaper in London."

"We can't do that, Theodore! There would be widespread panic."

"I hope so."

"I beg your pardon!" said Hughes heatedly.

"Try to understand, John," said Roosevelt. "Everyone in Whitechapel has been aware of the Ripper for more than a month. Prostitutes know that they're his quarry, and yet they continue to ply their trade and put themselves at risk. Maybe if they read this, if they get a brief peek into the mind of this madman, we can keep them off the streets until he's apprehended."

"Keep prostitutes off the streets?" laughed a nearby policeman. "You might as well try to keep the sun from rising."

"It's that, or prepare yourselves for more murders."

"It's not my decision to make," replied Hughes. "You've been working on this case at my request, and I've been your sole contact, so you can be forgiven for thinking that I'm in charge . . . but in point of fact we have more than 500 police officers working around the clock on the Ripper murders. I'll have to go through channels before we can get it published."

"What if I just took it to the papers, and said that I hadn't told you what I'd planned?"

"You'd be on the first ship back to America, and I doubt that your presence would ever be tolerated in England again."

*That's no great loss in a land that worships royalty and allows something like Whitechapel to exist,* thought Roosevelt. Aloud he said, "All right, John—but hurry! The sooner this is made known to the press, the better."

Hughes picked up the letter and stared at it. "I'll do what I can," he said.

"So will we all," replied Roosevelt.

Nothing happened.

A day passed, then a week, then three. The police again began suggesting that the Ripper might have been killed by some other member of the criminal class—there were enough stabbings and bludgeonings in Whitechapel and on the waterfront to write *fini* to a dozen Rippers.

Even Roosevelt relaxed his guard. He spent a day birding in the Cotswolds. He made a speech to the Royal Zoological Society, and another to Parliament. He found the time to write three articles and more than one hundred letters.

And still, he couldn't rid himself of the nagging feeling that this was the calm before the storm, and that he possessed some small but vital piece of the puzzle that could help him prevent another murder.

On the evening of November 8, he sat down to write a letter to his wife.

*My Dearest Edith:*

*It has been almost six weeks since the fiend last struck, and most of the authorities here have convinced themselves that he is dead, possibly by his own hand, possibly murdered. I don't agree. There was no pattern of regularity to his prior killings. The first and second were separated by nine days, the second and third by 22 days, the third and fourth by no more than an hour. Since there has been no pattern, I don't see how they can conclude that he's broken one.*

*As I mentioned in previous letters, some of the police still lean toward Prince Albert Victor, which is simply beyond the realm of possibility. All of their other suspects also seem to come from the upper classes: a doctor, a lawyer, a shipbuilder. They mean well, the London Metropolitan Police, but they simply lack American practicality as they go about this most important and onerous task.*

*I may not send this letter to you at all, because I do not want the details to cause you dismay, but I need to clarify my thinking by putting things down on paper.*

*I begin with the question: what do we know about Jack the Ripper?*

*It's true that there is an eyewitness account that makes him a head taller than myself, and thoroughly emaciated, but it was made by a hysterical woman whose veracity cannot be relied upon. Still, it's all the police have to go on, and that is the man they are searching for.*

*But that is all we know empirically. The rest comes from logic—or the science of deduction, to borrow from Sherlock Holmes, the fictional detective who has made such an impact here in the past year.*

*And what can I deduce?*

*First, he has at least a rudimentary knowledge of anatomy. The nature of the mutilations implies that he takes pleasure in removing certain internal organs—and he was able to tell a kidney from other organs in near-total darkness on the night of September 30.*

*Second, he is trying to delude us into thinking he is illiterate. That letter of his is a masterpiece of misdirection—for if he is a doctor, or if he has even studied medicine for a year, how could his spelling, diction and penmanship be so indicative of a barely literate man?*

*Third, he must possess an intimate knowledge of Whitechapel. The only time he was seen he eluded his pursuers, and being unseen the other times also implies familiarity with his surroundings.*

*Fourth, these murders must be planned in advance—a theory I have not shared with the police, because none of them would accept such a notion. But damn it, he had to know when and where he would kill each of his victims! Because if he didn't, then how did he get fresh clothing, and without fresh clothing, how did this man, who must have been soaked in the blood of his victims, escape detection as he walked through the streets of Whitechapel on his way back to wherever he goes when his foul work is done? He must have had a clean set of clothes hidden within yards of his victim, and that implies premeditation.*

*Fifth, and this is the one that I cannot begin to answer: even though they have been alerted, even though they know the Ripper is lurking in the darkness, he is nonetheless able to approach his victims with complete impunity. Do they know him? Does he appear so wealthy that they feel it is worth the risk? What leads otherwise cautious women to allow this fiend to approach them? There has been no sign of a struggle at any of the murder scenes. No victim has tried to run from him.*

*Why?*

Roosevelt pulled out his timepiece and opened it. It was 3:40 A.M., and he realized that he had fallen asleep.

He looked at the letter, read it over, frowned, and began writing again.

*Why? Why? Why?*

Suddenly there was a pounding on his door.

"Theodore, wake up!" shouted Hughes. "He's struck again! It's the worst yet!"

Room #13, 26 Dorset Street, was a scene straight out of hell.

Marie Jeanette Kelly—or what remained of her—lay on a blood-soaked bed. Her throat has been slashed. Her abdomen was sliced open. Both her breasts were cut off. Her liver and entrails had been ripped out and placed between her feet. Flesh from her thighs and her breasts had been put on a nearby table. Her right hand was stuck in her belly.

"My God!" exclaimed Hughes, covering his mouth and nose with a handkerchief.

"He was crazy to begin with, but this is past all imagining," said another officer. "He didn't cut her organs out, like the others. He reached in and *pulled* them out with his hands!"

"He had to be drenched in blood," said Roosevelt. "Surely someone saw him, if not here, then walking the street, or trying to hide until he could change into a clean outfit."

"Nobody saw a thing, sir," said the officer.

"They *had* to!" exclaimed Roosevelt. "They couldn't have missed him." He frowned and muttered: "But why didn't it register?"

Roosevelt paused, motionless—and then, slowly, a grin crossed the American's face. The officer stared at him as if he might soon start running amuck.

The American turned and walked to the door.

"Where are you going, Theodore?" asked Hughes.

"Back to my room," answered Roosevelt. "There's nothing more to see here."

"I'll be seeing it in my nightmares for the next thirty years," said Hughes grimly.

Roosevelt went to his desk, opened a drawer, pulled out his pistol, filled it with cartridges, and put it in the pocket of his buckskin coat.

Then he took his pen out, and added a few lines to the letter he had been writing to Edith.

*I curse my own blindness! I could have prevented this latest atrocity. I knew everything I had to know more than a month ago, but I didn't put it together until tonight.*

*I am going out now, to make sure this fiend never kills again.*

Roosevelt sat in the dark, his pistol on his lap, waiting.

Finally the knob turned, and a short, burly figure entered the room.

"Hello, Jack," said Roosevelt, pointing his pistol at the figure.

"Jack? Who's Jack?"

"We both know what I'm talking about," said Roosevelt calmly.

"I just come back from helping poor Liza Willoughby!"

"No," said Roosevelt, shaking his head. "You just got back from murdering Marie Jeanette Kelly."

"You're daft!"

"And you're Jack the Ripper."

"You've done lost your bloody mind!" yelled Irma the midwife, finally stepping out of the shadows.

"The Ripper had to live in Whitechapel," said Roosevelt, never lowering the pistol. "He had to know the area intimately. Who knows it better than a woman who lives and works here and makes dozens of house calls every week?"

He watched her reaction, then continued.

"The Ripper had to have some knowledge of anatomy. Not much—but enough to know one organ from another. Your letter fooled me for awhile. I thought *it* was the misdirection, but I was wrong: you need no formal schooling for your work." He paused. "Are you following me so far?"

She glared at him silently.

"There were two things that bothered me," continued Roosevelt. "Why would these women let the Ripper approach them when they knew he was killing prostitutes in Whitechapel? They'd been warned repeatedly to watch out for strange men. But then I realized that you're a trusted, even a necessary, member of the community. They were all looking for Jack, not Jane.

"The other thing I couldn't figure out," he said, "was how the Ripper could walk around in blood-spattered clothing without drawing everyone's attention. I made the false assumption that the killer had picked the spots for his murders and hidden fresh clothing nearby." Roosevelt grimaced. "I was wrong. Those murders were so deranged I should have known there couldn't be anything premeditated about them. Then, when I was at Marie Kelly's apartment tonight, I saw how you ripped out her intestines with your hands and I *knew* how much blood you had to have splashed on yourself, it occurred to me that I've never seen you when you *weren't* wearing blood-stained clothes. After all, you do nothing all day but deliver babies and perform abortions; there's nothing unusual about a midwife's clothing being bloody."

"So maybe a midwife killed all them women!" yelled Irma. "Do you know how many midwives there are in Whitechapel? Why pick on me?"

"That's what's been haunting me for six weeks," answered Roosevelt. "I knew everything I had to know right after you killed Catherine Eddowes, and yet I couldn't piece it together until I realized that a midwife was the likely killer. You made a major blunder, and it took me until tonight to realize what it was."

"What are you talking about?" demanded Irma, curiosity mingling with hatred on her chubby face.

"You told me you heard a woman scream, and then the Ripper knocked you over while he was escaping from the scene of the crime."

"He did!" said Irma. "He come running out of the darkness and—"

"You're lying," said Roosevelt. "I should have known it immediately."

"It's God's own truth!"

He shook his head. "I found you on the ground less than a minute after we heard Catherine Eddowes scream. The Ripper knocked you down just before I got there, right?"

"Yeah, right."

Roosevelt grinned in triumph. "*That's* what I missed. It would have taken the Ripper five minutes or more to disembowel poor Catherine and arrange her innards on the ground the way he did. Surely she couldn't have screamed four minutes into that. She was dead before he started." The grin vanished. "That was *you* screaming. What better way to escape from the scene of a murder than to have a solicitous policeman escort you to a hospital? If there were any contradictions in your statements, we would write it off to hysteria.

After all, you'd just come face to face with Jack the Ripper."

She glared at him balefully.

"Before we put an end to this, perhaps you'll tell me why you did it?"

"I told you before," said the midwife. "I honor the commandments. *They* broke 'em all! They were all sinners, and God told me to rid the world of 'em!"

"Did God tell you to disembowel them, too?" asked Roosevelt. "Or was that your own idea?"

Suddenly a butcher knife appeared in her hand. She held it above her head, screamed something unintelligible, and leaped toward him. Roosevelt never flinched. He kept the pistol trained on her and pulled the trigger.

She fell backward, a new red blotch appearing on the front of her blood-stained dress.

She tried to get up, and he fired once more. This time she lay still.

*My Dearest Edith:*

*Please destroy this letter after you have read it.*

*I have faked the symptoms of the malaria I contracted some years ago on a trip to the Everglades, and have been relieved of my unofficial duties here. I will be put aboard the next ship to America (quite possibly on a stretcher if you can imagine that!) and within a very few days I will once again be able to hold you and the children in my arms. And I'm pleased to see that Harrison defeated that fool Cleveland without my help.*

*My work here is done. I would have preferred to arrest the fiend, but I was given no choice in the matter. Jack the Ripper is no more.*

*If I make that fact public, two things will happen. First, I will probably be arrested for murder. Second (and actually more important, for no jury would convict me once they have heard my story), Whitechapel will remain a blight upon the face of England. Whereas a conversation I had a few days ago has convinced me that as long as the British authorities think the madman is still at large, they might do something positive about eradicating Whitechapel's intolerable conditions. If that is so, then it may actually be serendipitous that only I (and now you) know that the Ripper is dead.*

*At least I hope that is the outcome. One would like to think that if one's life didn't count for much, at least one's death did—and if Whitechapel can either be cleansed or raized to the ground, then perhaps, just perhaps, these five unfortunate women did not die totally in vain.*

*Your Theodore*

Theodore Roosevelt returned to London 22 years later, in 1910, on the way home from the year-long safari that followed his Presidency.

Whitechapel remained unchanged.

# BWANA

Ngai rules the universe from His throne atop Kirinyaga, which men call Mount Kenya, and on His sacred mountain the beasts of the field roam free and share the fertile green slopes with His chosen people.

To the first Maasai He gave a spear, and to the first Kamba He gave a bow, but to Gikuyu, who was the first Kikuyu, He gave a digging stick and told him to dwell on the slopes of Kirinyaga. The Kikuyu, said Ngai, could sacrifice goats to read their entrails, and they could sacrifice oxen to thank Him for sending the rains, but they must not molest any of His animals that dwelt on the mountain.

Then one day Gikuyu came to Him and said, "May we not have the bow and arrow, so that we may kill *fisi*, the hyena, in whose body dwell the vengeful souls of evil men?"

And Ngai said that no, the Kikuyu must not molest the hyena, for the hyena's purpose was clear: He had created it to feed upon the lions' leavings, and to take the sick and the elderly from the Kikuyu's *shambas*.

Time passed, and Gikuyu approached the summit of the mountain again. "May we not have the spear, so that we can kill the lion and the leopard, who prey upon our own animals?" he said.

And Ngai said that no, the Kikuyu could not kill the lion or the leopard, for He had created them to hold the population of the grass-eaters in check, so that they would not overrun the Kikuyu's fields.

Finally Gikuyu climbed the mountain one last time and

said, "We must at least be allowed to kill the elephant, who can destroy a year's harvest in a matter of minutes—but how are we to do so when you have allowed us no weapons?"

Ngai thought long and hard, and finally spoke. "I have decreed that the Kikuyu should till the land, and I will not stain your hands with the blood of my other creatures," announced Ngai. "But because you are my chosen people, and are more important than the beasts that dwell upon my mountain, I will see to it that others come to kill these animals."

"What tribe will these hunters come from?" asked Gikuyu. "By what name will we know them?"

"You will know them by a single word," said Ngai.

When Ngai told him the word by which the hunters would be known, Gikuyu thought He had made a joke, and laughed aloud, and soon forgot the conversation.

But Ngai never jokes when He speaks to the Kikuyu.


We have no elephants or lions or leopards on the Eutopian world of Kirinyaga, for all three species were extinct long before we emigrated from the Kenya that had become so alien to us. But we took the sleek impala, and the majestic kudu, and the mighty buffalo, and the swift gazelle—and because we were mindful of Ngai's dictates, we took the hyena and the jackal and the vulture as well.

And because Kirinyaga was designed to be a Utopia in climate as well as in social organization, and because the land was more fertile than Kenya's, and because Maintenance made the orbital adjustments that assured us that the rains would always come on schedule, the wild animals of Kirinyaga, like the domestic animals and the people themselves, grew fruitful and multiplied.

It was only a matter of time before they came into conflict

with us. Initially there would be sporadic attacks on our live-stock by the hyenas, and once old Koboki's entire harvest was destroyed by a herd of rampaging buffalo, but we took such setbacks with good grace, for Ngai had provided well for us and no one was ever forced to go hungry.

But then, as we reclaimed more and more of our terraformed veldt to be used as farmland, as the wild animals of Kirinyaga felt the pressure of our land-hungry people, the incidents grew more frequent and more severe.

I was sitting before the fire in my *boma,* waiting for the sun to burn the chill from the morning air and staring out across the acacia-dotted plains, when young Ndemi raced up the winding road from the village.

"Koriba!" he cried. "Come quickly!"

"What has happened?" I asked, rising painfully to my feet.

"Juma has been attacked by *fisi!*" he gasped, striving to regain his breath.

"By one hyena, or many?" I asked.

"One, I think. I do not know."

"Is he still alive?"

"Juma or *fisi?*" asked Ndemi.

"Juma."

"I think he is dead." Ndemi paused. "But you are the *mundumugu.* You can make him live again."

I was pleased that he placed so much faith in his *mundumugu*—his witch doctor—but of course if his companion was truly dead there was nothing I could do about it. I went into my hut, selected some herbs that were especially helpful in combatting infection, added a few *qat* leaves for Juma to chew (for we had no anesthetics on Kirinyaga, and the hallucinogenic trance caused by the *qat* leaves would at least make him forget his pain). All this I placed into a leather pouch that I hung about my neck. Then I emerged from my hut and nodded to Ndemi, who led the way to the *shamba* of Juma's father.

When we arrived, the women were already wailing the death chant, and I briefly examined what was left of poor little Juma's body. One bite from the hyena had taken away most of his face, and a second had totally removed his left arm. The hyena had then devoured most of Juma's torso before the villagers finally drove it away.

Koinnage, the paramount chief of the village, arrived a few moments later.

"*Jambo,* Koriba," he greeted me.

"*Jambo,* Koinnage," I replied.

"Something must be done," he said, looking at Juma's body, which was now covered by flies.

"I will place a curse on the hyena," I said, "and tonight I shall sacrifice a goat to Ngai, so that He will welcome Juma's soul."

Koinnage looked uneasy, for his fear of me was great, but finally he spoke: "It is not enough. This is the second healthy boy that the hyenas have taken this month."

"Our hyenas have developed a taste for men," I said. "It is because we leave the old and the infirm out for them."

"Then perhaps we should not leave the old and the sick out any longer."

"We have no choice," I replied. "The Europeans thought it was the mark of savages, and even Maintenance has tried to dissuade us—but we do not have medicine to ease their suffering. What seems barbarous to outsiders is actually an act of mercy. Ever since Ngai gave the first digging-stick to the first Kikuyu, it has always been our tradition to leave the old and the infirm out for the hyenas when it is time for them to die."

"Maintenance has medicines," suggested Koinnage, and I noticed that two of the younger men had edged closer to us and were listening with interest. "Perhaps we should ask them to help us."

"So that they will live a week or a month longer, and then be buried in the ground like Christians?" I said. "You cannot be part Kikuyu and part European. That is the reason we came to Kirinyaga in the first place."

"But how wrong could it be to ask only for medicine for our elderly?" asked one of the younger men, and I could see that Koinnage looked relieved now that he himself did not have to pursue the argument.

"If you accept their medicine today, then tomorrow you will be accepting their clothing and their machinery and their god," I replied. "If history has taught us nothing else, it has taught us that." They still seemed unconvinced, so I continued: "Most races look ahead to their Utopia, but the Kikuyu must look *back,* back to a simpler time when we lived in harmony with the land, when we were not tainted with the customs of a society to which we were never meant to belong. I have lived among the Europeans, and gone to school at their universities, and I tell you that you must not listen to the siren song of their technology. What works for the Europeans did not work for the Kikuyu when we lived in Kenya, and it will not work for us here on Kirinyaga."

As if to emphasize my statement, a hyena voiced its eerie laugh far off in the veldt. The women stopped wailing and drew closer together.

"But we must do something!" protested Koinnage, whose fear of the hyena momentarily overrode his fear of his *mundumugu.* "We cannot continue to let the beasts of the field destroy our crops and take our children."

I could have explained that there was a temporary imbalance as the grass-eaters lowered their birthrate to accommodate their decreased pasturage, and that the hyenas' birthrate would almost certainly adjust within a year, but they would not have understood or believed me. They wanted solutions, not explanations.

"Ngai is testing our courage, to see if we are truly worthy to live on Kirinyaga," I said at last. "Until the time of testing is over, we will arm our children with spears and have them tend the cattle in pairs."

Koinnage shook his head. "The hyenas have developed a taste for men—and two Kikuyu boys, even armed with spears, are no match for a pack of hyenas. Surely Ngai does not want His chosen people to become meals for *fisi*."

"No, He does not," I agreed. "It is the hyenas' nature to kill grass-eaters, just as it is our nature to till the fields. I am your *mundumugu*. You must believe me what I tell you that this time of testing will soon pass."

"How soon?" asked another man.

I shrugged. "Perhaps two rains. Perhaps three." The rains come twice a year.

"You are an old man," said the man, mustering his courage to contradict his *mundumugu*. "You have no children, and it is this that gives you patience. But those of us with sons cannot wait for two or three rains wondering each day if they will return from the fields. We must do something *now*."

"I am an old man," I agreed, "and this gives me not only patience, but wisdom."

"You are the *mundumugu*," said Koinnage at last, "and you must face the problem in your way. But I am the paramount chief, and I must face it in mine. I will organize a hunt, and we will kill all the hyenas in the area."

"Very well," I said, for I had foreseen this solution. "Organize your hunt."

"Will you cast the bones and see if we shall be successful?"

"I do not need to cast the bones to foresee the results of your hunt," I replied. "You are farmers, not hunters. You will not be successful."

"You will not give us your support?" demanded another man.

"You do not need my support," I replied. "I would give you my patience if I could, for that is what you need."

"We were supposed to turn this world into a Utopia," said Koinnage, who had only the haziest understanding of the word, but equated it with good harvests and a lack of enemies. "What kind of Utopia permits children to be devoured by wild animals?"

"You cannot understand what it means to be full until you have been hungry," I answered. "You cannot know what it means to be warm and dry until you have been cold and wet. And Ngai knows, even if you do not, that you cannot appreciate life without death. This is His lesson for you; it will pass."

"It must end *now*," said Koinnage firmly, now that he knew I would not try to prevent his hunt.

I made no further comment, for I knew that nothing I could say would dissuade him. I spent the next few minutes creating a curse for the individual hyena that had killed Juma, and that night I sacrificed a goat in the middle of the village and read in the entrails that Ngai had accepted the sacrifice and welcomed Juma's spirit.

Two days later Koinnage led ten of the village men out to the veldt to hunt the hyenas, while I stayed in my *boma* and prepared for what I knew was inevitable.

It was in late morning that Ndemi—the boldest of the boys in the village, whose courage had made him a favorite of mine—came up the long winding path to visit me.

"*Jambo,* Koriba," he greeted me unhappily.

"*Jambo,* Ndemi," I replied. "What is the matter?"

"They say that I am too young to hunt for *fisi,*" he complained, squatting down next to me.

"They are right."

"But I have practiced my bushcraft every day, and you yourself have blessed my spear."

"I have not forgotten," I said.

"Then why can I not join the hunt?"

"It makes no difference," I said. "They will not kill *fisi.* In fact, they will be very lucky if all of them return unharmed." I paused. "*Then* the troubles will begin."

"I thought they had already begun," said Ndemi, with no trace of sarcasm.

I shook my head. "What has been happening is part of the natural order of things, and hence it is part of Kirinyaga. But when Koinnage does not kill the hyenas, he will want to bring a hunter to Kirinyaga, and that is *not* part of the natural order."

"You know he will do this?" asked Ndemi, impressed.

"I know Koinnage," I answered.

"Then you will tell him not to."

"I will tell him not to."

"And he will listen to you."

"No," I said. "I do not think he will listen to me."

"But you are the *mundumugu.*"

"But there are many men in the village who resent me," I explained. "They see the sleek ships that land on Kirinyaga from time to time, and they hear stories about the wonders of Nairobi and Mombasa, and they forget why we have come here. They become unhappy with the digging-stick, and they long for the Maasai's spear or the Kamba's bow or the European's machines."

Ndemi sqautted in silence for a moment.

"I have a question, Koriba," he said at last.

"You may ask it."

"You are the *mundumugu*," he said. "You can change men into insects, and see in the darkness, and walk upon the air."

"That is true," I agreed.

"Then why do you not turn all the hyenas into honeybees and set fire to their hive?"

"Because *fisi* is not evil," I said. "It is his nature to eat flesh. Without him, the beasts of the field would become so plentiful that they would soon overrun our fields."

"Then why not kill just those *fisi* who kill us?"

"Do you not remember your own grandmother?" I asked. "Do you not recall the agony she suffered in her final days?"

"Yes."

"We do not kill our own kind. Were it not for *fisi*, she would have suffered for many more days. *Fisi* is only doing what Ngai created him to do."

"Ngai also created hunters," said Ndemi, casting me a sly look out of the corner of his eye.

"That is true."

"Then why do you not want hunters to come and kill *fisi?*"

"I will tell you the story of the Goat and the Lion, and then you will understand," I said.

"What do goats and lions have to do with hyenas?" he asked.

"Listen, and you will know," I answered. "Once there was a herd of black goats, and they lived a very happy life, for Ngai had provided them with green grass and lush plants and a nearby stream where they could drink, and when it rained they stood beneath the branches of large, stately trees where the raindrops could not reach them. Then one day a leopard came to their village, and because he was old and thin and weak, and could no longer hunt the impala and the waterbuck, he killed a goat and ate it.

" 'This is terrible!' said the goats. 'Something must be done.'

" 'He is an old leopard,' said the wisest of the goats. 'If he regains his strength from the flesh he has eaten, he will go back to hunting for the impala, for the impala's flesh is much more nourishing than ours, and if he does not regain his strength, he will soon be dead. All we need do is be especially alert while he walks among us.'

"But the other goats were too frightened to listen to his counsel, and they decided that they needed help.

" 'I would beware of anyone who is not a goat and offers to help you,' said the wisest goat, but they would not hear him, and finally they sought out a huge black-maned lion.

" 'There is a leopard that is eating our people,' they said, 'and we are not strong enough to drive him away. Will you help us?'

" 'I am always glad to help my friends,' answered the lion.

" 'We are a poor race,' said the goats. 'What tribute will you exact from us for your help?'

" 'None,' the lion assured them. 'I will do this solely because I am your friend.'

"And true to his word, the lion entered the village and waited until next the leopard came to feed, and then the lion pounced upon him and killed him.

" 'Oh, thank you, great saviour!' cried the goats, doing a dance of joy and triumph around the lion.

" 'It was my pleasure,' said the lion. 'For the leopard is my enemy as much as he is yours.'

" 'We shall sing songs and tell stories about you long after you leave,' continued the goats happily.

" 'Leave?' replied the lion, his eyes seeking out the fattest of the goats. 'Who is leaving?' "

Ndemi considered what I had said for a long moment, then looked up at me.

"You are not saying that the hunter will eat us as *fisi* does?"

"No, I am not."

He considered the implications further.

"Ah!" he said, smiling at last. "You are saying that if we cannot kill *fisi,* who will soon die or leave us, then we should not invite someone even stronger than *fisi,* someone who will not die or leave."

"That is correct."

"But why should a hunter of animals be a threat to Kirinyaga?" he continued thoughtfully.

"We are like the goats," I explained. "We live off the land, and we have not the power to kill our enemies. But a hunter is like the lion: It is his nature to kill, and he will be the only man on Kirinyaga who is skilled at killing."

"You think he will kill us, then?" asked Ndemi.

I shrugged. "Not at first. The lion had to kill the leopard before he could prey upon the goats. The hunter will kill *fisi* before he casts about for some other way to exercise his power."

"But you are our *mundumugu!*" protested Ndemi. "You will not let this happen!"

"I will try to prevent it," I said.

"If you try, you will succeed, and we will not send for a hunter."

"Perhaps."

"Are you not all-powerful?" asked Ndemi.

"I am all-powerful."

"Then why do you speak with such doubt?"

"Because I am not a hunter," I said. "The Kikuyu fear me because of my powers, but I have never knowingly harmed one of my people. I will not harm them now. I want what is best for Kirinyaga, but if their fear of *fisi* is greater than their fear of me, then I will lose."

Ndemi stared at the little patterns he had traced in the dirt with his finger.

"Perhaps, if a hunter does come, he will be a good man," he said at last.

"Perhaps," I agreed. "But he will still be a hunter." I paused. "The lion may sleep with the zebra in times of plenty. But in times of need, when both are starving, it is the lion who starves last."

Ten hunters had left the village, but only eight returned. Two had been attacked and killed by a pack of hyenas while they sat resting beneath the shade of an acacia tree. All day long the women wailed the death chant, while the sky turned black with the smoke, for it is our custom to burn the huts of our dead.

That very same night Koinnage called a meeting of the Council of Elders. I waited until the last rays of the sun had vanished, then painted my face and wrapped myself in my ceremonial leopardskin cloak, and made my way to his *boma*.

There was total silence as I approached the old men of the village. Even the night birds seemed to have taken flight, and I walked among them, looking neither right nor left, finally taking my accustomed place on a stool just to the left of Koinnage's personal hut. I could see his three wives clustered together inside his senior wife's hut, kneeling as close to the entrance as they dared while straining to see and hear what transpired.

The flickering firelight highlighted the faces of the elders, most of them grim and filled with fear. By precedent no one—not even the *mundumugu*—could speak until the paramount chief had spoken, and since Koinnage had still not emerged from his hut, I amused myself by withdrawing the bones from the leather pouch about my neck and casting them on the dirt. Three times I cast them, and three times I frowned at what I saw. Finally I put them back in my pouch, leaving those elders who were planning to disobey their *mundumugu* to wonder what I had seen.

At last Koinnage stepped forth from his hut, a long thin stick in his hand. It was his custom to wave the stick when he spoke to the Council, much as a conductor waves his baton.

"The hunt has failed," he announced dramatically, as if everyone in the village did not already know it. "Two more men have died because of *fisi*." He paused for dramatic effect, then shouted: "It must not happen again!"

"Do not go hunting again and it will not happen again," I said, for once he began to speak I was permitted to comment.

"You are the *mundumugu*," said one of the elders. "You should have protected them!"

"I told them not to go," I replied. "I cannot protect those who reject my counsel."

"*Fisi* must die!" screamed Koinnage, and as he turned to face me I detected a strong odor of *pombe* on his breath, and now I knew why he had remained in his hut for so long. He had been drinking *pombe* until his courage was up to the task at hand, that of opposing his *mundumugu*. "Never again will *fisi* dine upon the flesh of the Kikuyu, nor will we hide in our *bomas* like old women until Koriba tells us that it is safe to come out! *Fisi* must die!"

The elders took up the chant of "*Fisi* must die!" and Koinnage went through a pantomime of killing a hyena, using his stick as a spear.

"Men have reached the stars!" cried Koinnage. "They have built great cities beneath the sea. They have killed the last elephant and the last lion. Are we not men too—or are we old women to be terrified by unclean eaters of carrion?"

I got to my feet.

"What other men have achieved makes no difference to the Kikuyu," I said. "Other men did not cause our problem with *fisi;* other men cannot cure it."

"One of them can," said Koinnage, looking at the anxious faces which were distorted by the firelight. "A hunter."

The elders muttered their approval.

"We must send for a hunter," repeated Koinnage, waving his stick wildly.

"It must not be a European," said an elder.

"Nor can it be a Wakamba," said another.

"Nor a Luo," said a third.

"The Lumbwa and the Nandi are the enemies of our blood," added a fourth.

"It will be whoever can kill *fisi,*" said Koinnage.

"How will you find such a man?" asked an elder.

"Hyenas still live on Earth," answered Koinnage. "We will find a hunter or a control officer from one of the game parks, someone who has hunted and killed *fisi* many times."

"You are making a mistake," I said firmly, and suddenly there was absolute silence again.

"We must have a hunter," said Koinnage adamantly, when he saw that no one else would speak.

"You would only be bringing a greater killer to Kirinyaga to slay a lesser killer," I responded.

"I am the paramount chief," said Koinnage, and I could tell from the way he refused to meet my gaze that the effects of the *pombe* had left him now that he was forced to confront me before the elders. "What kind of chief would I be if I permitted *fisi* to continue to kill my people?"

"You can build traps for *fisi* until Ngai gives him back his taste for grass-eaters," I said.

"How many more of us will *fisi* kill before the traps have been set?" demanded Koinnage, trying to work himself up into a rage again. "How many of us must die before the *mundumugu* admits that he is wrong, and that this is not Ngai's plan?"

"Stop!" I shouted, raising my hands above my head, and even Koinnage froze in his tracks, afraid to speak or to move. "I am your *mundumugu*. I am the book of our collected wisdom; each sentence I speak is a page. I have brought the rains on time, and I have blessed the harvest. Never have I misled you. Now I tell you that you must not bring a hunter to Kirinyaga."

And then Koinnage, who was literally shaking from his fear of me, forced himself to stare into my eyes.

"I am the paramount chief," he said, trying to steady his voice, "and I say we must act before *fisi* hungers again. *Fisi* must die! I have spoken."

The elders began chanting "*Fisi* must die!" again, and Koinnage's courage returned to him as he realized that he was not the only one to openly disobey his *mundumugu*'s dictates. He led the frenzied chanting, walking from one elder to the next and finally to me, yelling "*Fisi* must die!" and punctuating it with wild gesticulations of his stick.

I realized that I had lost for the very first time in council, yet I made no threats, since it was important that any punishment for disobeying the dictates of their *mundumugu* must come from Ngai and not from me. I left in silence, walking through the circle of elders without looking at any of them, and returned to my *boma*.

The next morning two of Koinnage's cattle were found dead without a mark upon them, and each morning thereafter a different elder awoke to two dead cattle. I told the villagers that this was undoubtedly the hand of Ngai, and that the corpses must be burned, and that anyone who ate of them would die under a horrible *thahu,* or curse, and they followed my orders without question.

Then it was simply a matter of waiting for Koinnage's hunter to arrive.

He walked across the plain toward my *boma,* and it might have been Ngai Himself approaching me. He was tall, well over six and one-half feet, and slender, graceful as the gazelle and blacker than the darkest night. He was dressed in neither a *kikoi* nor in khakis, but in a lightweight pair of pants and a short-sleeved shirt. His feet were in sandals, and I could tell from the depth of their calluses and the straightness of his toes that he had spent most of his life without shoes. A small bag was slung over one shoulder, and in his left hand he carried a long rifle in a monogrammed gun case.

When he reached the spot where I was sitting he stopped, totally at ease, and stared unblinking at me. From the arrogance of his expression, I knew that he was a Maasai.

"Where is the village of Koriba?" he asked in Swahili.

I pointed to my left. "In the valley," I said.

"Why do you live alone, old man?"

Those were his exact words. Not *m'zee,* which is a term of respect for the elderly, a term that acknowledges the decades of accumulated wisdom, but *old man.*

*Yes,* I concluded silently, *there is no doubt that you are a Maasai.*

"The *mundumugu* always lives apart from other men," I answered aloud.

"So you are the witch doctor," he said. "I would have thought your people had outgrown such things."

133

"As yours have outgrown the need for manners?" I responded.

He chuckled in amusement. "You are not glad to see me, are you, old man?"

"No, I am not."

"Well, if your magic had been strong enough to kill the hyenas, I would not be here. *I* am not to blame for that."

"You are not to blame for anything," I said. "Yet."

"What is your name, old man?"

"Koriba."

He placed a thumb to his chest. "I am William."

"That is not a Maasai name," I noted.

"My full name is William Sambeke."

"Then I will call you Sambeke."

He shrugged. "Call me whatever you want." He shaded his eyes from the sun and looked off toward the village. "This isn't exactly what I expected."

"What did you expect, Sambeke?" I asked.

"I thought you people were trying to create a Utopia here."

"We are."

He snorted contemptuously. "You live in huts, you have no machinery, and you even have to hire someone from Earth to kill hyenas for you. That's not *my* idea of Utopia."

"Then you will doubtless wish to return to your home," I suggested.

"I have a job to do here first," he replied. "A job *you* failed to do."

I made no answer, and he stared at me for a long moment.

"Well?" he said at last.

"Well what?"

"Aren't you going to spout some mumbo-jumbo and make me disappear in a cloud of smoke, *mundumugu?*"

"Before you choose to become my enemy," I said in perfect English, "you should know that I am not as ineffectual as you may think, nor am I impressed by Maasai arrogance."

He stared at me in surprise, then threw back his head and laughed.

"There's more to you than meets the eye, old man!" he said in English. "I think we are going to become great friends!"

"I doubt it," I replied in Swahili.

"What schools did you attend back on Earth?" he asked, matching my change in languages again.

"Cambridge and Yale," I said. "But that was many years ago."

"Why does an educated man choose to sit in the dirt beside a grass hut?"

"Why does a Maasai accept a commission from a Kikuyu?" I responded.

"I like to hunt," he said. "And I wanted to see this Utopia you have built."

"And now you have seen it."

"I have seen Kirinyaga," he replied. "I have not yet seen Utopia."

"That is because you do not know how to look for it."

"You are a clever old man, Koriba, full of clever answers," said Sambeke, taking no offense. "Why have you not made yourself king of this entire planetoid?"

"The *mundumugu* is the repository of our traditions. That is all the power he seeks or needs."

"You could at least have had them build you a house, instead of living like this. No Maasai lives in a *manyatta* any longer."

"And after the house would come a car?" I asked.

"Once you built some roads," he agreed.

"And then a factory to build more cars, and another one to build more houses, and then an impressive building for our Parliament, and perhaps a railroad line?" I shook my head. "That is a description of Kenya, not of Utopia."

"You are making a mistake," said Sambeke. "On my way here from the landing field—what is it called?"

"Haven."

"On my way here from Haven, I saw buffalo and kudu and impala. A hunting lodge by the river overlooking the plains would bring in a lot of tourist money."

"We do not hunt our grass-eaters."

"You wouldn't have to," he said meaningfully. "And think of how much their money could help your people."

"May Ngai preserve us from people who want to help us," I said devoutly.

"You are a stubborn old man," he said. "I think I had better go talk to Koinnage. Which *shamba* is his?"

"The largest," I answered. "He is the paramount chief."

He nodded. "Of course. I will see you later, old man."

I nodded. "Yes, you will."

"And after I have killed your hyenas, perhaps we will share a gourd of *pombe* and discuss ways to turn this world into a Utopia. I have been very disappointed thus far."

So saying, he turned toward the village and began walking down the long, winding trail to Koinnage's *boma*.

He turned Koinnage's head, as I knew he would. By the time I had eaten and made my way to the village, the two of them were sitting beside a fire in front of the paramount chief's *boma*, and Sambeke was describing the hunting lodge he wanted to build by the river.

"*Jambo*, Koriba," said Koinnage, looking up at me as I approached them.

"*Jambo,* Koinnage," I responded, squatting down next to him.

"You have met William Sambeke?"

"I have met Sambeke," I said, and the Maasai grinned at my refusal to use his European name.

"He has many plans for Kirinyaga," continued Koinnage, as some of the villagers began wandering over.

"How interesting," I replied. "You asked for a hunter, and they have sent you a planner instead."

"Some of us," interjected Sambeke, an amused expression on his face, "have more than one talent."

"Some of us," I said, "have been here for half a day and have not yet begun to hunt."

"I will kill the hyenas tomorrow," said Sambeke, "when their bellies are full and they are too content to race away at my approach."

"How will you kill them?" I asked.

He carefully unlocked his gun case and pulled out his rifle, which was equipped with a telescopic sight. Most of the villagers had never seen such a weapon, and they crowded around it, whispering to each other.

"Would you care to examine it?" he asked me.

I shook my head. "The weapons of the Europeans hold no interest for me."

"This rifle was manufactured in Zimbabwe, by members of the Shona tribe," he corrected me.

I shrugged. "Then they are black Europeans."

"Whatever they are, they make a splendid weapon," said Sambeke.

"For those who are afraid to hunt in the traditional way," I said.

"Do not taunt me, old man," said Sambeke, and suddenly a hush fell over the onlookers, for no man speaks thus to the *mundumugu.*

"I do not taunt you, Maasai," I said. "I merely point out why you have brought the weapon. It is no crime to be afraid of *fisi.*"

"I fear nothing," he said heatedly.

"That is not true," I said. "Like all of us, you fear failure."

"I shall not fail with *this*," he said, patting the rifle.

"By the way," I asked, "was it not the Maasai who once proved their manhood by facing the lion armed only with a spear?"

"It was," he answered. "And it was the Maasai *and* the Kikuyu who lost most their babies at birth, and who succumbed to every disease that passed through their villages, and who lived in shelters that could protect them from neither the rain nor the cold nor even the flesh-eaters of the veldt. It was the Maasai and the Kikuyu who learned from the Europeans, and who took back their land from the white men, and who built great cities where once there was only dust and swamps. Or, rather," he added, "it was the Maasai and *most* of the Kikuyu."

"I remember seeing a circus when I was in England," I said, raising my voice so that all could hear me, though I directed my remarks at Sambeke. "In it there was a chimpanzee. He was a very bright animal. They dressed him in human clothing, and he rode a human bicycle, and he played human music on a human flute—but that did not make him a human. In fact, he amused the humans because he was such a grotesque mockery of them . . . just as the Maasai and Kikuyu who wear suits and drive cars and work in large buildings are not Europeans, but are instead a mockery of them."

"That is just your opinion, old man," said the Maasai, "and it is wrong."

"Is it?" I asked. "The chimpanzee had been tainted by his

association with humans, so that he could never survive in the wild. And *you,* I notice, must have the Europeans' weapon to hunt an animal that your grandfathers would have gone out and slain with a knife or a spear."

"Are you challenging me, old man?" asked Sambeke, once again amused.

"I am merely pointing out why you have brought your rifle with you," I answered.

"No," he said. "You are trying to regain the power you lost when your people sent for me. But you have made a mistake."

"In what way?"

"You have made me your enemy."

"Will you shoot me with your rifle, then?" I asked calmly, for I knew he would not.

He leaned over and whispered to me, so that only I could hear him.

"We could have made a fortune together, old man. I would have been happy to share it with you, in exchange for you keeping your people in line, for a safari company will need many workers. But now you have publicly opposed me, and I cannot permit that."

"We must learn to live with disappointments," I said.

"I am glad you feel that way," he said. "For I plan to turn this world into a Utopia, rather than some Kikuyu dreamland."

Then, suddenly, he stood up.

"Boy," he said to Ndemi, who was standing at the outskirts of the crowd. "Bring me a spear."

Ndemi looked to me, and I nodded, for I could not believe that the Maasai would kill me with *any* weapon.

Ndemi brought the spear to Sambeke, who took it from him and leaned it against Koinnage's hut. Then he stood before the fire and slowly began removing all his clothes.

When he was naked, with the firelight playing off his lean, hard body, looking like an African god, he picked up the spear and held it over his head.

"I go to hunt *fisi* in the dark, in the old way," he announced to the assembled villagers. "Your *mundumugu* has laid down the challenge, and if you are to listen to my counsel in the future, as I hope you will, you must know that I can meet any challenge he sets for me."

And before anyone could say a word or move to stop him, he strode boldly off into the night.

"Now he will die, and Maintenance will want to revoke our charter!" complained Koinnage.

"If he dies, it was his own decision, and Maintenance will not punish us in any way," I replied. I stared long and hard at him. "I wonder that you care."

"That I care if he should die?"

"That you care if Maintenance should revoke our charter," I answered. "If you listen to the Maasai, you will turn Kirinyaga into another Kenya, so why should you mind returning to the original Kenya?"

"He does not want to turn Kirinyaga into Kenya, but into Utopia," said Koinnage sullenly.

"We are already attempting to do that," I noted. "Does *his* Utopia include a big European house for the paramount chief?"

"We did not discuss it thoroughly," said Koinnage uneasily.

"And perhaps some extra cattle, in exchange for supplying him with porters and gunbearers?"

"He has good ideas," said Koinnage, ignoring my question. "Why should we carry our water from the river when he can create pumps and pipes to carry it for us?"

"Because if water is easy to obtain, it will become easy to

waste, and we have no more water to waste here than we had in Kenya, where all the lakes have dried up because of far-seeing men like Sambeke."

"You have answers for everything," said Koinnage bitterly.

"No," I said. "But I have answers for this Maasai, for his questions have been asked many times before, and always in the past the Kikuyu have given the wrong answer."

Suddenly we heard a hideous scream from perhaps half a mile away.

"It is finished," said Koinnage grimly. "The Maasai is dead, and now we must answer to Maintenance."

"It did not sound like a man," said Ndemi.

"You are just a *mtoto*—a child," said Koinnage. "What do you know?"

"I know what Juma sounded like when *fisi* killed him," said Ndemi defiantly. "That is what I know."

We waited in silence to see if there would be another sound, but none was forthcoming.

"Perhaps it is just as well that *fisi* has killed the Maasai," said old Njobe at last. "I saw the building that he drew in the dirt, the one he would make for visitors, and it was an evil building. It was not round and safe from demons like our own huts, but instead it had corners, and everyone knows that demons live in corners."

"Truly, there would be a curse upon it," agreed another of the elders.

"What can one expect from one who hunts *fisi* at night?" added another.

"One can expect a dead *fisi!*" said Sambeke triumphantly, as he stepped out of the shadows and threw the bloody corpse of a large male hyena onto the ground. Everyone backed away from him in awe, and he turned to me, the firelight flickering off his sleek black body. "What do you say now, old man?"

"I say that you are a greater killer than *fisi*," I answered.

He smiled with satisfaction.

"Now," he said, "let us see what we can learn from this particular *fisi*." He turned to a young man. "Boy, bring a knife."

"His name is Kamabi," I said.

"I have not had time to learn names," replied Sambeke. He turned back to Kamabi. "Do as I ask, boy."

"He is a man," I said.

"It is difficult to tell in the dark," said Sambeke with a shrug.

Kamabi returned a moment later with an ancient hunting knife; it was so old and so rusty that Sambeke did not care to touch it, and so he merely pointed to the hyena.

*"Kata hi ya tumbo,"* he said. "Slit the stomach here."

Kamabi knelt down and slit open the hyena's belly. The smell was terrible, but the Maasai picked up a stick and began prodding through the contents. Finally he stood up.

"I had hoped that we would find a bracelet or an earring," he said. "But it has been a long time since the boy was killed, and such things would have passed through *fisi* days ago."

"Koriba can roll the bones and tell if this is the one who killed Juma," said Koinnage.

Sambeke snorted contemptuously. "Koriba can roll the bones from now until the long rains come, but they will tell him nothing." He looked at the assembled villagers. "I have killed *fisi* in the old way to prove that I am no coward or European, to hunt only in the daylight and hide behind my gun. But now that I have shown you that I can do it, tomorrow I shall show you how many *fisi* I can kill in *my* way, and then you may decide which way is better, Koriba's or mine." He paused. "Now I need a hut to sleep in, so that I may be strong and alert when the sun rises."

Every villager except Koinnage immediately volunteered his hut. The Maasai looked at each man in turn, and then turned to the paramount chief. "I will take yours," he said.

"But—" began Koinnage.

"And one of your wives to keep me warm in the night." He stared directly into Koinnage's eyes. "Or would you deny me your hospitality after I have killed *fisi* for you?"

"No," said Koinnage at last. "I will not deny you."

The Maasai shot me a triumphant smile. "It is still not Utopia," he said. "But it is getting closer."

The next morning Sambeke went out with his rifle.

I walked down to the village in the morning to give Zindu ointment to help dry up her milk, for her baby had been stillborn. When I was finished, I went through the shambas, blessing the scarecrows, and before long I had my usual large group of children beside me, begging me to tell them a story.

Finally, when the sun was high in the sky and it was too hot to keep walking, I sat down beneath the shade of an acacia tree.

"All right," I said. "Now you may have your story."

"What story will you tell us today, Koriba?" asked one of the girls.

"I think I shall tell you the tale of the Unwise Elephant," I said.

"Why was he unwise?" asked a boy.

"Listen, and you shall know," I said, and they all fell silent.

"Once there was a young elephant," I began, "and because he was young, he had not yet acquired the wisdom of his race. And one day this elephant chanced upon a city in the middle of the savannah, and he entered it, and beheld its wonders, and thought it was quite the most marvelous thing he had ever seen. All his life he had labored day and night to fill his belly, and here, in the city, were wonderful machines that could make his life so much easier that he was determined to own some of them.

"But when he approached the owner of a digging stick, with which he could find buried acacia pods, the owner said, 'I am a poor man, and I cannot give my digging stick to you. But because you want it so badly, I will make a trade.'

" 'But I have nothing to trade,' said the elephant unhappily.

" 'Of course you do,' said the man. 'If you will let me have your ivory, so that I can carve designs on it, you may have the digging stick.'

"The elephant considered this offer, and finally agreed, for if he had a digging stick he would no longer need his tusks to root up the ground.

"And he walked a little farther, and he came to an old woman with a weaving loom, and he thought this was a wonderful thing, for with it he would be able to make a blanket for himself so that he could stay warm during the long nights.

"He asked the woman for her weaving loom, and she replied that she would not to give it away, but that she would be happy to trade it.

" 'All I have to trade is my digging stick,' said the elephant.

" 'But I do not need a digging stick,' said the old woman. 'You must let me cut off one of your feet, that I may make a stool of it.'

"The elephant thought for a long time, and he remembered how cold he had been the previous night, and finally he agreed, and the trade was made.

"Then he came to a man who had a net, and the elephant

thought that the net would be a wonderful thing to have, for now he could catch the fruits when he shook a tree, rather than having to hunt for them on the ground.

" 'I will not give you the net, for it took me many days to make it,' said the man, 'but I will trade it to you for your ears, which will make excellent sleeping mats.'

"Again the elephant agreed, and finally he went back to the herd to show them the wonders he had brought from the city of men.

" 'What need have we for digging sticks?' asked his brother. 'No digging stick will last as long as our tusks.'

" 'It might be nice to have a blanket,' said his mother, 'but to make a blanket with a weaving loom we would need fingers, which we do not have.'

" 'I cannot see the purpose of a net for catching fruit from the trees,' said his father. 'For if you hold the net in your trunk, how will you shake the fruits loose from the tree, and if you shake the tree, how will you hold the net?'

" 'I see now that the tools of men are of no use to elephants,' said the young elephant. 'I can never be a man, so I will go back to being an elephant.'

"His father shook his head sadly. 'It is true that you are not a man—but because you have dealt with men, you are no longer an elephant either. You have lost your foot, and cannot keep up with the herd. You have given away your ivory, and you cannot dig for water, or churn up the ground to look for acacia pods. You have parted with your ears, and now you cannot flap them to cool your blood when the sun is high in the sky.'

"And so the elephant spent the rest of his unhappy life halfway between the city and the herd, for he could not become part of one and he was no longer part of the other."

I stopped, and stared off into the distance, where a small

herd of impala was grazing just beyond one of our cultivated fields.

"Is that all?" asked the girl who had first requested the story.

"That is all," I said.

"It was not a very good story," she continued.

"Oh?" I asked, slapping a small insect that was crawling up my arm. "Why not?"

"Because the ending was not happy."

"Not all stories have happy endings," I said.

"I do not like unhappy endings," she said.

"Neither do I," I agreed. I paused and looked at her. "How do *you* think the story should end?"

"The elephant should not trade the things that make him an elephant, since he can never become a man."

"Very good," I said. "Would you trade the things that make you a Kikuyu, to try to be something you can never become?"

"Never!"

"Would any of you?" I asked my entire audience.

"No!" they cried.

"What if the elephant offered you his tusks, or the hyena offered you his fangs?"

"Never!"

I paused for just a moment before asking my next question.

"What if the Maasai offered you his gun?"

Most of the children yelled "No!" but I noticed that two of the older boys did not answer. I questioned them about it.

"A gun is not like tusks or teeth," said the taller of the two boys. "It is a weapon that men use."

"That is right," said the smaller boy, shuffling his bare feet in the dirt and raising a small cloud of dust. "The Maasai is not an animal. He is like us."

"He is not an animal," I agreed, "but he is not like us. Do the Kikuyu use guns, or live in brick houses, or wear European clothes?"

"No," said the boys in unison.

"Then if you were to use a gun, or live in a brick house, or wear European clothes, would you be a true Kikuyu?"

"No," they admitted.

"But would using a gun, or living in a brick house, or wearing European clothes, make you a Maasai or a European?"

"No."

"Do you see, then, why we must reject the tools and the gifts of outsiders? We can never become like them, but we can stop being Kikuyu, and if we stop being Kikuyu without becoming something else, then we are nothing."

"I understand, Koriba," said the taller boy.

"Are you sure?" I asked.

He nodded. "I am sure."

"Why are all your stories like this?" asked a girl.

"Like what?"

"They all have titles like the Unwise Elephant, or the Jackal and the Honeybird, or the Leopard and the Shrike, but when you explain them they are always about the Kikuyu."

"That is because I am a Kikuyu and you are a Kikuyu," I replied with a smile. "If we were leopards, then all my stories would really be about leopards."

I spent a few more minutes with them beneath the shade of the tree, and then I saw Ndemi approaching through the tall grass, his face alive with excitement.

"Well?" I said when he had joined us.

"The Maasai has returned," he announced.

"Did he kill any *fisi*?" I asked.

"*Mingi sana,*" replied Ndemi. "Very many."

"Where is he now?"

"By the river, with some of the young men who served as his gunbearers and skinners."

"I think I shall go visit them," I said, getting carefully to my feet, for my legs tend to get stiff when I sit in one position for too long. "Ndemi, you will come with me. The rest of you children are to go back to your *shambas,* and to think about the story of the Unwise Elephant."

Ndemi's chest puffed up like one of my roosters when I singled him out to accompany me, and a moment later we were walking across the sprawling savannah.

"What is the Maasai doing at the river?" I asked.

"He has cut down some young saplings with a *panga,*" answered Ndemi, "and he is instructing some of the men to build something, but I do not know what it is."

I peered through the haze of heat and dust, and saw a small party of men approaching us.

"*I* know what it is," I said softly, for although I had never seen a sedan chair, I knew what one looked like, and it was currently approaching us as four Kikuyu bore the weight of the sedan chair—and the Maasai—upon their sweating shoulders.

Since they were heading in our direction, I told Ndemi to stop walking, and we stood and waited for them.

"*Jambo,* old man!" said the Maasai when we were within earshot. "I have killed seven more hyenas this morning."

"*Jambo,* Sambeke," I replied. "You look very comfortable."

"It could use cushions," he said. "And the bearers do not carry it levelly. But I will make do with it."

"Poor man," I said, "who lacks cushions and thoughtful bearers. How did these oversights come to pass?"

148

"That is because it is not Utopia yet," he replied with a smile. "But it is getting very close."

"You will be sure to tell me when it arrives," I said.

"You will know, old man."

Then he directed his bearers to carry him to the village. Ndemi and I remained where we were, and watched him disappear in the distance.

That night there was a feast in the village to celebrate the slaying of the eight hyenas. Koinnage himself had slaughtered an ox, and there was much *pombe,* and the people were singing and dancing when I arrived, re-enacting the stalking and killing of the animals by their new saviour.

The Maasai himself was seated on a tall chair, taller even than Koinnage's throne. In one hand he held a gourd of *pombe,* and the leather case that held his rifle was laid carefully across his lap. He was clad now in the red robe of his people, his hair was neatly braided in his tribal fashion, and his lean body glistened with oils that had been rubbed onto it. Two young girls, scarcely past circumcision age, stood behind him, hanging upon his every word.

"*Jambo,* old man!" he greeted me as I approached him.

"*Jambo,* Sambeke," I said.

"That is no longer my name," he said.

"Oh? And have you taken a Kikuyu name instead?"

"I have taken a name that the Kikuyu will understand," he replied. "It is what the village will call me from this day forth."

"You are not leaving, now that the hunt is over?"

He shook his head. "I am not leaving."

"You are making a mistake," I said.

"Not as big a mistake as you made when you chose not to be my ally," he responded. Then, after a brief pause, he smiled and added: "Do you not wish to know my new name?"

"I suppose I should know it, if you are to remain here for any length of time," I agreed.

He leaned over and whispered the same word to me that Ngai had whispered to Gikuyu on the holy mountain millions of years earlier.

"Bwana?" I repeated.

He looked smugly at me, and smiled again.

"*Now,*" he said, "it is Utopia."

Bwana spent the next few weeks making Kirinyaga a Utopia—for Bwana.

He took three young wives for himself, and he had the villagers build him a large house by the river, a house with windows and corners and verandas such as the colonial Europeans might have built in Kenya two centuries earlier.

He went hunting every day, collecting trophies for himself and providing the village with more meat than they had ever had before. At nights he went to the village to eat and drink and dance, and then, armed with his rifle, he walked through the darkness to his own house.

Soon Koinnage was making plans to build a house similar to Bwana's, right in the village, and many of the young men wanted the Maasai to procure rifles for them. This he refused to do, explaining that there could be only one Bwana on Kirinyaga, and it was their job to serve as trackers and cooks and skinners.

He no longer wore European clothes, but always appeared in traditional Maasai dress, his hair meticulously pleated and braided, his body bright and glistening from the oils that his wives rubbed on him each night.

I kept my own counsel and continued my duties, caring for the sick, bringing the rains, reading the entrails of goats, blessing the scarecrows, alleviating curses. But I did not say another word to Bwana, nor did he speak to me.

Ndemi spent more and more time with me, tending my goats and chickens, and even keeping my *boma* clean, which is woman's work but which he volunteered to do.

Finally one day he approached me while I sat in the shade, watching the cattle grazing in a nearby field.

"May I speak, *mundumugu?*" he asked, squatting down next to me.

"You may speak, Ndemi," I answered.

"The Maasai has taken another wife," he said. "And he killed Karanja's dog because its barking annoyed him." He paused. "And he calls everyone 'Boy,' even the elders, which seems to me to be a term of disrespect."

"I know these things," I said.

"Why do you not do something, then?" asked Ndemi. "Are you not all-powerful?"

"Only Ngai is all-powerful," I said. "I am just the *mundumugu.*"

"But is not the *mundumugu* more powerful than a Maasai?"

"Most of the people in the village do not seem to think so," I said.

"Ah!" he said. "You are angry with them for losing faith in you, and *that* is why you have not turned him into an insect and stepped on him."

"I am not angry," I said. "Merely disappointed."

"When will you kill him?" asked Ndemi.

"It would do no good to kill him," I replied.

"Why not?"

"Because they believe in his power, and if he died, they would just send for another hunter, who would become another Bwana."

"Then will you do nothing?"

"I will do something," I answered. "But killing Bwana is not the answer. He must be humiliated before the people, so that they can see for themselves that he is not, after all, a *mundumugu* who must be listened to and obeyed."

"How will you do this?" asked Ndemi anxiously.

"I do not know yet," I said. "I must study him further."

"I thought you knew everything already."

I smiled. "The *mundumugu* does not know everything, nor does he have to."

"Oh?"

"He must merely know more than his people."

"But you already know more than Koinnage and the others."

"I must be sure I know more than the Maasai before I act," I said. "You may know how large the leopard is, and how strong, and how fast, and how cunning—but until you have studied him further, and learned how he charges, and which side he favors, and how he tests the wind, and how he signals an attack by moving his tail, you are at a disadvantage if you hunt him. I am an old man, and I cannot defeat the Maasai in hand-to-hand combat, so I must study him and discover his weakness."

"And what if he has none?"

"Everything has a weakness."

"Even though he is stronger than you?"

"The elephant is the strongest beast of all, and yet a handful of tiny ants inside his trunk can drive him mad with pain to the point where he will kill himself." I paused. "You do not have to be stronger than your opponent, for surely the ant is not stronger than the elephant. But the ant knows the elephant's weakness, and I must learn the Maasai's."

He placed his hand to his chest.

"*I* believe in you, Koriba," he said.

"I am glad," I said, shielding my eyes as a hot breeze blew a cloud of dust across my hill. "For you alone will not be disappointed when I finally confront the Maasai."

"Will you forgive the men of the village?" he asked.

I paused before answering. "When they remember once more why we came to Kirinyaga, I will forgive them," I said at last.

"And if they do not remember?"

"I must make them remember," I said. I looked out across the savannah, following its contours as it led up to the river and the woods. "Ngai has given the Kikuyu a second chance at Utopia, and we must not squander it."

"You and Koinnage, and even the Maasai, keep using that word, but I do not understand it."

"Utopia?" I asked.

He nodded. "What does it mean?"

"It means many things to many people," I replied. "To the true Kikuyu, it means to live as one with the land, to respect the ancient laws and rituals, and to please Ngai."

"That seems simple enough."

"It does, doesn't it?" I agreed. "And yet you cannot begin to imagine how many millions of men have died because their definition of Utopia differed from their neighbor's."

He stared at me. "Truly?"

"Truly. Take the Maasai, for example. His Utopia is to ride upon his sedan chair, and to shoot animals, and to take many wives, and to live in a big house by the river."

"It does not sound like a bad thing," observed Ndemi thoughtfully.

"It is not a bad thing—for the Maasai." I paused briefly. "But do you suppose it is Utopia for the men who must carry the chair, or the animals that he kills, or the young men of the village who cannot marry, or the Kikuyu who must build his house by the river?"

"I see," said Ndemi, his eyes widening. "Kirinyaga must be a Utopia for all of us, or it cannot be a Utopia at all." He brushed an insect from his cheek and looked at me. "Is that correct, Koriba?"

"You learn quickly, Ndemi," I said, reaching a hand out and rubbing the hair atop his head. "Perhaps some day you yourself will become a *mundumugu*."

"Will I learn magic then?"

"You must learn many things to be a *mungumugu*," I said. "Magic is the least of them."

"But it is the most impressive," he said. "It is what makes the people fear you, and fearing you, they are willing to listen to your wisdom."

As I considered his words, I finally began to get an inkling of how I would defeat Bwana and return my people to the Utopian existence that we had envisioned when we accepted our charter for Kirinyaga.

"Sheep!" growled Bwana. "All sheep! No wonder the Maasai preyed on the Kikuyu in the old days."

I had decided to enter the village at night, to further observe my enemy. He had drunk much *pombe,* and finally stripped off his red cloak and stood naked before Koinnage's *boma,* challenging the young men of the village to wrestle him. They stood back in the shadows, shaking like women, in awe of his physical prowess.

"I will fight three of you at once!" he said, looking around for any volunteers. There were none, and he threw back his head and laughed heartily.

"And you wonder why I am Bwana and you are a bunch of boys!"

Suddenly his eyes fell on me.

"*There* is a man who is not afraid of me," he announced.

"That is true," I said.

"Will *you* wrestle me, old man?"

I shook my head. "No, I will not."

"I guess you are just another coward."

"I do not fear the buffalo or the hyena, but I do not wrestle with *them*, either," I said. "There is a difference between courage and foolishness. You are a young man; I am an old one."

"What brings you to the village at night?" he asked. "Have you been speaking to your gods, plotting ways to kill me?"

"There is only one god," I replied, "and He disapproves of killing."

He nodded, an amused smile on his face. "Yes, it stands to reason that the god of sheep would disapprove of killing." Suddenly the smile vanished, and he stared contemptuously at me. "En-kai spits upon your god, old man."

"You call Him En-kai and we call him Ngai," I said calmly, "but it is the same god, and the day will come when we all must answer to Him. I hope you will be as bold and fearless then as you are now."

"I hope your Ngai will not tremble before *me*," he retorted, posturing before his wives, who giggled at his arrogance. "Did I not go naked into the night, armed with only a spear, and slay *fisi*? Have I not killed more than one hundred beasts in less than thirty days? Your Ngai had better not test my temper."

"He will test more than your temper," I replied.

"What does *that* mean?"

"It means whatever you wish it to mean," I said. "I am old and tired, and I wish to sit by the fire and drink *pombe*."

With that I turned my back on him and walked over to Njobe, who was warming his ancient bones by a small fire just outside Koinnage's *boma*.

Unable to find an opponent with which to wrestle, Bwana drank more *pombe* and finally turned to his wives.

"No one will fight me," he said with mock misery. "And yet my fighting blood is boiling within my veins. Set me a task—any task—that I may do for your pleasure."

The three girls whispered together and giggled again, and finally one of them stepped forward, urged by the other two.

"We have seen Koriba place his hand in the fire without being burned," she said. "Can you do that?"

He snorted contemptuously. "A magician's trick, nothing more. Set me a true task."

"Set him an *easier* task," I said. "Obviously the fire is too painful."

He turned and glared at me. "What kind of lotion did you place on your hand before putting it in the fire, old man?" he asked in English.

I smiled at him. "That would be an *illusionist's* trick, not a magician's," I answered.

"You think to humiliate me before my people?" he said. "Think again, old man."

He walked to the fire, stood between Njobe and myself, and thrust his hand into it. His face was totally impassive, but I could smell the burning flesh. Finally he withdrew it and held it up.

"There is no magic to it!" he shouted in Swahili.

"But you are burned, my husband," said the wife who had challenged him.

"Did I cry out?" he demanded. "Did I cringe from pain?"

"No, you did not."

"Can any other man place his hand in the fire without crying out?"

"No, my husband."

"Who, then, is the greater man—Koriba, who protects himself with magic, or I, who need no magic to place my hand in the fire?"

"Bwana," said his wives in unison.

He turned to me and grinned triumphantly.

"You have lost again, old man."

But I had not lost.

I had gone to the village to study my enemy, and I had learned much from my visit. Just as a Kikuyu cannot become a Maasai, this Maasai could not become a Kikuyu. There was an arrogance that had been bred into him, an arrogance so great that it had not only elevated him to his current high status, but would prove to be his downfall as well.

The next morning Koinnage himself came to my *boma*.

"*Jambo,*" I greeted him.

"*Jambo,* Koriba," he replied. "We must talk."

"About what?"

"About Bwana," said Koinnage.

"What about him?"

"He has overstepped himself," said Koinnage. "Last night, after you left, he decided that he had drunk too much *pombe* to return home, and he threw me out of my own hut—*me,* the paramount chief!" He paused to kick at a small lizard, that had been approaching his foot, and then continued. "Not only that, but this morning he announced that he was taking my youngest wife, Kibo, for his own!"

"Interesting," I remarked, watching the tiny lizard as it scurried under a bush, then turned and stared at us.

"Is that all you can say?" he demanded. "I paid twenty cows and five goats for her. When I told him that, do you know what he did?"

"What?"

Koinnage held up a small silver coin for me to see. "He gave me a *shilling* from Kenya!" He spat upon the coin and threw it onto the dry, rocky slope beyond my *boma*. "And now he says that whenever he stays in the village he will sleep in my hut, and that I must sleep elsewhere."

"I am very sorry," I said. "But I warned you against sending for a hunter. It is his nature to prey upon all things: the hyena, the kudu, even the Kikuyu." I paused, enjoying his discomfort. "Perhaps you should tell him to go away."

"He would not listen."

I nodded. "The lion may sleep with the goat, and he may feed upon him, but he very rarely listens to him."

"Koriba, we were wrong," said Koinnage, his face a mask of desperation. "Can you not rid of us this intruder?"

"Why?" I asked.

"I have already told you."

I shook my head slowly. "You have told me why *you* have cause to resent him," I answered. "That is not enough."

"What more must I say?" asked Koinnage.

I paused and looked at him. "It will come to you in the fullness of time."

"Perhaps we can contact Maintenance," suggested Koinnage. "Surely *they* have the power to make him leave."

I sighed deeply. "Have you learned nothing?"

"I do not understand."

"You sent for the Maasai because he was stronger than *fisi*. Now you want to send for Maintenance because they are stronger than the Maasai. If one man can so change our society, what do you think will happen when we invite many men? Already our young men talk of hunting instead of farming, and wish to build European houses with corners where demons can hide, and beg the Maasai to supply them with guns. What will they want when they have seen all the wonders that Maintenance possesses?"

"Then how are we to rid ourselves of the Maasai?"

"When the time comes, he will leave," I said.

"You are certain?"

"I am the *mundumugu*."

"When will this time be?" asked Koinnage.

"When you know *why* he must leave," I answered. "Now perhaps you should return to the village, lest you discover that he wants your other wives as well."

Panic spread across Koinnage's face, and he raced back down the winding trail to the village without another word.

I spent the next few days gathering bark from some of the trees at the edge of the savannah, and when I had gathered as much as I needed I added certain herbs and roots and mashed them to a pulp in an old turtle shell. I added some water, placed it in a cooking gourd, and began simmering the concoction over a small fire.

When I was done I sent for Ndemi, who arrived about half an hour later.

"*Jambo*, Koriba," he said.

"*Jambo*, Ndemi," I replied.

He looked at my cooking gourd and wrinkled his nose. "What is that?" he asked. "It smells terrible."

"It is not for eating," I replied.

"I hope not," he said devoutly.

"Be careful not to touch it," I said, walking over to the tree that grew within my *boma* and sitting down in its shade. Ndemi, giving the gourd a wide birth, joined me.

"You sent for me," he said.

"Yes, I did."

"I am glad. The village is not a good place to be."

"Oh?"

He nodded. "A number of the young men now follow Bwana everywhere. They take goats from the *shambas* and cloth from the huts, and nobody dares to stop them. Kanjara tried yesterday, but the young men hit him and made his mouth bleed while Bwana watched and laughed."

I nodded, for none of this surprised me.

"I think it is almost time," I said, waving my hand to scare away some flies that also sought shade beneath the tree and were buzzing about my face.

"Almost time for what?"

"For Bwana to leave Kirinyaga." I paused. "That is why I sent for you."

"The *mundumugu* wishes me to help him?" said Ndemi, his young face shining with pride.

I nodded.

"I will do anything you say," vowed Ndemi.

"Good. Do you know who makes the oils with which Bwana anoints himself?"

"Old Wambu makes them."

"You must bring me two gourds filled with them."

"I thought only the Maasai anoints himself," said Ndemi.

"Just do as I say. Now, have you a bow?"

"No, but my father does. He has not used it in many years, so he will not mind if I take it."

"I do not want anyone to know you have it."

Ndemi shrugged and idly drew a pattern in the dirt with his forefinger. "He will blame the young men who follow Bwana."

"And has your father any arrows with sharp tips?"

"No," said Ndemi. "But I can make some."

"I want you to make some this afternoon," I said. "Ten should be enough."

Ndemi drew an arrow in the dirt. "Like so?" he asked.

"A little shorter," I said.

"I can get the feathers for the arrows from the chickens in our *boma*," he suggested.

I nodded. "That is good."

"Do you want me to shoot an arrow into Bwana?"

"I told you once: the Kikuyu do not kill their fellow men."

"Then what do you want me to do with the arrows?"

"Bring them back here to my *boma* when you have made them," I said. "And bring ten pieces of cloth in which to wrap them."

"And then what?"

"And then we will dip them into the poison I have been making."

He frowned. "But you do not wish me to shoot an arrow into Bwana?" He paused. "What shall I shoot, then?"

"I will tell you when the time comes," I said. "Now return to the village and do what I have asked you to do."

"Yes, Koriba," he said, running out of my *boma* and down the hill on his strong young legs as a number of guinea fowl, squawking and screeching, moved resentfully out of his path.

It was less than an hour later that Koinnage once again climbed my hill, this time accompanied by Njobe and two other elders, all wearing their tribal robes.

"*Jambo*, Koriba," said Koinnage unhappily.

"*Jambo*," I replied.

"You told me to come back when I understood why Bwana must leave," said Koinnage. He spat on the ground, and a tiny spider raced away. "I have come."

"And what have you learned?" I asked, raising my hand to shade my eyes from the sun.

He lowered his eyes to the ground, uncomfortable as a child being questioned by his father.

"I have learned that a Utopia is a delicate thing which

requires protection from those who would force their will upon it."

"And you, Njobe?" I said. "What have you learned?"

"Our life here was very good," he answered. "And I believed that goodness was its own defense." He sighed deeply. "But it is not."

"Is Kirinyaga worth defending?" I asked.

"How can you, of all people, ask that?" demanded one of the other two elders.

"The Maasai can bring many machines and much money to Kirinyaga," I said. "He seeks only to improve us, not destroy us."

"It would not be Kirinyaga any longer," said Njobe. "It would be Kenya all over again."

"He has corrupted everything he has touched," said Koinnage, his face contorted with rage and humiliation. "My own son has become one of his followers. No longer does he show respect for his father, or for our women or our traditions. He speaks only of money and guns now, and he worships Bwana as if he were Ngai Himself." He paused. "You must help us, Koriba."

"Yes," added Njobe. "We were wrong not to listen to you."

I stared at each of their worried faces in turn, and finally I nodded.

"I will help you."

"When?"

"Soon."

"*How* soon?" persisted Koinnage, coughing as the wind blew a cloud of dust past his face. "We cannot wait much longer."

"Within a week the Maasai will be gone," I said.

"Within a week?" repeated Koinnage.

"That is my promise." I paused. "But if we are to purify our society, his followers may have to leave with him."

"You cannot take my son from me!" said Koinnage.

"The Maasai has already taken him," I pointed out. "I will have to decide if he will be allowed to return."

"But he is to be the paramount chief when I die."

"That is my price, Koinnage," I said firmly. "You must let me decide what to do with the Maasai's followers." I placed a hand to my heart. "I will make a just decision."

"I do not know," muttered Koinnage.

I shrugged. "Then live with the Maasai."

Koinnage stared intently at the ground, as if the ants and termites could tell him what to do. Finally he sighed.

"It will be as you say," he agreed unhappily.

"How will you rid us of the Maasai?" asked Njobe.

"I am the *mundumugu*," I answered noncommittally, for I wanted no hint of my plan to reach Bwana's ears.

"It will take powerful magic," said Njobe.

"Do you doubt my powers?" I asked.

Njobe would not meet my gaze. "No, but . . ."

"But what?"

"But he is like a god. He will be difficult to destroy."

"We have room for only one god," I said, "and His name is Ngai."

They returned to the village, and I went back to blending my poison.


While I waited for Ndemi to return, I took a thin piece of wood and carved a tiny hole in it. Then I took a long needle, stuck it lengthwise through the entire length of the wood, and withdrew it.

Finally I placed the wood to my lips and blew into the hole. I could hear no sound, but the cattle in the pasture suddenly raised their heads, and two of my goats began racing frantically in circles. I tried my makeshift whistle twice more, received the same reaction, and finally put it aside.

Ndemi arrived in mid-afternoon, carrying the oil gourds, his father's ancient bow and ten carefully crafted arrows. He had been unable to find any metal, but he had carved very sharp points at the end of each. I checked the bowstring, decided that it still had resiliency, and nodded my approval.

Then, very carefully making sure not to let any of the poison come in contact with my flesh, I dipped the head of each arrow into my solution, and wrapped them in the ten pieces of cloth Ndemi had brought.

"It is good," I said. "Now we are ready."

"What must I do, Koriba?" he asked.

"In the old days when we still lived in Kenya, only Europeans were allowed to hunt, and they used to be paid to take other Europeans on safari," I explained. "It was important to these white hunters that their clients killed many animals, for if they were disappointed, they would either not return or would pay a different white hunter to take them on their next safari." I paused. "Because of this, the hunters would sometimes train a pride of lions to come out and be killed."

"How would they do this, Koriba?" asked Ndemi, his eyes wide with wonder.

"The white hunter would send his tracker out ahead of the safari," I said, pouring the oil into six smaller gourds as I spoke. "The tracker would go into the veldt where the lions lived, and kill a wildebeest or a zebra, and slit open its belly, so that the odors wafted in the wind. Then he would blow a whistle. The lions would come, either because of the odors or because they were curious about the strange new sound.

"The tracker would kill another zebra the next day, and blow the whistle again, and the lions would come again. This went on every day until the lions knew that when they heard the whistle, there would be a dead animal waiting for them—and when the tracker had finally trained them to come at the sound of the whistle, he would return to the safari, and lead the hunter and his clients to the veldt where the lions dwelt, and then blow the whistle. The lions would run toward the sound, and the hunter's clients would collect their trophies."

I smiled at his delighted reaction, and wondered if anyone left on Earth knew that the Kikuyu had anticipated Pavlov by more than a century.

Then I handed Ndemi the whistle I had carved.

"This is your whistle," I said. "You must not lose it."

"I will place a thong around my neck and tie it to the thong," he said. "I will not lose it."

"If you do," I continued, "I will surely die a terrible death."

"You can trust me, *mundumugu*."

"I know I can." I picked up the arrows and handed them carefully to him. "These are yours," I said. "You must be very careful with them. If you cut your skin on them, or press them against a wound, you will almost certainly die, and not all of my powers will be able to save you."

"I understand," he said, taking the arrows gingerly and setting them on the ground next to his bow.

"Good," I said. "Do you know the forest that is half a mile from the house Bwana has built by the river?"

"Yes, Koriba."

"Each day I want you to go there and slay a grass-eater with one of your poisoned arrows. Do not try to kill the buffalo, because he is too dangerous—but you may kill any other grass-eater. Once it is dead, pour all the oil from one of these six gourds onto it."

165

"And then shall I blow the whistle for the hyenas?" he asked.

"Then you will climb a nearby tree, and only when you are safe in its branches are you to blow the whistle," I said. "They will come—slowly the first day, more rapidly the second and third, and almost instantly by the fourth. You will sit in the tree for a long time after they have eaten and gone, and then you will climb down and return to your *boma*."

"I will do as you ask, Koriba," he said. "But I do not see how this will make Bwana leave Kirinyaga."

"That is because you are not yet a *mundumugu*," I replied with a smile. "But I am not yet through instructing you."

"What else must I do?"

"I have one final task to set before you," I continued. "Just before sunrise on the seventh day, you will leave your *boma* and kill a seventh animal."

"I only have six gourds of oil," he pointed out.

"You will not need any on the seventh day. They will come simply because you whistle." I paused to make sure he was following my every word. "As I say, you will kill a grass-eater before sunrise, but this time you will not spread oil on him, and you will not blow your whistle immediately. You will climb a tree that affords you a clear view of the plains between the woods and the river. At some point you will see me wave my hand *thus*"—I demonstrated a very definite rotating motion with my right hand—"and then you must blow the whistle *immediately*. Do you understand?"

"I understand."

"Good."

"And what you have told me to do will rid Kirinyaga of Bwana forever?" he asked.

"Yes."

"I wish I knew how," persisted Ndemi.

"This much I will tell you," I said. "Being a civilized man, he will expect two things: that I will confront him on my own territory, and that—because I, too, have been educated by the Europeans—that I will use the Europeans' technology to defeat him."

"But you will not do what he expects?"

"No," I said. "He still does not understand that our traditions supply us with everything we need on Kirinyaga. I will confront him on his own battleground, and I will defeat him with the weapons of the Kikuyu and not the Europeans." I paused again. "And now, Ndemi, you must go slay the first of the grass-eaters, or it will be dark before you go home, and I do not want you walking across the savannah at night."

He nodded, picked up his whistle and his weapons, and strode off toward the woods by the river.

On the sixth night I walked down to the village, arriving just after dark.

The dancing hadn't started yet, though most of the adults had already gathered. Four young men, including Koinnage's son, tried to block my way, but Bwana was in a generous mood, and he waved them aside.

"Welcome, old man," he said, sitting atop his tall stool. "It has been many days since I have seen you."

"I have been busy."

"Plotting my downfall?" he asked with an amused smile.

"Your downfall was predetermined by Ngai," I replied.

"And what will cause *my* downfall?" he continued, signaling one of his wives—he had five now—to bring him a fresh gourd of *pombe*.

"The fact that you are not a Kikuyu."

"What is so special about the Kikuyu?" he demanded. "They are a tribe of sheep who stole their women from the

Wakamba and their cattle and goats from the Luo. Their sacred mountain, from which this world took its name, they stole from the Maasai, for *Kirinyaga* is a Maasai word."

"Is that true, Koriba?" asked one of the younger men.

I nodded. "Yes, it is true. In the language of the Maasai, *kiri* means *mountain,* and *nyaga* means *light.* But while it is a Maasai word, it is the Kikuyu's Mountain of Light, given to us by Ngai."

"It is the Maasai's mountain," said Bwana. "Even its peaks are named after Maasai chieftains."

"There has never been a Maasai on the holy mountain," said old Njobe.

"We owned the mountain first, or it would bear a Kikuyu name," responded Bwana.

"Then the Kikuyu must have slain the Maasai, or driven them away," said Njobe with a sly smile.

This remark angered Bwana, for he threw his gourd of *pombe* at a passing goat, hitting it on the flanks with such power that it bowled the goat over. The animal quickly got to its feet and raced through the village, bleating in terror.

"You are fools!" growled Bwana. "And if indeed the Kikuyu drove the Maasai from the mountain, then I will now redress the balance. I now proclaim myself Laibon of Kirinyaga, and declare that it is no longer a Kikuyu world."

"What is a Laibon?" asked one of the men.

"It is the Maasai word for king," I said.

"How can this not be a Kikuyu world, when everyone except you is a Kikuyu?" Njobe demanded of Bwana.

Bwana pointed at his five young henchmen. "I hereby declare these men to be Maasai."

"You cannot make them Maasai just by calling them Maasai."

Bwana grinned as the flickering firelight cast strange patterns on his sleek, shining body. "I can do anything I want. I am the Laibon."

"Perhaps Koriba has something to say about that," said Koinnage, for he knew that the week was almost up.

Bwana stared at me belligerently. "Well, old man, do you dispute my right to be king?"

"No," I said. "I do not."

"Koriba!" exclaimed Koinnage.

"You cannot mean that!" said Njobo.

"We must be realistic," I said. "Is he not our mightiest hunter?"

Bwana snorted. "I am your *only* hunter."

I turned to Koinnage. "Who else but Bwana could walk naked into the veldt, armed only with a spear, and slay *fisi?*"

Bwana nodded his head. "That is true."

"Of course," I continued, "none of us saw him do it, but I am sure he would not lie to us."

"Do you dispute that I killed *fisi* with a spear?" demanded Bwana heatedly.

"I do not dispute it," I said earnestly. "I have no doubt that you could do it again whenever you wished."

"That it true, old man," he said, somewhat assuaged.

"In fact," I continued, "perhaps we should celebrate your becoming Laibon with another such hunt—but this time in the daylight, so that your subjects may see for themselves the prowess and courage of their king."

He took another gourd from his youngest wife and stared at me intently. "Why are you saying this, old man? What do you really want?"

"Only what I have said," I replied, spitting on my hands to show my sincerity.

He shook his head. "No," he said. "You are up to some mischief."

I shrugged. "Well, if you would rather not . . ."

"Perhaps he is afraid to," said Njobe.

"I fear nothing!" snapped Bwana.

"Certainly he does not fear *fisi*," I said. "That much should be evident by now."

"Right," said Bwana, still staring at me.

"Then if he does not fear *fisi*, what *does* he fear about a hunt?" asked Njobe.

"He does not wish to hunt because *I* suggested it," I replied. "He still does not trust me, and that is understandable."

"Why is that understandable?" demanded Bwana. "Do you think I fear your mumbo-jumbo like the other sheep do?"

"I have not said that," I answered.

"You have no magic, old man," he said, getting to his feet. "You have only tricks and threats, and these mean nothing to a Maasai." He paused, and then raised his voice so that everyone could hear him. "I will spend the night in Koinnage's hut, and then I will hunt *fisi* tomorrow morning, in the old way, so that all my subjects can see the their Laibon in combat."

"Tomorrow morning?" I repeated.

He glared at me, his Maasai arrogance chiseled in every feature of his lean, handsome face.

"At sunrise."


I awoke early the next morning, as usual, but this time, instead of building a fire and sitting next to it until the chill had vanished from my aged bones, I donned my *kikoi* and walked immediately to the village. All of the men were gathered around Koinnage's *boma*, waiting for Bwana to emerge.

Finally he came out of his hut, his body anointed beneath his red cloak. He seemed clear-eyed despite the vast quantities of *pombe* he had imbibed the previous night, and in his right hand he clutched the same spear he had used during his very first hunt on Kirinyaga.

Contemptuous of us all, he looked neither right nor left, but began walking through the village and out onto the savannah toward the river. We fell into step behind him, and our little procession continued until we were perhaps a mile from his house. Then he stopped and held a hand up.

"You will come no farther," he announced, "or your numbers will frighten *fisi* away."

He let his red cloak fall to the ground and stood, naked and glistening, in the morning sunlight.

"Now watch, my sheep, and see how a true king hunts."

He hefted his spear once, to get the feel of it, and then he strode off into the waist-high grass.

Koinnage sidled up to me. "You promised that he would leave today," he whispered.

"So I did."

"He is still here."

"The day is not yet over."

"You're *sure* he will leave?" persisted Koinnage.

"Have I ever lied to my people?" I responded.

"No," he said, stepping back. "No, you have not."

We fell silent again, looking out across the plains. For a long time we could see nothing at all. Then Bwana emerged from a clump of bushes and walked boldly toward a spot about fifty yards ahead of him.

And then the wind shifted and suddenly the air was pierced by the ear-splitting laughter of hyenas as they caught scent of his oiled body. We could see grass swaying as the pack made their way toward Bwana, yelping and cackling as they approached.

For a moment he stood his ground, for he was truly a brave

man, but then, when he saw their number and realized that he could kill no more than one of them, he hurled his spear at the nearest hyena and raced to a nearby acacia tree, clambering up it just before the first six hyenas reached its base.

Within another minute there were fifteen full-grown hyenas circling the tree, snarling and laughing at him, and Bwana had no choice but to remain where he was.

"How disappointing," I said at last. "I believed him when he said he was a mighty hunter."

"He is mightier than you, old man," said Koinnage's son.

"Nonsense," I said. "Those are just hyenas around his tree, not demons." I turned to Koinnage's son and his companions. "I thought you were his friends. Why do you not go to help him?"

They shifted uneasily, and then Koinnage's son spoke: "We are unarmed, as you can see."

"What difference does that make?" I said. "You are almost Maasai, and they are just hyenas."

"If they are so harmless, why don't *you* make them go away?" demanded Koinnage's son.

"This is not my hunt," I replied.

"You cannot make them go away, so do not chide us for standing here."

"I can make them go away," I said. "Am I not the *mundumugu?*"

"Then do so!" he challenged me.

I turned to the men of the village. "The son of Koinnage has put a challenge to me. Do you wish me to save the Maasai?"

"No!" they said almost as one.

I turned to the young man. "There you have it."

"You are lucky, old man," he said, a sullen expression on his face. "You could not have done it."

"*You* are the lucky one," I said.

"Why?" he demanded.

"Because you called me old man, rather than *mundumugu* or *m'zee,* and I have not punished you." I stared unblinking at him. "But know that should you ever call me old man again, I will turn you into the smallest of rodents and leave you in the field for the jackals to feed upon."

I uttered my statement with such conviction that he suddenly seemed less sure of himself.

"You are bluffing, *mundumugu,*" he said at last. "You have no magic."

"You are a foolish young man," I said, "for you have seen my magic work in the past, and you know it will work again in the future."

"Then make the hyenas disperse," he said.

"If I do so, will you and your companions swear fealty to me, and respect the laws and traditions of the Kikuyu?"

He considered my proposition for a long moment, then nodded.

"And the rest of you?" I asked, turning to his companions.

There were mumbled assents.

"Very well," I said. "Your fathers and the village elders will bear witness to your agreement."

I began walking across the plain toward the tree where Bwana sat, glaring down at the hyenas. When I got within perhaps three hundred yards of them they noticed me and began approaching, constantly testing the wind and growling hungrily.

"In the name of Ngai," I intoned, "the *mundumugu* orders you to begone!"

As I finished the sentence, I waved my right arm at them in just the way I had demonstrated to Ndemi.

I heard no whistle, for it was above the range of human

hearing, but instantly the entire pack turned and raced off toward the woods.

I watched them for a moment, then turned back to my people.

"Now go back to the village," I said sternly. "I will tend to Bwana."

They retreated without a word, and I approached the tree from which Bwana had watched the entire pageant. He had climbed down and was waiting for me when I arrived.

"I have saved you with my magic," I said, "but now it is time for you to leave Kirinyaga."

"It was a trick!" he exclaimed. "It was not magic."

"Trick or magic," I said, "what difference does it make? It will happen again, and next time I will not save you."

"Why should I believe you?" he demanded sullenly.

"I have no reason to lie to you," I said. "The next time you go hunting they will attack you again, so many *fisi* that even your European gun cannot kill them all, and I will not be here to save you." I paused. "Leave while you can, Maasai. They will not be back for half an hour. You have time to walk to Haven by then, and I will use my computer to tell Maintenance that you are waiting to be taken back to Earth."

He looked deep into my eyes. "You are telling the truth," he said at last.

"I am."

"How did you do it, old man?" he asked. "I deserve to know that much before I leave."

I paused for a long moment before answering him.

"I am the *mundumugu*," I replied at last, and, turning my back on him, I returned to the village.

We tore his house down that afternoon, and in the evening I called down the rains, which purified Kirinyaga of the last taint of the corruption that had been in our midst.

The next morning I walked down the long, winding path to the village to bless the scarecrows, and the moment I arrived I was surrounded by the children, who asked for a story.

"All right," I said, gathering them in the shade of an acacia tree. "Today I shall tell you the story of the Arrogant Hunter."

"Has it a happy ending?" asked one of the girls.

I looked around the village and saw my people contentedly going about their daily chores, then stared out across the tranquil green plains.

"Yes," I said. "This time it has."

# SEVEN VIEWS OF OLDUVAI GORGE

The creatures came again last night.

The moon had just slipped behind the clouds when we heard the first rustlings in the grass. Then there was a moment of utter silence, as if they knew we were listening for them, and finally there were the familiar hoots and shrieks as they raced to within fifty meters of us and, still screeching, struck postures of aggression.

They fascinate me, for they never show themselves in the daylight, and yet they manifest none of the features of the true nocturnal animal. Their eyes are not oversized, their ears cannot move independently, they tread very heavily on their feet. They frighten most of the other members of my party, and while I am curious about them, I have yet to absorb one of them and study it.

To tell the truth, I think my use of absorption terrifies my companions more than the creatures do, though there is no reason why it should. Although I am relatively young by my race's standards, I am nevertheless many millennia older than any other member of my party. You would think, given their backgrounds, that they would know that any trait someone of my age possesses must by definition be a survival trait.

Still, it bothers them. Indeed, it *mystifies* them, much as my memory does. Of course, theirs seem very inefficient to me. Imagine having to learn everything one knows in a single lifetime, to be totally ignorant at the moment of birth! Far better to split off from your parent with his knowledge intact in your brain, just as *my* parent's knowledge came to him, and ultimately to me.

But then, that is why we are here: not to compare similarities, but to study differences. And never was there a race so different from all his fellows as Man. He was extinct barely seventeen millennia after he strode boldly out into the galaxy from this, the planet of his birth—but during that brief interval he wrote a chapter in galactic history that will last forever. He claimed the stars for his own, colonized a million worlds, ruled his empire with an iron will. He gave no quarter during his primacy, and he asked for none during his decline and fall. Even now, some forty-eight centuries after his extinction, his accomplishments and his failures still excite the imagination.

Which is why we are on Earth, at the very spot that was said to be Man's true birthplace, the rocky gorge where he first crossed over the evolutionary barrier, saw the stars with fresh eyes, and vowed that they would someday be his.

Our leader is Bellidore, an Elder of the Kragan people, orange-skinned, golden fleeced, with wise, patient ways. Bellidore is well versed in the behavior of sentient beings, and settles our disputes before we even know that we are engaged in them.

Then there are the Stardust Twins, glittering silver beings who answer to each other's names and finish each other's thoughts. They have worked on seventeen archaeological digs, but even *they* were surprised when Bellidore chose them for this most prestigious of all missions. They behave like life mates, though they display no sexual characteristics—but like all the others, they refuse to have physical contact with me, so I cannot assuage my curiosity.

Also in our party is the Moriteu, who eats the dirt as if it were a delicacy, speaks to no one, and sleeps upside-down while hanging from a branch of a nearby tree. For some reason, the creatures always leave it alone. Perhaps they think it is dead, possibly they know it is asleep and that only the rays of the sun can awaken it. Whatever the reason, we would be lost without it, for only the delicate tendrils that extend from its mouth can excavate the ancient artifacts we have discovered with the proper care.

We have four other species with us: one is an Historian, one an Exobiologist, one an Appraiser of human artifacts, and one a Mystic. (At least, I *assume* she is a Mystic, for I can find no pattern to her approach, but this may be due to my own shortsightedness. After all, what I do seems like magic to my companions and yet it is a rigorously applied science.)

And, finally, there is me. I have no name, for my people do not use names, but for the convenience of the party I have taken the name of He Who Views for the duration of the expedition. This is a double misnomer: I am not a *he,* for my race is not divided by gender; and I am not a viewer, but a Fourth Level Feeler. Still, I could intuit very early in the voyage that "feel" means something very different to my companions than to myself, and out of respect for their sensitivities, I chose a less accurate name.

Every day finds us back at work, examining the various strata. There are many signs that the area once teemed with living things, that early on there was a veritable explosion of life forms in this place, but very little remains today. There are a few species of insects and birds, some small rodents, and of course the creatures who visit our camp nightly.

Our collection has been growing slowly. It is fascinating to watch my companions perform their tasks, for in many ways they are as much of a mystery to me as my methods are to them. For example, our Exobiologist needs only to glide her tentacle across an object to tell us whether it was once living matter; the Historian, surrounded by its complex equipment, can date any object, carbon-based or otherwise, to within a decade of its origin, regardless of its state of preservation; and even the Moriteu is a thing of beauty and fascination as it gently separates the artifacts from the strata where they have rested for so long.

I am very glad I was chosen to come on this mission.

We have been here for two lunar cycles now, and the work goes slowly. The lower strata were thoroughly excavated eons ago (I have such a personal interest in learning about Man that I almost used the word *plundered* rather than *excavated,* so resentful am I at not finding more artifacts), and for reasons as yet unknown there is almost nothing in the more recent strata.

Most of us are pleased with our results, and Bellidore is particularly elated. He says that finding five nearly intact artifacts makes the expedition an unqualified success.

All the others have worked tirelessly since our arrival. Now it is almost time for me to perform my special function, and I am very excited. I know that my findings will be no more important that the others', but perhaps, when we put them all together, we can finally begin to understand what it was that made Man what he was.

"Are you . . ." asked the first Stardust Twin.

". . . ready?" said the second.

I answered that I was ready, that indeed I had been anxious for this moment.

"May we . . ."

". . . observe?" they asked.

"If you do not find it distasteful," I replied.

"We are . . ."

". . . scientists," they said. "There is . . ."

". . . very little . . ."

". . . that we cannot view . . ."

". . . objectively."

I ambulated to the table upon which the artifact rested. It was a stone, or at least that is what it appeared to be to my exterior sensory organs. It was triangular, and the edges showed signs of work.

"How old is this?" I asked.

"Three million . . ."

". . . five hundred and sixty-one thousand . . ."

". . . eight hundred and twelve years," answered the Stardust Twins.

"I see," I said.

"It is much . . ."

". . . the oldest . . ."

". . . of our finds."

I stared at it for a long time, preparing myself. Then I slowly, carefully, altered my structure and allowed my body to flow over and around the stone, engulfing it, and assimilating its history. I began to feel a delicious warmth as it became one with me, and while all my exterior senses had shut down, I knew that I was undulating and glowing with the thrill of discovery. I became one with the stone, and in that corner of my mind that is set aside for Feeling, I seemed to sense the Earth's moon looming low and ominous just above the horizon . . .

Enkatai awoke with a start just after dawn and looked up at the moon, which was still high in the sky. After all these weeks it still seemed far too large to hang suspended in the sky, and must surely crash down onto the planet any moment. The nightmare was still strong in her mind, and she tried to imagine the comforting sight of five small, unthreatening moons leapfrogging across the silver sky of her own world. She was able to hold the vision in her mind's eye for only a moment, and then it was lost, replaced by the reality of the huge satellite above her.

Her companion approached her.

"Another dream?" he asked.

"Exactly like the last one," she said uncomfortably. "The moon is visible in the daylight, and then we begin walking down the path . . ."

He stared at her with sympathy and offered her nourishment. She accepted it gratefully, and looked off across the veldt.

"Just two more days," she sighed, "and then we can leave this awful place."

"It is not such a terrible world," replied Bokatu. "It has many good qualities."

"We have wasted our time here," she said. "It is not fit for colonization."

"No, it is not," he agreed. "Our crops cannot thrive in this soil, and we have problems with the water. But we have learned many things, things that will eventually help us choose the proper world."

"We learned most of them the first week we were here," said Enkatai. "The rest of the time was wasted."

"The ship had other worlds to explore. They could not know we would be able to analyze this one in such a short time."

She shivered in the cool morning air. "I hate this place."

"It will someday be a fine world," said Bokatu. "It awaits only the evolution of the brown monkeys."

Even as he spoke, an enormous baboon, some 350 pounds in weight, heavily muscled, with a shaggy chest and bold, curious eyes, appeared in the distance. Even walking on all fours it was a formidable figure, fully twice as large as the great spotted cats.

"*We* cannot use this world," continued Bokatu, "but someday *his* descendants will spread across it."

"They seem so placid," commented Enkatai.

"They *are* placid," agreed Bokatu, hurling a piece of food at the baboon, which raced forward and picked it up off the ground. It sniffed at it, seemed to consider whether or not to taste it, and finally, after a moment of indecision, put it in its mouth. "But they will dominate this planet. The huge grass-eaters spend too much time feeding, and the predators sleep all the time. No, my choice is the brown monkey. They are fine, strong, intelligent animals. They have already developed thumbs, they possess a strong sense of community, and even the great cats think twice about attacking them. They are virtually without natural predators." He nodded his head, agreeing with himself. "Yes, it is they who will dominate this world in the eons to come."

"No predators?" said Enkatai.

"Oh, I suppose one falls prey to the great cats now and then, but even the cats do not attack when they are with their troop." He looked at the baboon. "That fellow has the strength to tear all but the biggest cat to pieces."

"Then how do you account for what we found at the bottom of the gorge?" she persisted.

"Their size has cost them some degree of agility. It is only natural that one occasionally falls down the slopes to its death."

"Occasionally?" she repeated. "I found seven skulls, each shattered as if from a blow."

"The force of the fall," said Bokatu with a shrug. "Surely you don't think the great cats brained them before killing them?"

"I wasn't thinking of the cats," she replied.

"What, then?"

"The small, tailless monkeys that live in the gorge."

Bokatu allowed himself the luxury of a superior smile. "Have you *looked* at them?" he said. "They are scarcely a quarter the size of the brown monkeys."

"I *have* looked at them," answered Enkatai. "And they, too, have thumbs."

"Thumbs alone are not enough," said Bokatu.

"They live in the shadow of the brown monkeys, and they are still here," she said. "*That* is enough."

"The brown monkeys are eaters of fruits and leaves. Why should they bother the tailless monkeys?"

"They do more than not bother them," said Enkatai. "They avoid them. That hardly seems like a species that will someday spread across the world."

Bokatu shook his head. "The tailless monkeys seem to be at an evolutionary dead end. Too small to hunt game, too large to feed themselves on what they can find in the gorge, too weak to compete with the brown monkeys for better territory. My guess is that they're an earlier, more primitive species, destined for extinction."

"Perhaps," said Enkatai.

"You disagree?"

"There is something about them . . ."

"What?"

Enkatai shrugged. "I do not know. They make me uneasy. It is something in their eyes, I think—a hint of malevolence."

"You are imagining things," said Bokatu.

"Perhaps," replied Enkatai again.

"I have reports to write today," said Bokatu. "But tomorrow I will prove it to you."

★ ★ ★ ★ ★

The next morning Bokatu was up with the sun. He prepared their first meal of the day while Enkatai completed her prayers, then performed his own while she ate.

"Now," he announced, "we will go down into the gorge and capture one of the tailless monkeys."

"Why?"

"To show you how easy it is. I may take it back with me as a pet. Or perhaps we shall sacrifice it in the lab and learn more about its life processes."

"I do not *want* a pet, and we are not authorized to kill any animals."

"As you wish," said Bokatu. "We will let it go."

"Then why capture one to begin with?"

"To show you that they are not intelligent, for if they are as bright as you think, I will not be able to capture one." He pulled her to an upright position. "Let us begin."

"This is foolish," she protested. "The ship arrives in mid-afternoon. Why don't we just wait for it?"

"We will be back in time," he replied confidently. "How long can it take?"

She looked at the clear blue sky, as if trying to urge the ship to appear. The moon was hanging, huge and white, just above the horizon. Finally she turned to him.

"All right, I will come with you—but only if you promise merely to observe them, and not to try to capture one."

"Then you admit I'm right?"

"Saying that you are right or wrong has nothing to do with the truth of the situation. I *hope* you are right, for the tailless monkeys frighten me. But I do not know you are right, and neither do you."

Bokatu stared at her for a long moment.

"I agree," he said at last.

"You agree that you cannot know?"

"I agree not to capture one," he said. "Let us proceed."

They walked to the edge of the gorge and then began climbing down the steep embankments, steadying themselves by wrapping their limbs around trees and other outgrowths. Suddenly they heard a loud screeching.

"What is that?" asked Bokatu.

"They have seen us," replied Enkatai.

"What makes you think so?"

"I have heard that scream in my dream—and always the moon was just as it appears now."

"Strange," mused Bokatu. "I have heard them many times before, but somehow they seem louder this time."

"Perhaps more of them are here."

"Or perhaps they are more frightened," he said. He glanced above him. "Here is the reason," he said, pointing. "We have company."

She looked up and saw a huge baboon, quite the largest she had yet seen, following them at a distance of perhaps fifty feet. When its eyes met hers it growled and looked away, but made no attempt to move any closer or farther away.

They kept climbing, and whenever they stopped to rest, there was the baboon, its accustomed fifty feet away from them.

"Does *he* look afraid to you?" asked Bokatu. "If these puny little creatures could harm him, would he be following us down into the gorge?"

"There is a thin line between courage and foolishness, and an even thinner line between confidence and over-confidence," replied Enkatai.

"If he is to die here, it will be like all the others," said Bokatu. "He will lose his footing and fall to his death."

"You do not find it unusual that every one of them fell on

its head?" she asked mildly.

"They broke every bone in their bodies," he replied. "I don't know why you consider only the heads."

"Because you do not get identical head wounds from different incidents."

"You have an overactive imagination," said Bokatu. He pointed to a small hairy figure that was staring up at them. "Does *that* look like something that could kill our friend here?"

The baboon glared down into the gorge and snarled. The tailless monkey looked up with no show of fear or even interest. Finally it shuffled off into the thick bush.

"You see?" said Bokatu smugly. "One look at the brown monkey and it retreats out of sight."

"It didn't seem frightened to me," noted Enkatai.

"All the more reason to doubt its intelligence."

In another few minutes they reached the spot where the tailless monkey had been. They paused to regain their strength, and then continued to the floor of the gorge.

"Nothing," announced Bokatu, looking around. "My guess is that the one we saw was a sentry, and by now the whole tribe is miles away."

"Observe our companion."

The baboon had reached the floor of the gorge and was tensely testing the wind.

"He hasn't crossed over the evolutionary barrier yet," said Bokatu, amused. "Do you expect him to search for predators with a sensor?"

"No," said Enkatai, watching the baboon. "But if there is no danger, I expect him to relax, and he hasn't done that yet."

"That's probably how he lived long enough to grow this large," said Bokatu, dismissing her remarks. He looked around. "What could they possibly find to eat here?"

"I don't know."

"Perhaps we should capture one and dissect it. The contents of its stomach might tell us a lot about it."

"You promised."

"It would be so simple, though," he persisted. "All we'd have to do would be bait a trap with fruits or nuts."

Suddenly the baboon snarled, and Bokatu and Enkatai turned to locate the source of his anger. There was nothing there, but the baboon became more and more frenzied. Finally it raced back up the gorge.

"What was that all about, I wonder?" mused Bokatu.

"I think we should leave."

"We have half a day before the ship returns."

"I am uneasy here. I walked down a path exactly like this in my dream."

"You are not used to the sunlight," he said. "We will rest inside a cave."

She reluctantly allowed him to lead her to a small cave in the wall of the gorge. Suddenly she stopped and would go no further.

"What is the matter?"

"This cave was in my dream," she said. "Do not go into it."

"You must learn not to let dreams rule your life," said Bokatu. He sniffed the air. "Something smells strange."

"Let us go back. We want nothing to do with this place."

He stuck his head into the cave. "New world, new odors."

"Please, Bokatu!"

"Let me just see what causes that odor," he said, shining his light into the cave. It illuminated a huge pile of bodies, many of them half-eaten, most in various states of decomposition.

"What are they?" he asked, stepping closer.

"Brown monkeys," she replied without looking. "Each with its head staved in."

"This was part of your dream, too?" he asked, suddenly nervous.

She nodded her head. "We must leave this place *now!*"

He walked to the mouth of the cave.

"It seems safe," he announced.

"It is never safe in my dream," she said uneasily.

They left the cave and walked about fifty yards when they came to a bend in the floor of the gorge. As they followed it, they found themselves facing a tailless monkey.

"One of them seems to have stayed behind," said Bokatu. "I'll frighten him away." He picked up a rock and threw it at the monkey, which ducked but held its ground.

Enkatai touched him urgently on the shoulder. "More than one," she said.

He looked up. Two more tailless monkeys were in a tree almost directly overhead. As he stepped aside, he saw four more lumbering toward them out of the bush. Another emerged from a cave, and three more dropped out of nearby trees.

"What have they got in their hands?" he asked nervously.

"You would call them the femur bones of grass-eaters," said Enkatai, with a sick feeling in her thorax. "*They* would call them weapons."

The hairless monkeys spread out in a semi-circle, then began approaching them slowly.

"But they're so *puny!*" said Bokatu, backing up until he came to a wall of rock and could go no farther.

"You are a fool," said Enkatai, helplessly trapped in the reality of her dream. "*This* is the race that will dominate this planet. Look into their eyes!"

Bokatu looked, and he saw things, terrifying things, that

he had never seen in any being or any animal before. He barely had time to offer a brief prayer for some disaster to befall this race before it could reach the stars, and then a tailless monkey hurled a smooth, polished, triangular stone at his head. It dazed him, and as he fell to the ground, the clubs began pounding down rhythmically on him and Enkatai.

At the top of the gorge, the baboon watched the carnage until it was over, and then raced off toward the vast savannah, where he would be safe, at least temporarily, from the tailless monkeys.

"A weapon," I mused. "It was a *weapon!*"

I was all alone. Sometime during the Feeling, the Stardust Twins had decided that I was one of the few things they could not be objective about, and had returned to their quarters.

I waited until the excitement of discovery had diminished enough for me to control my physical structure. Then I once again took the shape that I presented to my companions, and reported my findings to Bellidore.

"So even then they were aggressors," he said. "Well, it is not surprising. The will to dominate the stars had to have come from somewhere."

"It is surprising that there is no record of any race having landed here in their prehistory," said the Historian.

"It was a survey team, and Earth was of no use to them," I answered. "They doubtless touched down on any number of planets. If there is a record anywhere, it is probably in their archives, stating that Earth showed no promise as a colony world."

"But didn't they wonder what had happened to their team?" asked Bellidore.

"There were many large carnivores in the vicinity," I said. "They probably assumed the team had fallen prey to them.

189

Especially if they searched the area and found nothing."

"Interesting," said Bellidore. "That the weaker of the species should have risen to dominance."

"I think it is easily explained," said the Historian. "*As* the smaller species, they were neither as fast as their prey nor as strong as their predators, so the creation of weapons was perhaps the only way to avoid extinction . . . or at least the best way."

"Certainly they displayed the cunning of the predator during their millennia abroad in the galaxy," said Bellidore.

"One does not *stop* being aggressive simply because one invents a weapon," said the Historian. "In fact, it may *add* to one's aggression."

"I shall have to consider that," said Bellidore, looking somewhat unconvinced.

"I have perhaps over-simplified my train of thought for the sake of this discussion," replied the Historian. "Rest assured that I will build a lengthy and rigorous argument when I present my findings to the Academy."

"And what of you, He Who Views?" asked Bellidore. "Have you any observations to add to what you have told us?"

"It is difficult to think of a rock as being the precursor of the sonic rifle and the molecular imploder," I said thoughtfully, "but I believe it to be the case."

"A most interesting species," said Bellidore.

It took almost four hours for my strength to return, for Feeling saps the energy like no other function, drawing equally from the body, the emotions, the mind, and the empathic powers.

The Moriteu, its work done for the day, was hanging upside down from a tree limb, lost in its evening trance, and the Stardust Twins had not made an appearance since I had Felt the stone.

The other party members were busy with their own pursuits, and it seemed an ideal time for me to Feel the next object, which the Historian told me was approximately 23,300 years old.

It was a link of metallic chain, rusted and pitted, and before I assimilated it, I thought I could see a spot where it had been deliberately broken . . .

His name was Mtepwa, and it seemed to him that he had been wearing a metal collar around his neck since the day he had been born. He knew that couldn't be true, for he had fleeting memories of playing with his brothers and sisters, and of stalking the kudu and the bongo on the tree-covered mountain where he grew up.

But the more he concentrated on those memories, the more vague and imprecise they became, and he knew they must have happened a very long time ago. Sometimes he tried to remember the name of his tribe, but it was lost in the mists of time, as were the names of his parents and siblings.

It was at times like this that Mtepwa felt sorry for himself, but then he would consider his companions' situation, and he felt better, for while they were to be taken in ships and sent to the edge of the world to spend the remainder of their lives as slaves of the Arabs and the Europeans, he himself was the favored servant of his master, Sharif Abdullah, and as such his position was assured.

This was his eighth caravan—or was it his ninth?—from the Interior. They would trade salt and cartridges to the tribal chiefs who would in turn sell them their least productive warriors and women as slaves, and then they would march them out, around the huge lake and across the dry flat savannah.

191

They would circle the mountain that was so old that it had turned white on the top, just like a white-haired old man, and finally out to the coast, where dhows filled the harbor. There they would sell their human booty to the highest bidders, and Sharif Abdullah would purchase another wife and turn half the money over to his aged, feeble father, and they would be off to the Interior again on another quest for black gold.

Abdullah was a good master. He rarely drank—and when he did, he always apologized to Allah at the next opportunity—and he did not beat Mtepwa overly much, and they always had enough to eat, even when the cargo went hungry. He even went so far as to teach Mtepwa how to read, although the only reading matter he carried with him was the Koran.

Mtepwa spent long hours honing his reading skills with the Koran, and somewhere along the way he made a most interesting discovery: the Koran forbade a practitioner of the True Faith to keep another member in bondage.

It was at that moment that Mtepwa made up his mind to convert to Islam. He began questioning Sharif Abdullah incessantly on the finer points of his religion, and made sure that the old man saw him sitting by the fire, hour after hour, reading the Koran.

So enthused was Sharif Abdullah at this development that he frequently invited Mtepwa into his tent at suppertime, and lectured him on the subtleties of the Koran far into the night. Mtepwa was a motivated student, and Sharif Abdullah marveled at his enthusiasm.

Night after night, as lions prowled around their camp in the Serengeti, master and pupil studied the Koran together. And finally the day came when Sharif Abdullah could no longer deny that Mtepwa was indeed a true believer of Islam. It happened as they camped at the Olduvai Gorge, and that very day Sharif Abdullah had his smith remove the collar from Mtepwa's neck, and Mtepwa himself destroyed the chains link by link, hurling them deep into the gorge when he was finished. He kept a single link, which he wore around his neck as a charm.

Mtepwa was now a free man, but knowledgeable in only two areas: the Koran, and slave trading. So it was only natural that when he looked around for some means to support himself, he settled upon following in Sharif Abdullah's footsteps. He became a junior partner to the old man, and after two more trips to the Interior, he decided that he was ready to go out on his own.

To do that, he required a trained staff—warriors, smiths, cooks, trackers—and the prospect of assembling one from scratch was daunting, so, since his faith was less strong than his mentor's, he simply sneaked into Sharif Abdullah's quarters on the coast one night and slit the old man's throat.

The next day, he marched inland at the head of his own caravan.

He had learned much about the business of slaving, both as a practitioner and a victim, and he put his knowledge to full use. He knew that healthy slaves would bring a better price at market, and so he fed and treated his captives far better than Sharif Abdullah and most other slavers did. On the other hand, he knew which ones were fomenting trouble, and knew it was better to kill them on the spot as an example to the others, than to let any hopes of insurrection spread among the captives.

Because he was thorough, he was equally successful, and soon expanded into ivory trading as well. Within six years he had the biggest slaving and poaching operation in East Africa.

From time to time he ran across European explorers. It

was said that he even spent a week with Dr. David Livingstone and left without the missionary ever knowing that he had been playing host to the slaver he most wanted to put out of business.

After America's War Between the States killed his primary market, he took a year off from his operation to go to Asia and the Arabian Peninsula and open up new ones. Upon returning he found that Abdullah's son, Sharif Ibn Jad Mahir, had appropriated all his men and headed inland, intent on carrying on his father's business. Mtepwa, who had become quite wealthy, hired some 500 *askari*, placed them under the command of the notorious ivory poacher Alfred Henry Pym, and sat back to await the results.

Three months later Pym marched some 438 men back to the Tanganyikan coast. 276 were slaves that Sharif Ibn Jad Mahir had captured; the remainder were the remnants of Mtepwa's organization, who had gone to work for Sharif Ibn Jad Mahir. Mtepwa sold all 438 of them into slavery and built a new organization, composed of the warriors who had fought for him under Pym's leadership.

Most of the colonial powers were inclined to turn a blind eye to his practices, but the British, who were determined to put an end to slavery, issued a warrant for Mtepwa's arrest. Eventually he tired of continually looking over his shoulder, and moved his headquarters to Mozambique, where the Portuguese were happy to let him set up shop as long as he remembered that colonial palms needed constant greasing.

He was never happy there—he didn't speak Portuguese or any of the local languages—and after nine years he returned to Tanganyika, now the wealthiest black man on the continent.

One day he found among his latest batch of captives a young Acholi boy named Haradi, no more than ten years old, and decided to keep him as a personal servant rather than ship him across the ocean.

Mtepwa had never married. Most of his associates assumed that he had simply never had the time, but as the almost-nightly demands for Haradi to visit him in his tent became common knowledge, they soon revised their opinions. Mtepwa seemed besotted with his servant boy, though—doubtless remembering his own experience—he never taught Haradi to read, and promised a slow and painful death to anyone who spoke of Islam to the boy.

Then one night, after some three years had passed, Mtepwa sent for Haradi. The boy was nowhere to be found. Mtepwa awoke all his warriors and demanded that they search for him, for a leopard had been seen in the vicinity of the camp, and the slaver feared the worst.

They found Haradi an hour later, not in the jaws of a leopard, but in the arms of a young female slave they had taken from the Zaneke tribe. Mtepwa was beside himself with rage, and had the poor girl's arms and legs torn from her body.

Haradi never offered a word of protest, and never tried to defend the girl—not that it would have done any good—but the next morning he was gone, and though Mtepwa and his warriors spent almost a month searching for him, they found no trace of him.

By the end of the month Mtepwa was quite insane with rage and grief. Deciding that life was no longer worth living, he walked up to a pride of lions that were gorging themselves on a topi carcass and, striding into their midst, began cursing them and hitting them with his bare hands. Almost unbelievably, the lions backed away from him, snarling and growling, and disappeared into the thick bush.

The next day he picked up a large stick and began beating

a baby elephant with it. That should have precipitated a brutal attack by its mother—but the mother, standing only a few feet away, trumpeted in terror and raced off, the baby following her as best it could.

It was then that Mtepwa decided that he could not die, that somehow the act of dismembering the poor Zanake girl had made him immortal. Since both incidents had occurred within sight of his superstitious followers, they fervently believed him.

Now that he was immortal, he decided that it was time to stop trying to accommodate the Europeans who had invaded his land and kept issuing warrants for his arrest. He sent a runner to the Kenya border and invited the British to meet him in battle. When the appointed day came, and the British did not show up to fight him, he confidently told his warriors that word of his immortality had reached the Europeans and that from that day forth no white men would ever be willing to oppose him. The fact that he was still in German territory, and the British had no legal right to go there, somehow managed to elude him.

He began marching his warriors inland, openly in search of slaves, and he found his share of them in the Congo. He looted villages of their men, their women, and their ivory, and finally, with almost 600 captives and half that many tusks, he finally turned east and began the months-long trek to the coast.

This time the British were waiting for him at the Uganda border, and they had so many armed men there that Mtepwa turned south, not for fear for his own life, but because he could not afford to lose his slaves and his ivory, and he knew that his warriors lacked his invulnerability.

He marched his army down to Lake Tanganyika, then headed east. It took him two weeks to reach the western corridor of the Serengeti, and another ten days to cross it.

One night he made camp at the lip of the Olduvai Gorge, the very place where he had gained his freedom. The fires were lit, a wildebeest was slaughtered and cooked, and as he relaxed after the meal he became aware of a buzzing among his men. Then, from out of the shadows, stepped a strangely familiar figure. It was Haradi, now fifteen years old, and as tall as Mtepwa himself.

Mtepwa stared at him for a long moment, and suddenly all the anger seemed to drain from his face.

"I am very glad to see you again, Haradi," he said.

"I have heard that you cannot be killed," answered the boy, brandishing a spear. "I have come to see if that is true."

"We have no need to fight, you and I," said Mtepwa. "Join me in my tent, and all will be as it was."

"Once I tear your limbs from your body, *then* we will have no reason to fight," responded Haradi. "And even then, you will seem no less repulsive to me than you do now, or than you did all those many years ago."

Mtepwa jumped up, his face a mask of fury. "Do your worst, then!" he cried. "And when you realize that I cannot be harmed, I will do to you as I did to the Zanake girl!"

Haradi made no reply, but hurled his spear at Mtepwa. It went into the slaver's body, and was thrown with such force that the point emerged a good six inches on the other side. Mtepwa stared at Haradi with disbelief, moaned once, and tumbled down the rocky slopes of the gorge.

Haradi looked around at the warriors. "Is there any among you who dispute my right to take Mtepwa's place?" he asked confidently.

A burly Makonde stood up to challenge him, and within thirty seconds Haradi, too, was dead.

The British were waiting for them when they reached

Zanzibar. The slaves were freed, the ivory confiscated, the warriors arrested and forced to serve as laborers on the Mombasa/Uganda Railway. Two of them were later killed and eaten by lions in the Tsavo District.

By the time Lieutenant-Colonel J. H. Patterson shot the notorious Man-Eaters of Tsavo, the railway had almost reached the shanty town of Nairobi, and Mtepwa's name was so thoroughly forgotten that it was misspelled in the only history book in which it appeared.

"Amazing!" said the Appraiser. "I knew they enslaved many races throughout the galaxy—but to enslave *themselves!* It is almost beyond belief!"

I had rested from my efforts, and then related the story of Mtepwa.

"All ideas must begin somewhere," said Bellidore placidly. "This one obviously began on Earth."

"It is barbaric!" muttered the Appraiser.

Bellidore turned to me. "Man never attempted to subjugate *your* race, He Who Views. Why was that?"

"We had nothing that he wanted."

"Can you remember the galaxy when Man dominated it?" asked the Appraiser.

"I can remember the galaxy when Man's progenitors killed Bokatu and Enkatai," I replied truthfully.

"Did you ever have any dealings with Man?"

"None. Man had no use for us."

"But did he not destroy profligately things for which he had no use?"

"No," I said. "He took what he wanted, and he destroyed that which threatened him. The rest he ignored."

"Such arrogance!"

"Such practicality," said Bellidore.

"You call genocide on a galactic scale *practical?*" demanded the Appraiser.

"From Man's point of view, it was," answered Bellidore. "It got him what he wanted with a minimum of risk and effort. Consider that one single race, born not five hundred yards from us, at one time ruled an empire of more than a million worlds. Almost every civilized race in the galaxy spoke Terran."

"Upon pain of death."

"That is true," agreed Bellidore. "I did not say Man was an angel. Only that, if he was indeed a devil, he was an efficient one."

It was time for me to assimilate the third artifact, which the Historian and the Appraiser seemed to think was the handle of a knife, but even as I moved off to perform my function, I could not help but listen to the speculation that was taking place.

"Given his bloodlust and his efficiency," said the Appraiser, "I'm surprised that he lived long enough to reach the stars."

"It *is* surprising in a way," agreed Bellidore. "The Historian tells me that Man was not always homogenous, that early in his history there were several variations of the species. He was divided by color, by belief, by territory." He sighed. "Still, he must have learned to live in peace with his fellow man. That much, at least, accrues to his credit."

I reached the artifact with Bellidore's words still in my ears, and began to engulf it . . .

Mary Leakey pressed against the horn of the Landrover. Inside the museum, her husband turned to the young uniformed officer.

"I can't think of any instructions to give you," he said.

"The museum's not open to the public yet, and we're a good 300 kilometers from Kikuyuland."

"I'm just following my orders, Dr. Leakey," replied the officer.

"Well, I suppose it doesn't hurt to be safe," acknowledged Leakey. "There are a lot of Kikuyu who want me dead even though I spoke up for Kenyatta at his trial." He walked to the door. "If the discoveries at Lake Turkana prove interesting, we could be gone as long as a month. Otherwise, we should be back within ten to twelve days."

"No problem, sir. The museum will still be here when you get back."

"I never doubted it," said Leakey, walking out and joining his wife in the vehicle.

Lieutenant Ian Chelmswood stood in the doorway and watched the Leakeys, accompanied by two military vehicles, start down the red dirt road. Within seconds the car was obscured by dust, and he stepped back into the building and closed the door to avoid being covered by it. The heat was oppressive, and he removed his jacket and holster and laid them neatly across one of the small display cases.

It was strange. All the images he had seen of African wildlife, from the German Schillings' old still photographs to the American Johnson's motion pictures, had led him to believe that East Africa was a wonderland of green grass and clear water. No one had ever mentioned the dust, but that was the one memory of it that he would take home with him.

Well, not quite the only one. He would never forget the morning the alarm had sounded back when he was stationed in Nanyuki. He arrived at the settlers' farm and found the entire family cut to ribbons and all their cattle mutilated, most with their genitals cut off, many missing ears and eyes. But as horrible as that was, the picture he would carry to his grave was the kitten impaled on a dagger and pinned to the mailbox. It was the Mau Mau's signature, just in case anyone thought some madman had run berserk among the cattle and the humans.

Chelmswood didn't understand the politics of it. He didn't know who had started it, who had precipitated the war. It made no difference to him. He was just a soldier, following orders, and if those orders would take him back to Nanyuki so that he could kill the men who had committed those atrocities, so much the better.

But in the meantime, he had pulled what he considered Idiot Duty. There had been a very mild outburst of violence in Arusha, not really Mau Mau but rather a show of support for Kenya's Kikuyu, and his unit had been transferred there. Then the government found out that Professor Leakey, whose scientific finds had made Olduvai Gorge almost a household word among East Africans, had been getting death threats. Over his objections, they had insisted on providing him with bodyguards. Most of the men from Chelmswood's unit would accompany Leakey on his trip to Lake Turkana, but someone had to stay behind to guard the museum, and it was just his bad luck that his name had been atop the duty roster.

It wasn't even a museum, really, not the kind of museum his parents had taken him to see in London. *Those* were museums; this was just a two-room mud-walled structure with perhaps a hundred of Leakey's finds. Ancient arrowheads, some oddly-shaped stones that had functioned as prehistoric tools, a couple of bones that obviously weren't from monkeys but that Chelmswood was certain were not from any creature *he* was related to.

Leakey had hung some crudely drawn charts on the wall, charts that showed what he believed to be the evolution of

201

some small, grotesque, apelike beasts into *homo sapiens*. There were photographs, too, showing some of the finds that had been sent on to Nairobi. It seemed that even if this gorge was the birthplace of the race, nobody really wanted to visit it. All the best finds were shipped back to Nairobi and then to the British Museum. In fact, this wasn't a museum at all, decided Chelmswood, but rather a holding area for the better specimens until they could be sent elsewhere.

It was strange to think of life starting here in this gorge. If there was an uglier spot in Africa, he had yet to come across it. And while he didn't accept Genesis or any of that religious nonsense, it bothered him to think that the first human beings to walk the Earth might have been black. He'd hardly had any exposure to blacks when he was growing up in the Cotswolds, but he'd seen enough of what they could do since coming to British East, and he was appalled by their savagery and barbarism.

And what about those crazy Americans, wringing their hands and saying that colonialism had to end? If they had seen what *he'd* seen on that farm in Nanyuki, they'd know that the only thing that was keeping all of East Africa from exploding into an unholy conflagration of blood and butchery was the British presence. Certainly, there were parallels between the Mau Mau and America: both had been colonized by the British and both wanted their independence . . . but there all similarity ended. The Americans wrote a Declaration outlining their grievances, and then they fielded an army and fought the British *soldiers*. What did chopping up innocent children and pinning cats to mailboxes have in common with that? If he had his way, he'd march in half a million British troops, wipe out every last Kikuyu—except for the good ones, the loyal ones—and solve the problem once and for all.

He wandered over to the cabinet where Leakey kept his beer and pulled out a warm bottle. Safari brand. He opened it and took a long swallow, then made a face. If that's what people drank on safari, he'd have to remember never to go on one.

And yet he knew that someday he *would* go on safari, hopefully before he was mustered out and sent home. Parts of the country were so damned beautiful, dust or no dust, and he liked the thought of sitting beneath a shade tree, cold drink in hand, while his body servant cooled him with a fan made of ostrich feathers and he and his white hunter discussed the day's kills and what they would go out after tomorrow. It wasn't the shooting that was important, they'd both reassure themselves, but rather the thrill of the hunt. Then he'd have a couple of his black boys draw his bath, and he'd bathe and prepare for dinner. Funny how he had fallen into the habit of calling them boys; most of them were far older than he.

But while they weren't boys, they *were* children in need of guidance and civilizing. Take those Maasai, for example; proud, arrogant bastards. They looked great on postcards, but try *dealing* with them. They acted as if they had a direct line to God, that He had told them they were His chosen people. The more Chelmswood thought about it, the more surprised he was that it was the Kikuyu that had begun Mau Mau rather than the Maasai. And come to think of it, he'd notice four or five Maasai *elmorani* hanging around the museum. He'd have to keep an eye on them . . .

"Excuse, please?" said a high-pitched voice, and Chelmswood turned to see a small skinny black boy, no more than ten years old, standing in the doorway.

"What do you want?" he asked.

"Doctor Mister Leakey, he promise me candy," said the boy, stepping inside the building.

"Go away," said Chelmswood irritably. "We don't have any candy here."

"Yes yes," said the boy, stepping forward. "Every day."

"He gives you candy every day?"

The boy nodded his head and smiled.

"Where does he keep it?"

The boy shrugged. "Maybe in there?" he said, pointing to a cabinet.

Chelmswood walked to the cabinet and opened it. There was nothing in it but four jars containing primitive teeth.

"I don't see any," he said. "You'll have to wait until Dr. Leakey comes back."

Two tears trickled down the boy's cheek. "But Doctor Mister Leakey, he *promise!*"

Chelmswood looked around. "I don't know where it is."

The boy began crying in earnest.

"Be quiet!" snapped Chelmswood. "I'll look for it."

"Maybe next room," suggested the boy.

"Come along," said Chelmswood, walking through the doorway to the adjoining room. He looked around, hands on hips, trying to imagine where Leakey had hidden the candy.

"This place maybe," said the boy, pointing to a closet.

Chelmswood opened the closet. It contained two spades, three picks, and an assortment of small brushes, all of which he assumed were used by the Leakeys for their work.

"Nothing here," he said, closing the door.

He turned to face the boy, but found the room empty.

"Little bugger was lying all along," he muttered. "Probably ran away to save himself a beating."

He walked back into the main room—and found himself facing a well-built black man holding a machete-like *panga* in his right hand.

"What's going on here?" snapped Chelmswood.

"Freedom is going on here, Lieutenant," said the black man in near-perfect English. "I was sent to kill Dr. Leakey, but you will have to do."

"Why are you killing anyone?" demanded Chelmswood. "What did we ever do to the Maasai?"

"I will let the Maasai answer that. Any one of them could take one look at me and tell you that I am Kikuyu—but we are all the same to you British, aren't we?"

Chelmswood reached for his gun and suddenly realized he had left it on a display case.

"You all look like cowardly savages to me!"

"Why? Because we do not meet you in battle?" The black man's face filled with fury. "You take our land away, you forbid us to own weapons, you even make it a crime for us to carry spears—and then you call us savages when we don't march in formation against your guns!" He spat contemptuously on the floor. "We fight you in the only way that is left to us."

"It's a big country, big enough for both races," said Chelmswood.

"If we came to England and took away your best farmland and forced you to work for us, would you think England was big enough for both races?"

"I'm not political," said Chelmswood, edging another step closer to his weapon. "I'm just doing my job."

"And your job is to keep two hundred whites on land that once held a million Kikuyu," said the black man, his face reflecting his hatred.

"There'll be a lot less than a million when *we* get through with you!" hissed Chelmswood, diving for his gun.

Quick as he was, the black man was faster, and with a single swipe of his *panga* he almost severed the Englishman's right hand from his wrist. Chelmswood bellowed in pain, and spun around, presenting his back to the Kikuyu as he reached for the pistol with his other hand.

The *panga* came down again, practically splitting him open, but as he fell he managed to get his fingers around the handle of his pistol and pull the trigger. The bullet struck the black man in the chest, and he, too, collapsed to the floor.

"You've killed me!" moaned Chelmswood. "Why would anyone want to kill me?"

"You have so much and we have so little," whispered the black man. "Why must you have what is ours, too?"

"What did I ever do to you?" asked Chelmswood.

"You came here. That was enough," said the black man. "Filthy English!" He closed his eyes and lay still.

"Bloody nigger!" slurred Chelmswood, and died.

Outside, the four Maasai paid no attention to the tumult within. They let the small Kikuyu boy leave without giving him so much as a glance. The business of inferior races was none of their concern.

"These notions of superiority among members of the same race are very difficult to comprehend," said Bellidore. "Are you *sure* you read the artifact properly, He Who Views?"

"I do not *read* artifacts," I replied. "I *assimilate* them. I become one with them. Everything *they* have experienced, *I* experience." I paused. "There can be no mistake."

"Well, it is difficult to fathom, especially in a species that would one day control most of the galaxy. Did they think *every* race they met was inferior to them?"

"They certainly behaved as if they did," said the Historian. "They seemed to respect only those races that stood up to them—and even then they felt that militarily defeating them was proof of their superiority."

"And yet we know from ancient records that primitive

man worshipped non-sentient animals," put in the Exobiologist.

"They must not have been survived for any great length of time," suggested the Historian. "If Man treated the races of the galaxy with contempt, how much worse must he have treated the poor creatures with whom he shared his home world?"

"Perhaps he viewed them much the same as he viewed my own race," I offered. "If they had nothing he wanted, if they presented no threat . . ."

"They would have had something he wanted," said the Exobiologist. "He was a predator. They would have had meat."

"And land," added the Historian. "If even the galaxy was not enough to quench Man's thirst for territory, think how unwilling he would have been to share his own world."

"It is a question I suspect will never be answered," said Bellidore.

"Unless the answer lies in one of the remaining artifacts," agreed the Exobiologist.

I'm sure the remark was not meant to jar me from my lethargy, but it occurred to me that it had been half a day since I had assimilated the knife handle, and I had regained enough of my strength to examine the next artifact.

It was a metal stylus . . .

*February 15, 2103:*

*Well, we finally got here! The Supermole got us through the tunnel from New York to London in just over four hours. Even so we were twenty minutes late, missed our connection, and had to wait another five hours for the next flight to Khartoum. From there our means of transport got increasingly more primitive—jet planes to Nairobi and Arusha—and then a quick shuttle to our campsite, but we've finally put civilization behind us. I've never seen open spaces like this before; you're barely aware of the sky-scrapers of Nyerere, the closest town.*

*After an orientation speech telling us what to expect and how to behave on safari, we got the afternoon off to meet our traveling companions. I'm the youngest member of the group: a trip like this just costs too much for most people my age to afford. Of course, most people my age don't have an Uncle Reuben who dies and leaves them a ton of money. (Well, it's probably about eight ounces of money, now that the safari is paid for. Ha ha.)*

*The lodge is quite rustic. They have quaint microwaves for warming our food, although most of us will be eating at the restaurants. I understand the Japanese and Brazilian ones are the most popular, the former for the food—real fish—and the latter for the entertainment. My roommate is Mr. Shiboni, an elderly Japanese gentleman who tells me he has been saving his money for fifteen years to come on this safari. He seems pleasant and good-natured; I hope he can survive the rigors of the trip.*

*I had really wanted a shower, just to get in the spirit of things, but water is scarce here, and it looks like I'll have to settle for the same old chemical dry-shower. I know, I know, it disinfects as well as cleanses, but if I wanted all the comforts of home, I'd have stayed home and saved $150,000.*

*February 16:*

*We met our guide today. I don't know why, but he doesn't quite fit my preconception of an African safari guide. I was expecting some grizzled old veteran who had a wealth of stories to tell, who had maybe even seen a civet cat or a duiker before they became extinct. What we got was Kevin Ole Tambake, a young Maasai who can't be 25 years old and dresses in a suit while we all wear our khakis. Still, he's lived here all his life, so I suppose he knows his way around.*

*And I'll give him this: he's a wonderful storyteller. He spent half an hour telling us myths about how his people used to live in huts called* manyattas, *and how their rite of passage to manhood was to kill a lion with a spear. As if the government would let anyone kill an animal!*

*We spent the morning driving down into the Ngorongoro Crater. It's a collapsed* caldara, *or volcano, that was once taller than Kilimanjaro itself. Kevin says it used to teem with game, though I can't see how, since any game standing atop it when it collapsed would have been instantly killed.*

*I think the real reason we went there was just to get the kinks out of our safari vehicle and learn the proper protocol. Probably just as well. The air-conditioning wasn't working right in two of the compartments, the service mechanism couldn't get the temperature right on the iced drinks, and once, when we thought we saw a bird, three of us buzzed Kevin at the same time and jammed his communication line.*

*In the afternoon we went out to Serengeti. Kevin says it used to extend all the way to the Kenya border, but now it's just a 20-square-mile park adjacent to the Crater. About an hour into the game run we saw a ground squirrel, but he disappeared into a hole before I could adjust my holo camera. Still, he was very impressive. Varying shares of brown, with dark eyes and a fluffy tail. Kevin estimated that he went almost three pounds, and says he hasn't seen one that big since he was a boy.*

*Just before we returned to camp, Kevin got word on the radio from another driver that they had spotted two starlings nesting in a tree about eight miles north and east of us. The vehicle's computer told us we wouldn't be able to reach it before dark, so Kevin had it lock the spot in its memory and promised us that we'd go there first thing in the morning.*

*I opted for the Brazilian restaurant, and spent a few pleasant hours listening to the live band. A very nice end to the first full day of safari.*

*February 17:*

*We left at dawn in search of the starlings, and though we found the tree where they had been spotted, we never did see them. One of the passengers—I think it was the little man from Burma, though I'm not sure—must have complained, because Kevin soon announced to the entire party that this was a* safari, *that there was no guarantee of seeing any particular bird or animal, and that while he would do his best for us, one could never be certain where the game might be.*

*And then, just as he was talking, a banded mongoose almost a foot long appeared out of nowhere. It seemed to pay no attention to us, and Kevin announced that we were killing the motor and going into hover mode so the noise wouldn't scare it away.*

*After a minute or two everyone on the right side of the vehicle had gotten their holographs, and we slowly spun on our axis so that the left side could see him—but the movement must have scared him off, because though the maneuver took less than thirty seconds, he was nowhere to be seen when we came to rest again.*

*Kevin announced that the vehicle had captured the mongoose on its automated holos, and copies would be made available to anyone who had missed their holo opportunity.*

*We were feeling great—the right side of the vehicle, anyway— when we stopped for lunch, and during our afternoon game run we saw three yellow weaver birds building their spherical nests in a tree. Kevin let us out, warning us not to approach closer than thirty yards, and we spent almost an hour watching and holographing them.*

*All in all, a very satisfying day.*

*February 18:*

*Today we left camp about an hour after sunrise, and went to a new location: Olduvai Gorge.*

*Kevin announced that we would spend our last two days here, that with the encroachment of the cities and farms on all the flat land, the remaining big game was pretty much confined to the gulleys and slopes of the gorge.*

*No vehicle, not even our specially-equipped one, was capable of navigating its way through the gorge, so we all got out and began walking in single file behind Kevin.*

*Most of us found it very difficult to keep up with Kevin. He clambered up and down the rocks as if he'd been doing it all his life, whereas I can't remember the last time I saw a stair that didn't move when I stood on it. We had trekked for perhaps half an hour when I heard one of the men at the back of our strung-out party give a cry and point to a spot at the bottom of the gorge, and we all looked and saw something racing away at phenomenal speed.*

*"Another squirrel?" I asked.*

*Kevin just smiled.*

*The man behind me said he thought it was a mongoose.*

*"What you saw," said Kevin, "was a dik-dik, the last surviving African antelope."*

*"How big was it?" asked a woman.*

*"About average size," said Kevin. "Perhaps ten inches at the shoulder."*

*Imagine anything ten inches high being called* average!

*Kevin explained that dik-diks were very territorial, and that this one wouldn't stray far from his home area. Which meant that if we were patient and quiet—and lucky—we'd be able to spot him again.*

*I asked Kevin how many dik-diks lived in the gorge, and he scratched his head and considered it for a moment and then guessed that there might be as many as ten. (And Yellowstone has only nineteen rabbits left! Is it any wonder that all the serious animal buffs come to Africa?)*

*We kept walking for another hour, and then broke for lunch, while Kevin gave us the history of the place, telling us all about Dr. Leakey's finds. There were probably still more skeletons to be dug up, he guessed, but the government didn't want to frighten any animals away from what had become their last refuge, so the bones would have to wait for some future generation to unearth them. Roughly translated, that meant that Tanzania wasn't going to give up the revenues from 300 tourists a week and turn over the crown jewel in their park system to a bunch of anthropologists. I can't say that I blame them.*

*Other parties had begun pouring into the gorge, and I think the entire safari population must have totaled almost 70 by the time lunch was over. The guides each seemed to have "their" areas marked out, and I noticed that rarely did we get within a quarter mile of any other parties.*

*Kevin asked us if we wanted to sit in the shade until the heat of the day had passed, but since this was our next-to-last day on safari we voted overwhelmingly to proceed as soon as we were through eating.*

*It couldn't have been ten minutes later that the disaster occurred. We were clambering down a steep slope in single file, Kevin in the lead as usual, and me right behind him, when I heard a grunt and then a surprised yell, and I looked back to see Mr. Shiboni tumbling down the path. Evidently he'd lost his footing, and we could hear the bones in his leg snap as he hurtled toward us.*

*Kevin positioned himself to stop him, and almost got knocked down the gorge himself before he finally stopped poor Mr. Shiboni. Then he knelt down next to the old gentleman to tend to his broken leg—but as he did so his keen eyes spotted something we all had missed, and suddenly he was bounding up the slopes like a monkey. He stopped where Mr. Shiboni had initially stumbled, squatted down, and examined something. Then, looking like Death itself, he picked up the object and brought it back down the path.*

*It was a dead lizard, fully-grown, almost eight inches long, and smashed flat by Mr. Shiboni. It was impossible to say whether his fall was caused by stepping on it, or whether it simply couldn't get out of the way once he began tumbling . . . but it made no difference: he was responsible for the death of an animal in a National Park.*

*I tried to remember the release we had signed, giving the Park System permission to instantly withdraw money from our accounts should we destroy an animal for any reason, even self-protection. I knew that the absolute minimum penalty was $50,000, but I think that was for two of the more common birds, and that ugaama and gecko lizards were in the $70,000 range.*

*Kevin held the lizard up for all of us to see, and told us that should legal action ensue, we were all witnesses to what had happened.*

*Mr. Shiboni groaned in pain, and Kevin said that there was no sense wasting the lizard, so he gave it to me to hold while he splinted Mr. Shiboni's leg and summoned the paramedics on the radio.*

*I began examining the little lizard. Its feet were finely-shaped, its tail long and elegant, but it was the colors that made the most lasting impression on me: a reddish head, a blue body, and grey legs, the color growing lighter as it reached the claws. A beautiful, beautiful thing, even in death.*

*After the paramedics had taken Mr. Shiboni back to the lodge, Kevin spent the next hour showing us how the ugaama lizard functioned: how its eyes could see in two directions at once, how its claws allowed it to hang upside down from any uneven surface, and how efficiently its jaws could crack the carapaces of the insects it caught. Finally, in view of the tragedy, and also because he wanted to check on Mr. Shiboni's condition, Kevin suggested that we call it a day.*

*None of us objected—we knew Kevin would have hours of ex-*

*tra work, writing up the incident and convincing the Park Department that his safari company was not responsible for it—but still we felt cheated, since there was only one day left. I think Kevin knew it, because just before we reached the lodge he promised us a special treat tomorrow.*

*I've been awake half the night wondering what it could be? Can he possibly know where the other dik-diks are? Or could the legends of a last flamingo possibly be true?*

*February 19:*
*We were all excited when we climbed aboard the vehicle this morning. Everyone kept asking Kevin what his "special treat" was, but he merely smiled and kept changing the subject. Finally we reached Olduvai Gorge and began walking, only this time we seemed to be going to a specific location, and Kevin hardly stopped to try to spot the dik-dik.*

*We climbed down twisting, winding paths, tripping over tree roots, cutting our arms and legs on thorn bushes, but nobody objected, for Kevin seemed so confident of his surprise that all these hardships were forgotten.*

*Finally we reached the bottom of the gorge and began walking along a flat winding path. Still, by the time we were ready to stop for lunch, we hadn't seen a thing. As we sat beneath the shade of an acacia tree, eating, Kevin pulled out his radio and conversed with the other guides. One group had seen three dik-diks, and another had found a lilac-breasted roller's nest with two hatchlings in it. Kevin is very competitive, and ordinarily news like that would have had him urging everyone to finish eating quickly so that we would not return to the lodge having seen less than everyone else, but this time he just smiled and told the other guides that we had seen nothing on the floor of the gorge and that the game seemed to have moved out, perhaps in search of water.*

*Then, when lunch was over, Kevin walked about 50 yards*

*away, disappeared into a cave, and emerged a moment later with
a small wooden cage. There was a little brown bird in it, and while
I was thrilled to be able to see it close up, I felt somehow disappointed that this was to be the special treat.*

*"Have you ever seen a honey guide?" he asked.*

*We all admitted that we hadn't, and he explained that that
was the name of the small brown bird.*

*I asked why it was called that, since it obviously didn't produce
honey, and seemed incapable of replacing Kevin as our guide, and
he smiled again.*

*"Do you see that tree?" he asked, pointing to a tree perhaps 75
yards away. There was a huge beehive on a low-hanging branch.*

*"Yes," I said.*

*"Then watch," he said, opening the cage and releasing the
bird. It stood still for a moment, then fluttered its wings and took
off in the direction of the tree.*

*"He is making sure there is honey there," explained Kevin,
pointing to the bird as it circled the hive.*

*"Where is he going now?" I asked, as the bird suddenly flew
down the river bed.*

*"To find his partner."*

*"Partner?" I asked, confused.*

*"Wait and see," said Kevin, sitting down with his back
propped against a large rock.*

*We all followed suit and sat in the shade, our binoculars and
holo cameras trained on the tree. After almost an hour nothing
had happened, and some of us were getting restless, when Kevin
tensed and pointed up the river bed.*

*"There!" he whispered.*

*I looked in the direction he was pointing, and there, following
the bird, which was flying just ahead of him and chirping frantically, was an enormous black-and-white animal, the largest I
have ever seen.*

*"What is it?" I whispered.*

*"A honey badger," answered Kevin softly. "They were thought to be extinct twenty years ago, but a mated pair took sanctuary in Olduvai. This is the fourth generation to be born here."*

*"Is he going to eat the bird?" asked one of the party.*

*"No," whispered Kevin. "The bird will lead him to the honey, and after he has pulled down the nest and eaten his fill, he will leave some for the bird."*

*And it was just as Kevin said. The honey badger climbed the bole of the tree and knocked off the beehive with a forepaw, then climbed back down and broke it apart, oblivious to the stings of the bees. We caught the whole fantastic scene on our holos, and when he was done he did indeed leave some honey for the honey guide.*

*Later, while Kevin was recapturing the bird and putting it back in its cage, the rest of us discussed what we had seen. I thought the honey badger must have weighed 45 pounds, though less excitable members of the party put its weight at closer to 36 or 37. Whichever it was, the creature was enormous. The discussion then shifted to how big a tip to leave for Kevin, for he had certainly earned one.*

*As I write this final entry in my safari diary, I am still trembling with the excitement that can only come from encountering big game in the wild. Prior to this afternoon, I had some doubts about the safari—I felt it was overpriced, or that perhaps my expectations had been too high—but now I know that it was worth every penny, and I have a feeling that I am leaving some part of me behind here, and that I will never be truly content until I return to this last bastion of the wilderness.*

The camp was abuzz with excitement. Just when we were sure that there were no more treasures to unearth, the Stardust Twins had found three small pieces of bone, attached together with a wire—obviously a human artifact.

"But the dates are wrong," said the Historian, after examining the bones thoroughly with its equipment. "This is a primitive piece of jewelry—for the adornment of savages, one might say—and yet the bones and wire both date from centuries after Man discovered space travel."

"Do you . . ."

". . . deny that we . . ."

". . . found it in the . . ."

". . . gorge?" demanded the Twins.

"I believe you," said the Historian. "I simply state that it seems to be an anachronism."

"It is our find, and . . ."

". . . it will bear our name."

"No one is denying your right of discovery," said Bellidore. "It is simply that you have presented us with a mystery."

"Give it to . . ."

". . . He Who Views, and he . . ."

". . . will solve the mystery."

"I will do my best," I said. "But it has not been long enough since I assimilated the stylus. I must rest and regain my strength."

"That is . . ."

". . . acceptable."

We let the Moriteu go about brushing and cleaning the artifact, while we speculated on why a primitive fetish should exist in the starfaring age. Finally the Exobiologist got to her feet.

"I am going back into the gorge," she announced. "If the Stardust Twins could find this, perhaps there are other things we have overlooked. After all, it is an enormous area." She paused and looked at the rest of us. "Would anyone care to come with me?"

It was nearing the end of the day, and no one volunteered,

and finally the Exobiologist turned and began walking toward the path that led down into the depths of Olduvai Gorge.

It was dark when I finally felt strong enough to assimilate the jewelry. I spread my essence about the bones and the wire and soon became one with them . . .

His name was Joseph Meromo, and he could live with the money but not the guilt.

It had begun with the communication from Brussels, and the veiled suggestion from the head of the multi-national conglomerate headquartered there. They had a certain commodity to get rid of. They had no place to get rid of it. Could Tanzania help?

Meromo had told them he would look into it, but he doubted that his government could be of use.

Just *try,* came the reply.

In fact, more than the reply came. The next day a private courier delivered a huge wad of large-denomination bills, with a polite note thanking Meromo for his efforts on their behalf.

Meromo knew a bribe when he saw one—he'd certainly taken enough in his career—but he'd never seen one remotely the size of this one. And not even for helping them, but merely for being willing to explore possibilities.

Well, he had thought, why not? What could they conceivably have? A couple of containers of toxic waste? A few plutonium rods? You bury them deep enough in the earth and no one would ever know or care. Wasn't that what the Western countries did?

Of course, there was the Denver Disaster, and that little accident that made the Thames undrinkable for almost a century, but the only reason they popped so quickly to mind is because they were the *exceptions,* not the rule. There were thousands of dumping sites around the world, and 99% of them caused no problems at all.

Meromo had his computer cast a holographic map of Tanzania above his desk. He looked at it, frowned, added topographical features, then began studying it in earnest.

*If* he decided to help them dump the stuff, whatever it was—and he told himself that he was still uncommitted—where would be the best place to dispose of it?

Off the coast? No, the fishermen would pull it up two minutes later, take it to the press, and raise enough hell to get him fired, and possibly even cause the rest of the government to resign. The party really couldn't handle any more scandals this year.

The Selous Province? Maybe five centuries ago, when it was the last wilderness on the continent, but not now, not with a thriving, semi-autonomous city-state of fifty-two million people where once there had been nothing but elephants and almost-impenetrable thorn bush.

Lake Victoria? No. Same problem with the fishermen.

Dar es Salaam? It was a possibility. Close enough to the coast to make transport easy, practically deserted since Dodoma had become the new capital of the country.

But Dar es Salaam had been hit by an earthquake twenty years ago, when Meromo was still a boy, and he couldn't take the chance of another one exposing or breaking open whatever it was that he planned to hide.

He continued going over the map: Gombe, Ruaha, Iringa, Mbeya, Mtwara, Tarengire, Olduvai . . .

He stopped and stared at Olduvai, then called up all available data.

Almost a mile deep. That was in its favor. No animals left. Better still. No settlements on its steep slopes. Only a handful of Maasai still living in the area, no more than two dozen families, and they were too arrogant to pay any attention to what the government was doing. Of that Meromo was sure: he himself was a Maasai.

So he strung it out for as long as he could, collected cash gifts for almost two years, and finally gave them a delivery date.

Meromo stared out the window of his 34th floor office, past the bustling city of Dodoma, off to the east, to where he imagined Olduvai Gorge was.

It had seemed so simple. Yes, he was paid a lot of money, a disproportionate amount—but these multi-nationals had money to burn. It was just supposed to be a few dozen pluto-nium rods, or so he had thought. How was he to know that they were speaking of forty-two *tons* of nuclear waste?

There was no returning the money. Even if he wanted to, he could hardly expect them to come back and pull all that deadly material back out of the ground. Probably it was safe, probably no one would ever know . . .

But it haunted his days, and even worse, it began haunting his nights as well, appearing in various guises in his dreams. Sometimes it was as carefully sealed containers, sometimes it was as ticking bombs, sometimes a disaster had already occurred and all he could see were the charred bodies of Maasai children spread across the lip of the gorge.

For almost eight months he fought his devils alone, but eventually he realized that he must have help. The dreams not only haunted him at night, but invaded the day as well. He would be sitting at a staff meeting, and suddenly he would imagine he was sitting among the emaciated, sore-covered bodies of the Olduvai Maasai. He would be reading a book, and the words seemed to change and he would be reading that Joseph Meromo had been sentenced to death for his greed. He would watch a holo of the Titanic disaster, and suddenly he was viewing some variation of the Olduvai Disaster.

Finally he went to a psychiatrist, and because he was a Maasai, he chose a Maasai psychiatrist. Fearing the doctor's contempt, Meromo would not state explicitly what was causing the nightmares and intrusions, and after almost half a year's worth of futile attempts to cure him, the psychiatrist announced that he could do no more.

"Then am I to be cursed with these dreams forever?" asked Meromo.

"Perhaps not," said the psychiatrist. "*I* cannot help you, but just possibly there is one man who can."

He rummaged through his desk and came up with a small white card. On it was written a single word: MULEWO.

"This is his business card," said the psychiatrist. "Take it."

"There is no address on it, no means of communicating with him," said Meromo. "How will I contact him?"

"He will contact you."

"You will give him my name?"

The psychiatrist shook his head. "I will not have to. Just keep the card on your person. He will know you require his services."

Meromo felt like he was being made the butt of some joke he didn't understand, but he dutifully put the card in his pocket and soon forgot about it.

Two weeks later, as he was drinking at a bar, putting off going home to sleep as long as he could, a small woman approached him.

"Are you Joseph Meromo?" she asked.

"Yes."

"Please follow me."

"Why?" he asked suspiciously.

"You have business with Mulewo, do you not?" she said.

Meromo fell into step behind her, at least as much to avoid going home as from any belief that this mysterious man with no first name could help him. They went out to the street, turned left, walked in silence for three blocks, and turned right, coming to a halt at the front door to a steel-and-glass skyscraper.

"The 63rd floor," she said. "He is expecting you."

"You're not coming with me?" asked Meromo.

She shook her head. "My job is done." She turned and walked off into the night.

Meromo looked up at the top of the building. It seemed residential. He considered his options, finally shrugged, and walked into the lobby.

"You're here for Mulewo," said the doorman. It was not a question. "Go to the elevator on the left."

Meromo did as he was told. The elevator was paneled with an oiled wood, and smelled fresh and sweet. It operated on voice command and quickly took him to the 63rd floor. When he emerged he found himself in an elegantly decorated corridor, with ebony wainscoting and discreetly placed mirrors. He walked past three unmarked doors, wondering how he was supposed to know which apartment belonged to Mulewo, and finally came to one that was partially open.

"Come in, Joseph Meromo," said a hoarse voice from within.

Meromo opened the door the rest of the way, stepped into the apartment, and blinked.

Sitting on a torn rug was an old man, wearing nothing but a red cloth gathered at the shoulder. The walls were covered by reed matting, and a noxious-smelling caldron bubbled in the fireplace. A torch provided the only illumination.

"What *is* this?" asked Meromo, ready to step back into the

corridor if the old man appeared as irrational as his surroundings.

"Come sit across from me, Joseph Meromo," said the old man. "Surely this is less frightening than your nightmares."

"What do you know about my nightmares?" demanded Meromo.

"I know why you have them. I know what lies buried at the bottom of Olduvai Gorge."

Meromo shut the door quickly.

"Who told you?"

"No one told me. I have peered into your dreams, and sifted through them until I found the truth. Come sit."

Meromo walked to where the old man indicated and sat down carefully, trying not to get too much dirt on his freshly pressed outfit.

"Are you Mulewo?" he asked.

The old man nodded. "I am Mulewo."

"How do you know these things about me?"

"I am a *laibon*," said Mulewo.

"A witch doctor?"

"It is a dying art," answered Mulewo. "I am the last practitioner."

"I thought *laibons* cast spells and created curses."

"They also remove curses—and your nights, and even your days, are cursed, are they not?"

"You seem to know all about it."

"I know that you have done a wicked thing, and that you are haunted not only by the ghost of it, but by the ghosts of the future as well."

"And you can end the dreams?"

"That is why I have summoned you here."

"But if I did such a terrible thing, why do you *want* to help me?"

223

"I do not make moral judgments. I am here only to help the Maasai."

"And what about the Maasai who live by the gorge?" asked Meromo. "The ones who haunt my dreams?"

"When *they* ask for help, then I will help them."

"Can you cause the material that's buried there to vanish?"

Mulewo shook his head. "I cannot undo what has been done. I cannot even assuage your guilt, for it is a just guilt. All I can do is banish it from your dreams."

"I'll settle for that," said Meromo.

There was an uneasy silence.

"What do I do now?" asked Meromo.

"Bring me a tribute befitting the magnitude of the service I shall perform."

"I can write you a check right now, or have money transferred from my account to your own."

"I have more money than I need. I must have a tribute."

"But—"

"Bring it back tomorrow night," said Mulewo.

Meromo stared at the old *laibon* for a long minute, then got up and left without another word.

He called in sick the next morning, then went to two of Dodoma's better antique shops. Finally he found what he was looking for, charged it to his personal account, and took it home with him. He was afraid to nap before dinner, so he simply read a book all afternoon, then ate a hasty meal and returned to Mulewo's apartment.

"What have you brought me?" asked Mulewo.

Meromo laid the package down in front of the old man. "A headdress made from the skin of a lion," he answered. "They told me it was worn by Sendayo himself, the greatest of all *laibons*."

"It was not," said Mulewo, without unwrapping the package. "But it is a sufficient tribute nonetheless." He reached beneath his red cloth and withdrew a small necklace, holding it out for Meromo.

"What is this for?" asked Meromo, examining the necklace. It was made of small bones that had been strung together.

"You must wear it tonight when you go to sleep," explained the old man. "It will take all your visions unto itself. Then, tomorrow, you must go to Olduvai Gorge and throw it down to the bottom, so that the visions may lay side by side with the reality."

"And that's all?"

"That is all."

Meromo went back to his apartment, donned the necklace, and went to sleep. That night his dreams were worse than they had ever been before.

In the morning he put the necklace into a pocket and had a government plane fly him to Arusha. From there he rented a ground vehicle, and two hours later he was standing on the edge of the gorge. There was no sign of the buried material.

He took the necklace in his hand and hurled it far out over the lip of the gorge.

His nightmares vanished that night.

134 years later, mighty Kilimanjaro shuddered as the long-dormant volcano within it came briefly to life.

One hundred miles away, the ground shifted on the floor of Olduvai Gorge, and three of the lead-lined containers broke open.

Joseph Meromo was long dead by that time; and, unfortunately, there were no *laibons* remaining to aid those people who were now compelled to live Meromo's nightmares.

\* \* \* \* \*

I had examined the necklace in my own quarters, and when I came out to report my findings, I discovered that the entire camp was in a tumultuous state.

"What has happened?" I asked Bellidore.

"The Exobiologist has not returned from the gorge," he said.

"How long has she been gone?"

"She left at sunset last night. It is now morning, and she has not returned or attempted to use her communicator."

"We fear . . ."

". . . that she might . . ."

". . . have fallen and . . ."

". . . become immobile. Or perhaps even . . ."

". . . unconscious . . ." said the Stardust Twins.

"I have sent the Historian and the Appraiser to look for her," said Bellidore.

"I can help, too," I offered.

"No, you have the last artifact to examine," he said. "When the Moriteu awakens, I will send it as well."

"What about the Mystic?" I asked.

Bellidore looked at the Mystic and sighed. "She has not said a word since landing on this world. In truth, I do not understand her function. At any rate, I do not know how to communicate with her."

The Stardust Twins kicked at the earth together, sending up a pair of reddish dust clouds.

"It seems ridiculous . . ." said one.

". . . that we can find the tiniest artifact . . ." said the other.

". . . but we cannot find . . ."

". . . an entire exobiologist."

"Why do you not help search for it?" I asked.

"They get vertigo," explained Bellidore.

"We searched . . ."

". . . the entire camp," they added defensively.

"I can put off assimilating the last piece until tomorrow, and help with the search," I volunteered.

"No," replied Bellidore. "I have sent for the ship. We will leave tomorrow, and I want all of our major finds examined by then. It is *my* job to find the Exobiologist; it is *yours* to read the history of the last artifact."

"If that is your desire," I said. "Where is it?"

He led me to a table where the Historian and the Appraiser had been examining it.

"Even *I* know what this is," said Bellidore. "An unspent cartridge." He paused. "Along with the fact that we have found no human artifacts on any higher strata, I would say this in itself is unique: a bullet that a man chose *not* to fire."

"When you state it in those terms, it *does* arouse the curiosity," I acknowledged.

"Are you . . ."

". . . going to examine it . . ."

". . . now?" asked the Stardust Twins apprehensively.

"Yes, I am," I said.

"Wait!" they shouted in unison.

I paused above the cartridge while they began backing away.

"We mean . . ."

". . . no disrespect . . ."

". . . but watching you examine artifacts . . ."

". . . is too unsettling."

And with that, they raced off to hide behind some of the camp structures.

"What about you?" I asked Bellidore. "Would you like me to wait until you leave?"

"Not at all," he replied. "I find diversity fascinating. With your permission, I would like to stay and observe."

"As you wish," I said, allowing my body to melt around the cartridge until it had become a part of myself, and its history became my own history, as clear and precise as if it had all occurred yesterday . . .

"They are coming!"

Thomas Naikosiai looked across the table at his wife.

"Was there ever any doubt that they would?"

"This was foolish, Thomas!" she snapped. "They will force us to leave, and because we made no preparations, we will have to leave all our possessions behind."

"Nobody is leaving," said Naikosiai.

He stood up and walked to the closet. "You stay here," he said, donning his long coat and his mask. "I will meet them outside."

"That is both rude and cruel, to make them stand out there when they have come all this way."

"They were not invited," said Naikosiai. He reached deep into the closet and grabbed the rifle that leaned up against the back wall, then closed the closet, walked through the airlock and emerged on the front porch.

Six men, all wearing protective clothing and masks to filter the air, confronted him.

"It is time, Thomas," said the tallest of them.

"Time for *you*, perhaps," said Naikosiai, holding the rifle casually across his chest.

"Time for all of us," answered the tall man.

"I am not going anywhere. This is my home. I will not leave it."

"It is a pustule of decay and contamination, as is this whole country," came the answer. "We are all leaving."

Naikosiai shook his head. "My father was born on this land, and his father, and his father's father. *You* may run from danger, if you wish; I will stay and fight it."

"How can you make a stand against radiation?" demanded the tall man. "Can you put a bullet through it? How can you fight air that is no longer safe to breathe?"

"Go away," said Naikosiai, who had no answer to that, other than the conviction that he would never leave his home. "I do not demand that you stay. Do not demand that I leave."

"It is for your own good, Naikosiai," urged another. "If you care nothing for your own life, think of your wife's. How much longer can she breathe the air?"

"Long enough."

"Why not let *her* decide?"

"*I* speak for our family."

An older man stepped forward. "She is *my* daughter, Thomas," he said severely. "I will not allow you to condemn her to the life you have chosen for yourself. Nor will I let my grandchildren remain here."

The old man took another step toward the porch, and suddenly the rifle was pointing at him.

"That's far enough," said Naikosiai.

"They are Maasai," said the old man stubbornly. "They must come with the other Maasai to our new world."

"You are not Maasai," said Naikosiai contemptuously. "Maasai did not leave their ancestral lands when the rinderpest destroyed their herds, or when the white man came, or when the governments sold off their lands. Maasai never surrender. *I* am the last Maasai."

"Be reasonable, Thomas. How can you not surrender to a world that is no longer safe for people to live on? Come with us to New Kilimanjaro."

"The Maasai do not run from danger," said Naikosiai.

"I tell you, Thomas Naikosiai," said the old man, "that I cannot allow you to condemn my daughter and my grandchildren to live in this hellhole. The last ship leaves tomorrow morning. They will be on it."

"They will stay with me, to build a new Maasai nation."

The six men whispered among themselves, and then their leader looked up at Naikosiai.

"You are making a terrible mistake, Thomas," he said. "If you change your mind, there is room for you on the ship."

They all turned to go, but the old man stopped and turned to Naikosiai.

"I will be back for my daughter," he said.

Naikosiai gestured with his rifle. "I will be waiting for you."

The old man turned and walked off with the others, and Naikosiai went back into his house through the airlock. The tile floor smelled of disinfectant, and the sight of the television set offended his eyes, as always. His wife was waiting for him in the kitchen, amid the dozens of gadgets she had purchased over the years.

"How can you speak with such disrespect to the Elders!" she demanded. "You have disgraced us."

"No!" he snapped. "*They* have disgraced us, by leaving!"

"Thomas, you cannot grow anything in the fields. The animals have all died. You cannot even breathe the air without a filtering mask. *Why* do you insist on staying?"

"This is our ancestral land. We will not leave it."

"But all the others—"

"They can do as they please," he interrupted. "Enkai will judge them, as He judges us all. I am not afraid to meet my creator."

"But why must you meet him so soon?" she persisted. "You have seen the tapes and disks of New Kilimanjaro. It is a beautiful world, green and gold and filled with rivers and lakes."

"Once Earth was green and gold and filled with rivers and lakes," said Naikosiai. "They ruined this world. They will ruin the next one."

"Even if they do, we will be long dead," she said. "I want to go."

"We've been through all this before."

"And it always ends with an order rather than an agreement," she said. Her expression softened. "Thomas, just once before I die, I want to see water that you can drink without adding chemicals to it. I want to see antelope grazing on long green grasses. I want to walk outside without having to protect myself from the very air I breathe."

"It's settled."

She shook her head. "I love you, Thomas, but I cannot stay here, and I cannot let our children stay here."

"No one is taking my children from me!" he yelled.

"Just because you care nothing for *your* future, I cannot permit you to deny our sons *their* future."

"Their future is here, where the Maasai have always lived."

"Please come with us, Papa," said a small voice behind him, and Naikosiai turned to see his two sons, eight and five, standing in the doorway to their bedroom, staring at him.

"What have you been saying to them?" demanded Naikosiai suspiciously.

"The truth," said his wife.

He turned to the two boys. "Come here," he said, and they trudged across the room to him.

"What are you?" he asked.

"Boys," said the younger child.

"What *else?*"

"Maasai," said the older.

"That is right," said Naikosiai. "You come from a race of giants. There was a time when, if you climbed to the very top of Kilimanjaro, all the land you could see in every direction belonged to us."

"But that was long ago," said the older boy.

"Someday it will be ours again," said Naikosiai. "You must remember who you are, my son. You are the descendant of Leeyo, who killed 100 lions with just his spear; of Nelion, who waged war against the whites and drove them from the Rift; of Sendayo, the greatest of all the *laibons*. Once the Kikuyu and the Wakamba and the Lumbwa trembled in fear at the very mention of the word Maasai. This is your heritage; do not turn your back on it."

"But the Kikuyu and the other tribes have all left."

"What difference does that make to the Maasai? We did not make a stand only against the Kikuyu and the Wakamba, but against *all* men who would have us change our ways. Even after the Europeans conquered Kenya and Tanganyika, they never conquered the Maasai. When Independence came, and all the other tribes moved to cities and wore suits and aped the Europeans, we remained as we had always been. We wore what we chose and we lived where we chose, for we were proud to be Maasai. Does that not *mean* something to you?"

"Will we not still be Maasai if we go to the new world?" asked the older boy.

"No," said Naikosiai firmly. "There is a bond between the Maasai and the land. We define it, and it defines us. It is what we have always fought for and always defended."

"But it is diseased now," said the boy.

"If I were sick, would you leave me?" asked Naikosiai.

"No, Papa."

"And just as you would not leave me in my illness, so we

will not leave the land in *its* illness. When you love something, when it is a part of what you are, you do not leave it simply because it becomes sick. You stay, and you fight even harder to cure it than you fought to win it."

"But—"

"Trust me," said Naikosiai. "Have I ever misled you?"

"No, Papa."

"I am not misleading you now. We are Enkai's chosen people. We live on the ground He has given us. Don't you see that we *must* remain here, that we must keep our covenant with Enkai?"

"But I will never see my friends again!" wailed his younger son.

"You will make new friends."

"Where?" cried the boy. "Everyone is gone!"

"Stop that at once!" said Naikosiai harshly. "Maasai do not cry."

The boy continued sobbing, and Naikosiai looked up at his wife.

"This is *your* doing," he said. "You have spoiled him."

She stared unblinking into his eyes. "Five-year-old boys are allowed to cry."

"Not Maasai boys," he answered.

"Then he is no longer Maasai, and you can have no objection to his coming with me."

"I want to go too!" said the eight-year-old, and suddenly he, too, forced some tears down his face.

Thomas Naikosiai looked at his wife and his children—really *looked* at them—and realized that he did not know them at all. This was not the quiet maiden, raised in the traditions of his people, that he had married nine years ago. These soft sobbing boys were not the successors of Leeyo and Nelion.

He walked to the door and opened it.

"Go to the new world with the rest of the black Europeans," he growled.

"Will you come with us?" asked his oldest son.

Naikosiai turned to his wife. "I divorce you," he said coldly. "All that was between us is no more."

He walked over to his two sons. "I disown you. I am no longer your father, you are no longer my sons. Now go!"

His wife put coats and masks on both of the boys, then donned her own.

"I will send some men for my things before morning," she said.

"If any man comes onto my property, I will kill him," said Naikosiai.

She stared at him, a look of pure hatred. Then she took the children by the hands and led them out of the house and down the long road to where the ship awaited them.

Naikosiai paced the house for a few minutes, filled with nervous rage. Finally he went to the closet, donned his coat and mask, pulled out his rifle, and walked through the airlock to the front of his house. Visibility was poor, as always, and he went out to the road to see if anyone was coming.

There was no sign of any movement. He was almost disappointed. He planned to show them how a Maasai protected what was his.

And suddenly he realized that this was *not* how a Maasai protected his own. He walked to the edge of the gorge, opened the bolt, and threw his cartridges into the void one by one. Then he held the rifle over his head and hurled it after them. The coat came next, then the mask, and finally his clothes and shoes.

He went back into the house and pulled out that special trunk that held the memorabilia of a lifetime. In it he found what he was looking for: a simple piece of red cloth. He attached it at his shoulder.

Then he went into the bathroom, looking among his wife's cosmetics. It took almost half an hour to hit upon the right combinations, but when he emerged his hair was red, as if smeared with clay.

He stopped by the fireplace and pulled down the spear that hung there. Family tradition had it that the spear had once been used by Nelion himself; he wasn't sure he believed it, but it was definitely a Maasai spear, blooded many times in battle and hunts during centuries past.

Naikosiai walked out the door and positioned himself in front of his house—his *manyatta*. He planted his bare feet on the diseased ground, placed the butt of his spear next to his right foot, and stood at attention. Whatever came down the road next—a band of black Europeans hoping to rob him of his possessions, a lion out of history, a band of Nandi or Lumbwa come to slay the enemy of their blood, they would find him ready.

They returned just after sunrise the next morning, hoping to convince him to emigrate to New Kilimanjaro. What they found was the last Maasai, his lungs burst from the pollution, his dead eyes staring proudly out across the vanished savannah at some enemy only he could see.

I released the cartridge, my strength nearly gone, my emotions drained.

So that was how it had ended for Man on earth, probably less than a mile from where it had begun. So bold and so foolish, so moral and so savage. I had hoped the last artifact would prove to be the final piece of the puzzle, but instead it merely added to the mystery of this most contentious and fascinating race.

Nothing was beyond their ability to achieve. One got the

feeling that the day the first primitive man looked up and saw the stars, the galaxy's days as a haven of peace and freedom were numbered. And yet they came out to the stars not just with their lusts and their hatred and their fears, but with their technology and their medicine, their heroes as well as their villains. Most of the races of the galaxy had been painted by the Creator in pastels; Men were primaries.

I had much to think about as I went off to my quarters to renew my strength. I do not know how long I lay, somnolent and unmoving, recovering my energy, but it must have been a long time, for night had come and gone before I felt prepared to rejoin the party.

As I emerged from my quarters and walked to the center of camp, I heard a yell from the direction of the gorge, and a moment later the Appraiser appeared, a large sterile bag balanced atop an air trolly.

"What have you found?" asked Bellidore, and suddenly I remembered that the Exobiologist was missing.

"I am almost afraid to guess," replied the Appraiser, laying the bag on the table.

All the members of the party gathered around as he began withdrawing items: a blood-stained communicator, bent out of shape; the floating shade, now broken, that the Exobiologist used to protect her head from the rays of the sun; a torn piece of clothing; and finally, a single gleaming white bone.

The instant the bone was placed on the table, the Mystic began screaming. We were all shocked into momentary immobility, not only because of the suddenness of her reaction, but because it was the first sign of life she had shown since joining our party. She continued to stare at the bone and scream, and finally, before we could question her or remove the bone from her sight, she collapsed.

"I don't suppose there can be much doubt about what

happened," said Bellidore. "The creatures caught up with the Exobiologist somewhere on her way down the gorge and killed her."

"Probably ate . . ."

". . . her too," said the Stardust Twins.

"I am glad we are leaving today," continued Bellidore. "Even after all these millennia, the spirit of Man continues to corrupt and degrade this world. Those lumbering creatures can't possibly be predators: there are no meat animals left on Earth. But given the opportunity, they fell upon the Exobiologist and consumed her flesh. I have this uneasy feeling that if we stayed much longer, we, too, would become corrupted by this world's barbaric heritage."

The Mystic regained consciousness and began screaming again, and the Stardust Twins gently escorted her back to her quarters, where she was given a sedative.

"I suppose we might as well make it official," said Bellidore. He turned to the Historian. "Would you please check the bone with your instruments and make sure that this is the remains of the Exobiologist?"

The Historian stared at the bone, horror-stricken. "She was my *friend!*" it said at last. "I cannot touch it as if it were just another artifact."

"We must know for sure," said Bellidore. "If it is not part of the Exobiologist, then there is a chance, however slim, that your friend might still be alive."

The Historian reached out tentatively for the bone, then jerked its hand away. "I can't!"

Finally Bellidore turned to me.

"He Who Views," he said. "Have you the strength to examine it?"

"Yes," I answered.

They all moved back to give me room, and I allowed my

mass to slowly spread over the bone and engulf it. I assimilated its history and ingested its emotional residue, and finally I withdrew from it.

"It is the Exobiologist," I said.

"What are the funeral customs of her race?" asked Bellidore.

"Cremation," said the Appraiser.

"Then we shall build a fire and incinerate what remains of our friend, and we will each offer a prayer to send her soul along the Eternal Path."

And that is what we did.

The ship came later that day, and took us off the planet, and it is only now, safely removed from its influence, that I can reconstruct what I learned on that last morning.

I lied to Bellidore—to the entire party—for once I made my discovery I knew that my primary duty was to get them away from Earth as quickly as possible. Had I told them the truth, one or more of them would have wanted to remain behind, for they are scientists with curious, probing minds, and I would never be able to convince them that a curious, probing mind is no match for what I found in my seventh and final view of Olduvai Gorge.

The bone was *not* a part of the Exobiologist. The Historian, or even the Moriteu, would have known that had they not been too horrified to examine it. It was the tibia of a *man*.

Man has been extinct for five thousand years, at least as we citizens of the galaxy have come to understand him. But those lumbering, ungainly creatures of the night, who seemed so attracted to our campfires, are what Man has become. Even the pollution and radiation he spread across his own planet could not kill him off. It merely changed him to the extent that we were no longer able to recognize him.

I could have told them the simple facts, I suppose: that a tribe of these pseudo-Men stalked the Exobiologist down the gorge, then attacked and killed and, yes, ate her. Predators are not unknown throughout the worlds of the galaxy.

But as I became one with the tibia, as I felt it crashing down again and again upon our companion's head and shoulders, I felt a sense of power, of exultation I had never experienced before. I suddenly seemed to see the world through the eyes of the bone's possessor. I saw how he had killed his own companion to create the weapon, I saw how he planned to plunder the bodies of the old and the infirm for more weapons, I saw visions of conquest against other tribes living near the gorge.

And finally, at the moment of triumph, he and I looked up at the sky, and we knew that someday all that we could see would be ours.

And this is the knowledge that I have lived with for two days. I do not know who to share it with, for it is patently immoral to exterminate a race simply because of the vastness of its dreams or the ruthlessness of its ambition.

But this is a race that refuses to die, and somehow I must warn the rest of us, who have lived in harmony for almost five millennia.

*It's not over.*